When the Bough Breaks

When the Bough Breaks

by STUART ROSENBERG

THOMAS Y. CROWELL COMPANY
NEW YORK / ESTABLISHED 1834

Designed by Ingrid Beckman

Manufactured in the United States of America

Library of Congress Cataloging in Publication Data
Rosenberg, Stuart.
 When the bough breaks.

 I. Title.
PZ4.R81156Wh   [PS3568.07883] 813'.5'4   75-33277
ISBN 0-690-01027-3

1 2 3 4 5 6 7 8 9 10

To Jacqueline

Acknowledgments

I WISH TO EXPRESS my appreciation for the assistance in certain technical matters I received from my brother-in-law, Laurence F. Harding. My brother, Philip, not only suggested the idea for this book to me but also served throughout the writing as an attentive critic, editor and friend. I cannot thank him adequately. Finally, I must thank Jackie, my wife, who helped me in ways too numerous and too important to specify here.

When the Bough Breaks

CHAPTER 1

R O G E R   M A P E S   S Q U I N T E D into the morning sunlight as the station wagon hung into the curve. The car was seven years old and the compression was shot. He had to keep his foot jammed to the floor to maintain his speed on the grade. He should have taken care of it before, when he had the chance.

Jimmy sat all the way over on the passenger side leaning against the door. He and his father had barely said a word to each other since they left the house over two hours ago.

The boy was slouched down too low to see the road. Most of the time he gazed absently out the side window at the endless procession of soft green hills. Broken lines of dairy cattle straggled by in the distance, seeming to undulate in the heat rising from the soil.

Occasionally he glanced at his father, then turned away uneasily. Roger still gripped the steering wheel tightly in both hands and stared straight ahead, his lips drawn white against his teeth. It confused the boy when his father looked like that, so cold and angry he didn't dare speak to him. Jimmy never understood what really set him off. It could be almost anything. Mom never started their fights but something she did probably started them. At any rate he could pretty much tell by watching her when she thought one was coming.

Along the road the evenly spaced trees flickered sunlight over the car. Jimmy was tired and the pulsing glare began to give him a headache. For a while he tried squinting like his father did but that only made it worse. Several times during the night he had been awakened by his parents' voices, first from the bedroom and then from the kitchen. His door was closed but he could still hear them yelling. He was afraid—even more, for some reason, when he couldn't make out all their words. He tried to shut out their voices altogether but it was as if they had gotten inside him. He heard them even when he managed to doze off. Certain phrases went round and round in his mind, softly, until they lost all meaning.

Suddenly his father was standing over him holding his gym bag and some clothes crumpled up in one hand. It seemed as if it had been quiet for a long time. At first the boy thought he was dreaming. His father was so far away. His face floated above him, bloodless, his eyes burning in the cool darkness of the room. He knew he had to get up but he couldn't force himself to move.

Then Roger grabbed him by the shoulder with his free hand, almost lifting him out of the bed. Jimmy threw his legs out to keep his balance. His father dropped the clothes on the floor and stalked away. The boy dressed quickly and followed him, carrying his socks and sneakers in his hand. In the hall he heard his mother breathing heavily through her mouth and the rustle of sheets as she tossed on the bed. He paused for a moment. Her muffled sobs reminded him of something odd, the sound the refrigerator sometimes made at night.

His father was waiting for him on the porch. The sun had not yet cleared the trees.

"You want to come?" Roger said.

"Sure."

They got in the car, closing the doors quietly. It was Saturday and the only sound on the street was the hum of a power mower a few blocks away. Jimmy asked, "What about Mom?" He knew it was a mistake as soon as he said it.

Roger started the engine without answering. They drove to town and stopped at Grantland's for breakfast. Roger ordered for both of them without consulting Jimmy—orange juice, scrambled eggs and hashed browns, coffee for himself.

The waitress said, "That's the number four, isn't it?"

"Is it?" Roger said.

They drove west at first, then circled back to Route 63. It was a county highway, a winding two-lane road that picked its way among the small, misshapen dairy farms of eastern Iowa. This was the first hot weekend of the year, going to be a scorcher, so traffic was heavier than usual. A lot of people were headed for Lake Barrett or the state park further north.

Roger passed them effortlessly. The old station wagon didn't have much power but it could still get rolling pretty good once it built up a head of steam. He kept it close to eighty. Once he let himself get almost on top of a horse-drawn surrey before swerving hard to go around it. On these old trough roads there was no shoulder for it to drive on. Not that it mattered—the Amish always drove on the pavement, even on interstates. Every so often you'd hear on the news about a car plowing into one of them from the rear.

The swaying of the car pressed the boy's forehead against the window, bringing him suddenly alert. He caught just a glimpse of the Amish driver with his somber face and beard and black hat. He sat rigidly on a plank seat high above the road, the reins motionless in his hand. Then he was gone. There was something forbidding in his appearance that struck Jimmy to the heart. The man's face looked like it had been carved in weathered wood and it said, *You have no business with me. Stay away.*

Jimmy spun around to watch the carriage out the rear window. Even when Roger veered back right in front of the horse's nose the driver never moved, never changed his expression. Indifferent, patriarchal eyes filtered out the alien world of automobiles.

In a moment the surrey and its driver disappeared around a bend in the road. Jimmy wasn't certain but he thought his father had cut in on them on purpose. When he was mad, he was mad at everyone. The boy couldn't help smiling. The Amish man had acted as if he hadn't even noticed. Sometimes that was the only way to deal with his father but it wasn't always easy to do it.

Jimmy tipped his head back for a minute while the picture of the Amish father faded gradually from his mind. Then he turned and studied Roger, not knowing what to think. He wanted to ask where they were going and whether they would do anything special. But he was scared to say anything. His father held the steering wheel all the tighter, it seemed, and grinned mirthlessly at some private reflection.

⊂≒   ⊂≒   ⊂≒

The sun woke Kay Orben a little before seven. She had left her shade up intentionally last night to watch the heat lightning. It was supposed to mean hot weather the next day. About time too. It was already May and there hadn't been one nice weekend all year.

Now she climbed out of bed and went to the window. It was going to be hot all right. A heavy mist rose from the still-black land. You could smell it in the air, the earth rising with the ground fog, nearly hiding the windbreak at their property line. Only the tops of the trees floated above it.

She took her summer robe off its hanger in the closet and was still pulling it on over her pajamas as she reached the bottom of the stairs. Her mother was in the kitchen. It didn't seem to matter what time Kay woke up, when she got downstairs Mom was in the kitchen.

Kay sneaked up behind her on her bare feet and kissed her on the back of the neck. Mrs. Orben turned, a little startled.

"Kay! How come you're up so early?"

"It's too sunny to sleep. Looks like a fantastic day."

Mrs. Orben smiled. "It's never too sunny on school days," she said, opening the refrigerator door.

Kay shrugged and sat down sideways to the table. That was her mother's way of teasing. She didn't mean anything by it.

In fact Mrs. Orben was in particularly fine spirits this morning. Perhaps the hint of summer contributed to her mood. She thrived on hot weather. And she had just been thinking what a milestone this summer would be. Her youngest daughter was a few weeks away from graduating high school. Soon she'd be getting ready for college. All her worrying, thank God, had been wasted, just as it had for Margaret, her eldest. You do the best you can for your children and pray it's enough. But the papers these days are full of kids who get in trouble. Sometimes you lie awake at night, wondering if it might happen to yours. There's so much about them you never know—where they go sometimes, and who their friends are. Fortunately, both of her daughters were trustworthy. She felt confident of that.

"Can I fix you some breakfast, Honey?" she asked.

"Okay. But what about Daddy?"

"I suspect he'll be in pretty soon."

"Do you want me to wait?"

"No, don't be silly."

Kay wandered around the kitchen listlessly while her mother scrambled two eggs. "Do you have any plans today?" Mrs. Orben asked as soon as she had set Kay's breakfast on the table. "It'd be a shame to waste a day like this."

"Uh-huh. Marian and I thought we might go to Lake Barrett if the weather's nice."

"You couldn't ask for nicer. Only be careful not to get too much sun. It's your first time."

Kay nodded.

"Do you need the car?" her mother asked a minute later.

Kay knew what the question meant. "It's an awful long walk, Mother," she said. "Why? Do you need it?"

"Well, I was going into town this afternoon. I suppose I could take your father's but it's such a boat. Why don't you see if Marian can get her folks' car?"

"What if she can't?"

"That's all right, Dear. I'll take Daddy's if there's no choice."

"*I'll* take it," Kay volunteered brightly. "I'd do anything for my Mom."

Mrs. Orben laughed. Harold was so finicky about that Lincoln of his. "You're a sweet child," she said, "but I doubt your father would accept that solution."

Kay clucked her tongue knowingly. "Okay. I'll go call Marian." She pushed away from the table, having finished eating already. "Do you want me to do the dishes?" she asked from the door.

"It's not necessary. I'll do them . . . " Her voice trailed off. Kay hadn't waited for an answer. Mrs. Orben shook her head and completed her sentence for herself. "When I do your father's."

"I'm not making any fucking plans!" Roger said, spitting the words through his teeth. "How many times do I have to tell you that?"

Jimmy subsided, whimpering. He had asked when they'd be going home, that was all.

This wasn't the first time Roger had to get away from the house. He'd disappear for a few days, occasionally as long as a week, not doing much except driving around until he got it worked out of his system. Once, when Marty was still alive, he took the boys with him.

That was during the winter. It happened exactly the same way. Days of endless squabbling with Mom finally exploded in a night of screaming and blows. The next morning Roger came into the boys' room and took them away. They were frightened at first, not knowing what their father had in mind. But they stuck close together and tried to steer clear of him when he got in his foul moods. In the end they had a great time.

That trip became very important to Jimmy. He still remembered almost everything they did as though it happened yesterday. The first night they put up at a cheap cabin, all three in a single bed, but then Roger bought camping gear and they hardly ever stopped driving. Roger and Marty took turns at the wheel. Even with the sleeping bags it got too cold at night if the motor was shut for long. Near a town called Hibbing a deer came close to their car when they stopped to cook breakfast. Thick snow lay on the ground and she must have been hungry to venture so close to people. But then she ran away. Roger told Marty to get his carbine from the trunk and they all chased after her. Marty fired a shot. Then they followed her blood in the snow. When they found her she was lying on her side, a good-sized doe with huge, vacant eyes that somehow still seemed alive. Since they didn't have a hunting license they left her where she fell. She was so thin she would have died in any case, Roger said.

Jimmy remembered other things too, like the special, eerie stillness inside the speeding car with all the windows rolled up. But they were only details, handles to bring it all back. It didn't really matter what they did or where they went. No, the important thing was that for the first time in his life he felt he was a part of his father's world. He couldn't even explain it to Marty but it gave him a strange sense of wholeness like nothing he had ever known before. It more than made up for always being at least a little frightened.

And so this morning, ever since his father had come to get him again, he had been alive to the possibility that they'd be going on another long journey. Finally he got up the nerve to broach the subject.

"I don't know," Roger said, making the boy wait for even that much of an answer. "We'll see."

"I mean are we gonna go home tonight, or like that other time?"

"What other time?"

"You remember."

"No. What other time?"

Jimmy ran his tongue over his lips. He couldn't believe that his father didn't know what he was talking about. "When we went to Minnesota and slept in the car," he said, his voice edging toward a whine. "With Marty. You remember. You bought all that camping stuff at that store in Rochester."

Roger remembered all right. He stopped pretending he didn't. "Minnesota," he said doubtfully. "What do you want to go all the way up there again for?"

That wasn't the point. Jimmy didn't want them to go back home, not so soon at any rate. He longed to say, C'mon, Dad, let's keep driving—just the two of us. But he couldn't say it. His father didn't care, not the way he did.

A few miles later he asked again, timidly, and his father blew up at him. "I'm not making any fucking plans!" he shouted. Jimmy withdrew even further toward the corner of the seat.

Roger seemed to back down. His eyes darted in the boy's direction a few times, carrying a hint of an apology. But Jimmy wasn't looking. Roger lit a cigarette and pushed the incident to the back of his mind.

Where the sign pointed to the Lake Barrett Recreation Area he slowed down and turned right. It wasn't but a couple hundred yards to the familiar dirt road that led to the parking lot. He turned right again and didn't bother to accelerate on the choppy, tree-shaded path.

Jimmy sat up and turned anxiously toward his father.

"Let's go for a swim," Roger said, his voice surprisingly light and even.

Jimmy shrugged. "All right," he mumbled, making sure his father heard his lack of enthusiasm. He usually liked the beach but he was in no mood for it now. If they spent the day at the lake they'd probably go home afterwards. He still hoped they'd do something exciting. Besides, there'd be a big crowd and they'd barely have room to lie down.

Roger let the car coast to a stop under the stand of cottonwoods that guarded the entrance to the parking lot. They could see the water from there. "Something eating you?" he asked. "I thought you liked the beach." He wanted to please the boy but the words came out as an ultimatum.

Jimmy didn't answer right away. He knew that it wouldn't matter what he said. Why couldn't his father understand that he only wanted to share the car with him—that he cherished, despite everything, their private times together—and let it go at that?

Roger ground out his cigarette in the ashtray. "Jim?" he said.

"We don't even have bathing suits, do we?"

"No. Wear your cut-offs. I'll hang them on the antenna and they'll dry."

"That's stupid. I'm not gonna go swimming in cut-offs," Jimmy muttered petulantly.

"Then sit in the car if that's what you want." Roger took his foot off the brake and the car rolled forward.

"Dad?"

Roger stopped the car again.

"We're not going home afterwards?"

Roger raised his eyebrows. "And if I say we're not . . . ?"

"Then I'll sit on your fucking beach."

Roger snorted sharply. The answer took him by surprise. The kid was spunky, he had to give him that. He reached over and tousled the boy's hair roughly.

He gunned the engine the few remaining yards, then stopped abruptly beside the parking attendant's kiosk. No one came out. The lot looked full. A few cars were even parked in the aisles. While they waited for the attendant Roger began tapping impatiently on the steering wheel. Then he slid into a regular tempo, bobbing his head in time and letting his ring slap randomly against the wheel rim to punctuate the rhythm. Jimmy grinned and joined in on the dashboard but his father picked up the beat, drumming more and more frantically until the boy broke up and couldn't follow him. He threw up his hands in submission, which only encouraged his father. The metallic clatter of his ring grew louder and more insistent.

Finally a portly man wearing a baseball cap stuck his head out of the kiosk and glowered at them. Roger snapped to attention like a comedy drunk trying to act sober.

"We're full up," the attendant said, shaking his head.

"It's only ten-thirty," Roger said.

The fat man bent down and peered into the car. There were always too many rowdies at the beach, ruining it for everyone. But these weren't high school kids. They were a father and son, even if they did make a lot of noise. "See for yourself," he said, gesturing toward the parking area.

"What about right there? I'll leave the keys in case that guy wants to get out."

"Sorry. Can't do it, pal."

Roger stared at him a few seconds. "Now that's a shame," he said with exaggerated solemnity. "The boy's gonna be awful disappointed."

On cue Jimmy frowned and lowered his head despondently.

The man stooped down and narrowed his eyes toward Jimmy again. The kid really looked unhappy. "I'll tell you what you can do," he drawled. "Get yourself some lunch, come back in an hour or so. I'll hold a space for you. I'm not supposed to. That sound fair enough?"

"No," Roger said decisively, "but I'll tell you what *you* can do." He jerked his left hand out the window, the middle finger extended, and waved it in the attendant's face. The man's jaw dropped. Roger stomped down savagely on the accelerator and the station wagon bolted forward between two rows of parked cars. Jimmy flung himself back against the seat and squealed with delight. At the end of the row Roger cut the wheel hard to his left, kicking up an enormous cloud of dust. On the loose dirt and gravel the car fishtailed through a U-turn and roared back toward the kiosk down the next aisle. The fat man scurried to the other side of the booth to intercept them but the car raced by in the exit lane. This time it was Jimmy who gave him the finger, leaning as far out of the car as he could. His hand came within inches of the man's nose. The attendant, furious, shook his fist at them in helpless rage. Afterwards he remembered the peculiar intensity that twisted the driver's features and the way the boy—who couldn't have been more than twelve—was laughing deliriously.

⊂⊃ ⊂⊃ ⊂⊃

Sheila Mapes stumbled into the bathroom and pulled open the door to the medicine cabinet, holding onto it for support. The blinds in the house were tightly drawn. In the windowless bathroom it was pitch black. She took a deep breath and tried to clear her mind.

Why had she come in here? The aspirin—yes. She felt around on the bottom shelf of the cabinet, hoping to find the bottle without having to turn the light on. It should have been right next to the

Listerine. She finally located it. Taking it from the shelf she brushed a pair of tweezers into the sink. They made a high tinny noise against the porcelain that felt like a shot going off inside her head.

She filled the sink with cold water and groped for a washcloth to put on her face. Cold water would make the throbbing go away. But when she dipped the cloth in the water the chill went right through her and she couldn't bring herself to do it. She left the washcloth in the standing water and made her way back to the bedroom, drying her hands on her robe.

As soon as she lay down she realized she didn't get any water to wash down the pills. She rolled onto her side to get the cool of the pillow against her cheek, her lips soundlessly forming the word, "Shit." The pain wasn't going away.

In a few minutes she made up her mind to take the pills anyway. She wrestled with the safety cap on the bottle until she thought she would go out of her mind. Why wouldn't the damn thing open? Then, telling herself to relax, she rotated the cap until she could feel the flange lined up with the notch on the bottle and peeled it back. Good. She dumped a few in her hand without counting them and stuffed them in her mouth.

It was harder to swallow the pills than she had expected. They began to dissolve in her mouth and turn gummy. The acrid, powdery taste almost made her gag. She swallowed hard a few times, forcing the tablets back into her throat, and finally felt them go down. The taste would stay with her for hours.

What time was it now anyway?

It didn't matter. Roger was gone. She heard him in Jimmy's room just before she dozed off. But he was gone now, she was sure of that. If she was lucky he wouldn't come back till Sunday night. Please, don't let him come back until then. What made him think that no matter what they did to each other they could just walk away from it and then everything would be all right? If he was crazy, she was even crazier to stay with him.

No, it was a dead end thinking along those lines. She had argued it out with herself so many thousands of times—ever since they were married. It was one thing to think things through rationally, to reach a decision and stick to it, but she didn't know of anyone who actually lived his life that way. There were men who beat their wives and women who fooled around, and sometimes a marriage went on like that for thirty years. Her parents' did.

And some women left their husbands after putting up with everything till the kids were grown and even the grandchildren. They left them after they really stopped caring. That's what Mrs. McAuliffe had done, and no one seemed to understand why.

Roger would be back, not until Sunday night, please God, and not a damn thing was going to be different . . . unless it got worse.

She probed her cheek gingerly under the eye. It was puffy and tender but there wasn't any blood and it didn't feel broken. There was blood back under her ear though. Strange, it didn't really hurt there. Her fingers picked idly at the clot and found it was still sticky underneath. She wiped her hand as best she could on the pillowcase. Fuck it, the bed needed changing anyway.

She thought back. The first time Roger had struck her was while they were still dating. He hit her once and apologized immediately, she couldn't remember why.

Sometimes their life together wasn't so bad. He was fun to be with when he wasn't angry and he had quiet periods when they didn't fight for months at a time. Like after that terrible business with his son last summer. Marty had hardly been back a week from R.O.T.C. summer camp. He left the house one night and the next thing they knew they found his body in the river. It had floated all the way down to the railroad bridge at the University. She had never been close to the boy, who wasn't her son, and she felt guilty about it in the following months. She knew that in a confused way he meant a great deal to Roger, depending, it seemed, on how much of the mother he saw in him at any moment. Roger brooded around the house for a few weeks acting strangely childish. He tried to help her with the cleaning and cooking and generally got in her hair. But when he went back to work he was like a different person. Into the new year he didn't miss a day. He put in a lot of overtime and came home tired but apparently contented. She didn't understand it but he finally seemed at peace with himself. He hardly ever raised his voice the entire period. This is how most women live, she remembered thinking. But then he gradually went back to being Roger again.

Anyway, that was all beside the point. Roger could be gentle when he wanted but that wasn't what kept her from leaving. No, there was something about him. She couldn't put her finger on it. It was this force in him, this sense of energy you felt around him, of driving to break loose. He was too alive. That was his cross, why he would never amount to anything, why he would always drift from job to job and collect unemployment in between. But it was also why she held on to him.

The day they got married Roger's mother took her aside. She said, Roger can be somebody. Make him harness his energy and there's no stopping that boy. Sheila didn't understand what she meant at the time but over the years those words, whether they were right or not, took on a kind of special significance for her. Sometimes she blamed herself for Roger's shortcomings. Another woman might have helped him. But most of the time she felt that helping or changing or turning this into that wasn't really the issue. Roger could have helped her too, but he never did.

Recently she had been seeing a man named Glen, who had been Roger's foreman when he worked at the garage. They met once or twice a week, on their lunch hours, and neither pretended it was any more than it was. After this she'd probably have to stop seeing him.

Nonetheless she toyed with the idea of calling him. He'd come over later and she'd fix him a good dinner, something extra nice that she never bothered to make normally. They'd spend the evening together. By evening she'd feel up to it.

Fuck it, she thought, it's Saturday.

It must all be some kind of joke, she thought. Roger wasn't the jealous type, not actually, and sex meant so little to her that she sometimes worried there was something physically the matter. If she didn't have any for the next ten years it wouldn't especially bother her. Yet here they were—to look at them you'd swear it was the old story of the possessive husband and the promiscuous wife. Yet you'd miss the point completely.

What *was* the point? That was the question Sheila kept coming back to. Why do we do this to each other? What makes us do this to each other?

It was no use, going over things like that in your mind. Did it ever make them any better?

She needed a cigarette desperately but she lay on the bed, trying not to let herself think any more. What if Roger had taken the last pack with him? The idea paralyzed her. Jimmy must have gone with his father. At last she put on the light over the bed and got up to look for the cigarettes. As she passed the dresser she glanced at her face in the mirror. It was like seeing a stranger—she felt no connection with the image in the glass. Her left eye was purple, swollen almost shut. Her jaw and neck were badly swollen and there were maroon streaks of blood on her cheek where her fingers had painted them. Oh, she thought dispassionately, is that the way I look?

There were almost two packs in the living room, enough at least until evening. She sat down on the sofa and lit one. After dark she could call Mason's and ask them to deliver some cough medicine or something for Jimmy and, oh, yes, a carton of cigarettes. She'd meet the boy at the door with the porch light out and he wouldn't see anything.

It was funny, she had learned that trick from her mother. Thinking about it as she inhaled the first warm drags of tobacco she began crying until her body shook with convulsions. All the lessons she could have learned from her mother, and that was the one she had chosen.

CHAPTER 2

R O S E   T A L I A F E R R O   S H O O E D the boys out the door as soon as she could, telling them to stay at the playground until she called them for lunch. She liked Walt to be able to sleep late on Saturdays.

After clearing the breakfast dishes she sat down in the den with the morning paper and her second cup of coffee. Why couldn't the children realize that their father needed his rest? He wasn't a strong man.

No, that wasn't true. He had the constitution of a horse when you got right down to it. But the angina meant he had to be handled with kid gloves. Unfortunately, a sheriff can't take it easy whenever he feels like it. With summer coming it was bound to get worse. His deputies went on vacation, leaving him shorthanded just when special details were needed for the lakes and parks. Traffic was heavier too. On top of everything, Walt was never one to delegate or say it couldn't be done. When work piled up he put in the extra hours himself. It was sheer stubbornness on his part. After all the years he had given the force, no one could complain if he didn't push himself so hard.

Rose lit a cigarette and folded the paper back to the movie listings. Maybe she could talk Walt into taking her to a show tonight. He'd enjoy it. She couldn't really blame the kids. At five and seven they don't know what it means to be quiet, to sit still for even a minute. Sometimes she got fed up with having to shush them all weekend long.

It had been a mistake having children so late in life. Walt was forty-two when Danny was born; she was thirty-six. After they had finally accepted the fact that they could never have children, he was like a gift from heaven. She could never truly be sorry. But then, while she was pregnant with Wally, Walt started getting chest pains. Angina, the doctor said. He could live to be a hundred but he had to be careful. One of the arteries to his heart was obstructed. Overexertion or aggravation could trigger an attack. And he tired easily.

So the boys became a problem, or at least a potential danger. Rose couldn't do anything about the tensions that went along with her husband's job—short of asking him to retire, which was out of the question. But she could see to it that the children disturbed him as little as possible.

That was the sad part, that Walter couldn't get the pleasure out of his sons that a man was entitled to. And Rose, because she had to be a watchdog, protecting him from the million and one intrusions the boys would otherwise make on his peace and quiet— Rose didn't get very much pleasure out of them either.

She sighed and turned the paper back to the front page. The movies they made these days—she wouldn't pay money to see that kind of filth. Well, there was so much to be thankful for. In all honesty she could say she loved Walter more now than on the day they were married. Not many women could say that. She looked up to him. He was a good man and in the long run that counted for more than the other qualities she used to think were important.

Rose Taliaferro lit a second cigarette and drained her cup of coffee. Putting the cup back on the end table, she cocked her head to one side and listened. Was that Walt walking around upstairs? No, it was only a beam shifting somewhere in the house, the kind of noise you always hear when you're up alone at night. But on this summery weekend morning, the kids at the playground, all the windows open and not a breeze to stir the curtains, it was so quiet she heard it now.

⊂╪   ⊂╪   ⊂╪

Past Lake Barrett the road veered to the northwest, following the course of one of the feeder rivers. Roger drove with one arm out the window, enjoying the sun and the rush of moist air against his skin. The heat, stupifying when they had to stop, wasn't so bad when the car was in motion.

Jimmy had curled up contentedly on the front seat with his head against the door. Despite the bouncing of the car he quickly fell asleep.

After a while they came to a trestle bridge that led to a small market town on the other side of the river. Roger crossed over and parked in front of the drugstore. Without waking Jimmy he went in and bought a carton of cigarettes and a packet of Tiparillos.

When he came out Jimmy was still fast asleep with his mouth open, his head now hanging down. He didn't look comfortable. Roger stretched him out and threw the packages in the back. He had a few things he wanted to do. The kid would be okay where he was. The car was heating up like a sauna but there was nothing he could do about it. Close to midday there wasn't an inch of shade anywhere along the street. Jimmy's hair was already plastered down with sweat. Roger brushed it back from his forehead and shut the door, smiling sardonically at the perverse impulse that had prompted him to take the boy along.

Not that he'd be much trouble, but what did he need a twelve-year-old kid for?

He strode aimlessly down the one main street, eight or ten blocks long. Except for a few farmers in town for Saturday shopping, the street was deserted. Almost every business was named after the town—Timmons Hardware, Timmons Pharmacy, Timmons Feed and Grain Supply. He felt bottled up, like he was going around in circles. It was more than being out of work. Shit, he could get another job whenever he wanted—there was always someone looking for an experienced mechanic. That wasn't the problem. But whatever he did, it turned out to be a trap.

Sheila was another trap. In the back of his mind he planned vaguely on going away somewhere, making a fresh start. Without her and without the kid. Sure. He didn't know exactly what he would do but he had to do something. When was it?—a couple years ago—he told her he was leaving and she laughed in his face. Don't say it if you don't mean it, she screamed.

Maybe she was right. Why had he gone into the boy's room this morning? Well, it was too late to do anything about it now. At least it would piss off Sheila, he thought. She sometimes resented the way Jimmy tried to cling to him.

He turned around and headed for the department store he had seen across from the car. It was a cavernous, old-fashioned building, one floor and a mezzanine. Inside it was cool and dank. He bought an extra can of kerosene for the Coleman stove, which was still in the car, and a few packages of Jockey shorts and T-shirts for Jimmy, guessing his size. Everything else he could get at the market.

On his way out he noticed a table piled up with bathing suits on sale. They must have been last year's styles left over. He pawed through them desultorily, finally deciding on a suit for himself in a stretch fabric, cut like a pair of briefs without any legs, and a boxer style for Jimmy in an American flag design.

Looking for a cash register, he saw two salesgirls talking together behind the men's furnishings counter. They had been watching him pick out the suits. As he approached them they tittered self-consciously. One whispered to the other behind her hand, then nudged her forward and melted off into the corner. They were just high school kids and the prospect of selling a man a bathing suit either amused or embarrassed them.

His salesgirl glanced toward her friend a few times as if looking for encouragement. Something in this pantomime got under Roger's skin, the way they flaunted their innocence. Who do they think they're kidding? he wondered bitterly, surprising himself by the strength of his annoyance.

Impulsively, he held up his suit by the corners of the waistband, stretching it out in front of him. "Does that look like it would fit me, miss?" he asked, making sure she heard the innuendo in the question.

The girl blushed slightly. "I don't know, sir," she said softly. "Is it your size?"

"Yeah."

He laid the suits on the counter. While she wrote up the sale, not raising her eyes, he stared fixedly at the top of her head. "Aren't you supposed to ask me if it's cash or charge?" he asked flatly.

"I'm sorry. I forgot."

Roger waited.

"Will that be cash or charge? . . . sir."

"Cash."

A puzzled frown crossed her face. "That'll be eight . . ."

"Hmmh?" Roger cut in sharply. In a strange way it excited him, toying with this girl.

"Will there . . . will there be anything else, sir?"

Roger smiled faintly. He leaned forward and lowered his voice confidentially. "As a matter of fact, yes," he said. "I need an athletic supporter. Could you get me one?"

Her eyes darted to her friend again, but the other girl had her back turned and was pretending to arrange stock on the shelf. She's not gonna help you, Roger thought. When her face came back to him he grinned at her cruelly. It didn't take a genius to see how her hot little imagination worked. He felt he could see right through her. Just mention a jock strap and she started to come unglued. You think I don't know about your raunchy little fantasies? he said with his eyes.

The corners of her mouth twitched perceptibly, exposing pink gums. "I'm sorry, sir," she stammered. "I don't usually work in this department. The salesman is out. Couldn't you . . . please, I don't . . ."

Couldn't I leave you alone? Roger thought, completing her sentence. No, I couldn't. Her discomfiture gratified him enormously. "I'm only asking for an athletic supporter, miss," he said, struggling to keep his tone as normal as possible. "I'm sure you or your little friend can find one for me."

The girl hesitated and then dutifully went to look. Roger's eyes followed her as she stooped down to search the cases below the counter. Her skirt came halfway up her thighs. She knows I'm watching, he thought. She wants more, I'll give it to her.

The other girl checked him out over her shoulder, then returned hurriedly to her busywork as though she were afraid of getting caught doing something she shouldn't. Her movement drew his attention. He winked at her but she had turned away already.

The salesgirl kept riffling through the same boxes over and over. She had found the supporters but hadn't realized before that they came in different sizes. Roger chortled involuntarily. Sooner or later she'd have to ask—she couldn't stay down there forever. Now if it had been Sheila behind that counter she wouldn't mind finding out what size jock a guy wore. Old Sheil had a little machine that would measure him. Old Sheil never missed a chance to use her little machine.

When she stood up the color was drained from her face and her upper lip glistened with sweat. "There are . . . uh . . . different sizes." The last two words were barely audible.

Roger raised his eyebrows suggestively as if to say, How about that! Look, it was a game and she loved it as much as he did. The second girl whirled around. "I'll get it, Alice," she said sharply.

Well, he had pushed a little too hard, tripped the safety valve. At least he knew her name now. Alice. She bolted from behind the counter and ran across the floor, her shoulders hunched and her hands in front of her face.

"Size thirty-four, medium," Roger said calmly, as if nothing had happened. He had no interest in starting in with this one. Alice was probably bawling to the manager already, telling him there was a maniac on the loose trying to buy a jock strap. Christ, it was easy to find the raw nerve.

The girl slapped down the package in front of him. Then she checked the register tape to see what had been rung up already and completed the sale. Roger read the total in the register window and handed her a twenty. She counted his change into his hand and put the items in a bag, folding over the top and laying it on the counter.

⊂⊱   ⊂⊱   ⊂⊱

Kay wrapped a bathtowel around herself, tucking the end in tightly under her arm, and dashed down the hall to her bedroom. As the door clicked shut behind her, her mother shouted from downstairs. "Marian's here, Kay."

"I'll be down in two minutes."

She stood in the middle of the room biting her thumb as she puzzled over what to wear. Marian had said that Robert and his roommate were coming down from Iowa City for the weekend. They were all going to meet at the beach.

It was dumb to worry about how she looked for a blind date, she finally decided. She grabbed a pair of old jeans and her S.U.I. sweatshirt from the drawer. Plenty good enough.

Marian was sitting with Kay's father at the kitchen table while he finished his breakfast. She was telling him how much trouble she was having deciding on a college, and soliciting his advice. He took the implicit flattery in stride, wearing the role of trusted adviser as comfortably as an old shoe. Kay turned a chair around and sat down straddling it. She didn't say anything, but listened to the conversation in a curious frame of mind. There was never this kind of give-and-take in *her* discussions with her father.

The small talk dragged on long after the table had been cleared. "C'mon," Kay said as soon as she saw a chance, "or we won't be able to get in."

"Do you have your suit and towel?" Mrs. Orben asked. She had been hovering around the table like a mother hen. "Just let me run get the beach blanket. Do you need a blanket? Anything else you need?"

"I got everything." Her tote bag and a blanket were on the step-stool.

Mr. Orben held out his key case, dangling it by one of the keys. Kay looked puzzled. "We're taking Marian's car," she said.

"I couldn't get it," Marian said, looking significantly at Kay. "My brother needed it after all."

Kay got the message. Robert and Marian wouldn't have to chauffeur her around if she had her own car. As she reached for the keys, her father drew them back.

"Now you'll drive carefully," he said. "You're not used to such a big car."

Kay's eyes lit up. "Can I have *your* car, Daddy?" she squealed, her voice cracking with excitement.

"If it's okay with your mother."

"It's fine with me," Mrs. Orben said, as surprised by this development as her daughter. "I'd rather have the Ford anyway. But are you sure it's a good idea, Harold?"

He nodded, trying not to show the pleasure he took in Kay's reaction.

"I'll be careful," she promised solemnly.

"I know you will."

He led the way out to the garage and raised the door for her. The chrome, even the body of the car, glistened magnificently as the sunlight streamed in. Kay opened the driver's door, then came back and kissed her father gratefully on the cheek. "Thanks, Daddy," she said in her little-girl voice.

She let the car inch back carefully without giving it any gas. My God, the garage seemed so narrow! She had driven the Lincoln a few times before but never by herself. When she was safely in the driveway she let out a deep breath she hadn't realized she had been holding. Her mother came out to the lawn and told her to have a good time. Kay eased the car into the street and drove off at a crawl, concentrating too intently on the road ahead to wave goodbye to her parents.

C⊨   C⊨   C⊨

Roger found an A & P two blocks away and bought a load of groceries, the kind of stuff that required no preparation or could be cooked easily over a camp stove. He also got toothpaste, soap, toilet paper and two six-packs of cold beer. He asked the clerk if he

could write a check in the amount of the purchase but the clerk said
no, not without a card on file in the store. He paid cash but then
decided he'd better drive back to Arlington to get more money.

Jimmy opened his eyes slowly. They were moving again. Roger
had propped him more or less upright to get his legs off the driver's
seat.

"Where are we?" the boy asked hazily, still groggy from sleeping in the broiling sun.

Roger didn't answer. He held a Tiparillo clenched firmly in his
teeth but he didn't seem mad any more, just preoccupied. Jimmy
didn't bother repeating the question. He leaned across his father,
turning his wrist to get a look at his watch. It was only one-thirty.

Roger said, "You hungry, Jim? There's some food in the back."

Jimmy clambered over the seat to investigate. He'd had no dinner last night but hadn't realized how famished he was until his father mentioned it. There was a bag of potato chips on top of the
bundle. He tore it open and started eating ravenously.

"Get me a beer, will you?" Roger said. "Have one yourself if
you want."

Far out, Jimmy thought. He found the beer and twisted two cans
out of the plastic template that held them together. Handing one to
his father, he stretched out with his head resting against the back of
the front seat. The rear seats were folded down and it was cool
lying on the metal flooring. He broke off the tab and began sipping
the beer. A few drops trickled down his chin and into his jersey. It
felt refreshing. He rolled the frosty can over his cheeks and brow
until his skin tingled painfully.

With lowered eyes he watched the highway unravel out the
tailgate. Fragments of landscape popped up at the edge of his vision, centered themselves, and receded steadily until they were
sucked in an instant below the crest of a hill or vanished around a
turning in the road. It was so peaceful in the back of the car, like
living in another world. Even the irregular *whoosh, whoosh,
whoosh* of traffic going the other way, so intrusive at first, grew
distant and comforting. He and his father floated in a giant balloon
high over the countryside. Far below them, people they knew raced

after them, calling them back. They just soared higher and higher, into the clouds, until they couldn't hear them anymore.

Maybe they'd never go home, he thought.

He smiled inwardly. Deep inside him something dark and familiar uncoiled and slithered away. Suddenly he felt safe. His father's temper couldn't hurt him, he realized, as long as they were together. He thought of the way Marty used to lash back furiously when Roger had been unfair, and how depressed he got afterward. Sometimes Jimmy hated his father too and it frightened him, that he was becoming just like Marty. But it didn't have to be that way. He was really a part of his father, so close to him they were almost one person. Roger had wanted him along, hadn't he? That was all that counted.

Roger tossed his empty beer can out the window. Jimmy watched it bounce crazily along the white line until it rolled to a stop against the curb. Narrowing his eyes and concentrating hard, he was sure he could still see it for more than a mile. When he finally lost sight of it, he handed his father another beer without being asked.

"Thanks," Roger said. "Hey, Jim, d'you still want that swim? If I can find it, there's a trail near here that goes down to an old pier at the lake. I'll cook some of those hot dogs too."

"What lake?" Jimmy asked bewilderedly.

"Lake Barrett."

Jimmy sat up quickly, his eyes wide with a sense of betrayal. He had no idea they were going back toward Arlington.

Roger noticed his expression in the rear view mirror. "Take it easy," he laughed before Jimmy could say anything. "I gotta cash a check at Rademacher's. Then I figure we might head down toward Missouri—sort of follow the river. But we got plenty of time. D'you want that swim or don't you?"

Jimmy felt his heart leap inside him. "It sounds okay," he said, sliding back down against the rear of the seat. The words fell oddly short of what he meant them to say.

CHAPTER 3

B E N H A R G R O V E, the parking lot attendant, waddled out of his kiosk and rested his arm on top of the car, bending down to speak to the driver. "Sorry, Kay," he said, "but we're all full up. You should've got here sooner."

Kay turned questioningly to Marian. "Do you want to wait for someone to leave?" she asked, curling her lip. "I can let you out here if you want."

Marian thought a second, then shook her head. "No, let's go."

"Are you sure?"

"Yes," she said firmly.

"You can turn around in there," Ben Hargrove said. "But tell me. Your father trade in that old Ford for a Mer-say-deez Benz or something? How come he let you have his car?"

Kay laughed. "He trusts me, I guess."

As soon as they rounded the stand of cottonwoods and were out of sight of the parking lot, Marian started babbling excitedly about an old access road that led to a clearing right by the lake. It was private property but no one would mind if they parked the car there. In fact there were hundreds of these little-used trails if you knew where to look for them. This one would take them less than half a mile from the beach.

Kay was willing to try it but when Marian showed her where to turn she had second thoughts. The path was no more than a pair of wheel ruts thickly choked with grass and brambles. It looked as if she would virtually have to pick her way among the trees.

"Oh, come on," Marian pleaded. "A couple of twigs won't hurt the paint."

Kay frowned doubtfully. She had no business taking the car down a trail like that. Besides, they hadn't told her parents they'd be meeting Robert and his roommate. If it was up to her, she'd just as soon forget the whole thing.

"Robert says he's really cute," Marian said, practically reading her mind. "He's from Connecticut or someplace."

"Terrific," Kay said petulantly. "A blind date." It dawned on her that Marian was simply using her so that she and Robert wouldn't be stuck with the roommate.

"Look, we can't sit here all day. If you want to go home, drive me back to the parking lot."

Kay wavered, easing her foot off the brake without really making a decision. The car rolled forward. She followed the meager trail as best she could, gritting her teeth at the sound of branches brushing over the car. Marian knew enough not to say anything for fear Kay might change her mind.

Finally they came to a tiny clearing around the crumbling relic of a firepit. The trees had all been felled years ago, their places taken by wild blackberry bushes growing in stunted clumps. They weren't in full leaf yet.

At least there'd be room to turn around, Kay thought. She'd been afraid she would have to back all the way out to the road. After locking the doors she examined the car carefully. There were numerous lines that looked at first like scratches but she was able to rub them away with her finger.

The clearing opened right to the waterfront. There was no beach, only a bank of dark clay rising vertically a foot or so above the level of the lake.

"Isn't this a fantastic place!" Marian gushed.

Kay smiled appreciatively. It *was* beautiful. Leave it to Marian to know about a place like this, she thought. It must be the greatest make-out spot in Iowa. From where they were standing there wasn't a sign of human life anywhere to be seen. The public beach was hidden around the curving shoreline and the opposite bank had never been developed. Everything was perfectly still. For a few seconds the breeze shifted to the north, carrying faint traces of the jubilant cries of children playing in the water, but when it turned again the voices faded away.

The wild grandeur of the scene was almost eerie. Kay momentarily surrendered herself to the sense of isolation. "I bet it's scary coming down here at night," she murmured. Her shoulders trembled involuntarily.

Marian laughed impishly. "Well, don't come alone," she said.

Kay's eyes twinkled, breaking her pensive mood. "Right," she said, cocking a finger and pointing it at Marian. "Let's go. I want to take a swim."

Doug Eddy was kneeling above her, saying her name softly. "Kay . . . Kay . . . We must have dozed off. You're gonna get an awful burn if you don't get up. Let's go in the water."

She offered him her hand and he pulled her upright. They ran into the lake together holding hands, not letting go until they both dived under the surface. She paddled along the silty bottom as long as her breath held out, then shot to the top. Doug was only a few yards away. Though the water was shallow enough for her to stand, she fell over on her back and floated up to him. He put out his hand, letting the top of her head bump against it. She rested there, looking up at his face against the pale blue sky, kicking easily to stay afloat. The movement of her legs pushed her forward, maintaining a slight pressure where he touched her.

"That wasn't so bad," she said. "I usually go in one inch at a time."

He hesitated before making his confession. "Yeah. So do I."

She laughed and rolled onto her stomach. Then she started swimming, leading Doug briskly out to the chain of plastic buoys that marked the safety perimeter. They draped themselves over it to talk. She had begun to like him.

At first she had been wary. He was certainly attractive—tall and strongly built. From the moment they met he seemed perfectly at ease with her, like they were old friends. But something gave her the uncomfortable impression that such familiarity came readily to him, that it was merely a skill he had mastered. With no way to gauge what he really thought of her, she held aloof for a while, reserving judgment.

He struck her as being much older than Robert or other boys she knew in college. They never had more than the vaguest notion of what they would do with their lives. Doug knew what he wanted. He hoped to be a novelist some day but he was prepared to do other things—other kinds of writing—until his career was established. In fact, he came to Iowa—it was the only conceivable reason, he said—because the atmosphere at the University's Writers' Workshop was supposed to stimulate people like him.

That note of irony, so frequent with him, appealed to her. It touched even his own ambitions, as if he were reluctant to take anything, even himself, too seriously. She liked the way he radiated self-confidence but never seemed cocky. It was an attitude, she thought, peculiar to people from the East, and she worried that he might regard her as—what?—provincial. When he talked about his writing she really didn't know what to say, and she winced whenever he poked fun at Iowa.

Now, as they swam together, she wondered at the frivolousness of her earlier reservations.

When they came out of the water, Doug went with Robert to the refreshment stand to get something to eat. They returned with a pizza, Cokes and ice creams on a stick, which melted faster than they could eat them.

Later Kay and Doug went swimming again. Then she said she had better get dressed. She had been out in the sun too long already.

Doug said, "All right. But let's not go back to the beach. Do you feel like taking a walk?"

"Sure."

In the bathhouse she had to wait over fifteen minutes for a dressing room. It was almost three o'clock and the families that had come out early were more than ready to go home. Harried mothers stood in line, smoking cigarettes and commiserating with each other. They made no effort to control their children. Little girls, exhausted and cranky, ran wild all over the place, rattling lockers and yanking open the stalls. When Kay's turn finally came she changed quickly into her sweatshirt but decided to leave on her bikini pants. She stuffed her jeans and everything else into her tote bag, ran a comb hastily through her wet hair and rushed out to find Doug.

Robert and Marian were gone. "How long does it take you to put on a sweatshirt?" Doug teased. He was dressed too.

Kay shrugged. "Do you know where they went?"

"Not exactly. They took Bob's car but they said they'd be back in a couple hours. I think they're planning to stay late."

Kay thought that sounded like an invitation. "Why don't we walk around the lake?" she suggested. "I'm parked down there. I could give you a ride back."

"Do you have to go home?"

"Uh-huh. Dinner."

"Can you get out after?"

"No."

"Saturday night? You have to stay home?"

She grimaced. "You know. I can't tell my folks I just met a boy at the beach and now I'm going out with him again."

"Oh . . . why not?" Behind the question she detected his playful sarcasm, aimed at her midwestern proprieties.

"I can't."

He seemed to accept that. He picked up the blanket and signaled her to lead the way. She decided to go the long way around the lake. Even walking slowly she'd be in plenty of time for supper.

When they came to the head of the trail, he said, "What if you don't tell your folks you met me this afternoon? Evidently they don't mind if you go out with me, just as long as you don't do it twice."

Kay laughed, then pursed her lips thoughtfully. "We'll see," she said.

They walked in silence for about half an hour along trails too narrow for two people to go side by side. Doug followed a few steps behind her. At a tiny rivulet that fed fresh water into the lake Kay sat down, slipped her shoes off and put her feet in the water. It was icy cold and just deep enough to cover her ankles. Doug sat on the bank, his shoulder lightly nudging her back. It was wonderful, she thought, to feel they didn't have to make conversation.

"Katherine? Is that your name?"

"Uh-huh. With a K."

She gazed dreamily into the rivulet. Beneath her legs was a tiny pool so still a waterskate, balanced on the surface, remained in exactly the same spot. Doug began tickling the back of her neck with a small twig. She reached up to brush it away and he stopped.

"Does anyone ever call you Kate?"

"No."

"Do you mind if I do?"

"Why?"

" 'Cause no one else does."

She shrugged her shoulders noncommittally. He had struck a false note and she drew away from him inside, feeling that strange emptiness she always felt in the evening when the last quarter inch of the sun dropped below the horizon. What was happening here? She had been hooked by the smoothest boy she ever met, that was all. "Can I call you Kate because no one else does?" People didn't say things like that.

Then she thought, I'm stupid to be so analytical, so careful all the time. If I like him, why look for things to dislike?

Doug slid away from her and leaned her backward until her head was in his lap. She lifted her arm and wrapped it around his waist, squeezing a little so that her cheek pressed against the hard muscles of his stomach. But when she tried to smile at him it didn't feel right.

"Is anything the matter?" he said.

"No." She told herself to relax. It was childish to worry about stopping things before they got started.

"Good," Doug said. "Will you really be going to Iowa next fall?" He was looking at her sweatshirt.

"I'm not sure. I might go to Southern Illinois. They have a good speech therapy program."

"Is that what you want to do? Be a speech therapist?"

"I guess so."

He traced the outline of the S.U.I. emblem lightly with his finger, starting at the bottom. The top of it was between her breasts. She felt her body tense but forced herself to squeeze him again with her arm. Don't be such a baby, a voice pleaded inside her. He hasn't even touched you yet.

She let him continue drawing his circles, his fingertip crossing and recrossing the band under her bra. "Don't go to Southern Illinois," he said. "I bet they don't even have sweatshirts."

She laughed soundlessly. Doug placed his hand flat on her stomach, on the bare skin between her bathing suit and the hem of her sweatshirt. It felt cool against her sunburn. She put her right hand over his, gently stroking his fingers. For once she would just let things happen. She had this system built inside her that told her when to say yes and when to say no. She trusted her instincts to tell her when to stop.

He took the bottom of her sweatshirt and began drawing it up until it caught where she was lying on it. She arched her back, her head digging into his thighs, and he pulled it up the rest of the way so that it was all bunched under her arms. "Lift your head," he said. "Do you want me to take it off?"

"No. Is that okay?"

He didn't answer. She was wearing a mesh bra and her tiny, dark nipples showed through the fabric. She watched his hand as it slowly covered one of her breasts and then she closed her eyes thinking, He hasn't even kissed me yet.

The way he did it felt so natural. His hand hardly moved at all. She wasn't prepared to feel such contentment, such happiness. Always before when she let boys go this far she had been in a state of feverish excitement so that afterward it was hard to remember why she had let them do it.

A light breeze had sprung up, rustling the leaves softly overhead and darting specks of sunlight over her body. She raised her head slightly and watched his hand slide down to cradle her breast. It had never been anything like this before.

She sat up and leaned back against him without removing his hand. Her sweatshirt fell down and covered it. He pressed harder on her breast and her body turned toward him until he bent down and kissed her. His hand was on her back now as he held her tightly. Their tongues met, sliding back and forth deliciously against each other. She knew when he wanted her to lie down and she felt the damp grass fresh and cool against her bare skin and Doug lying beside her, his hand now moving to her belly and slowly downward until his finger slipped under the elastic of her bathing suit.

And she thought, No, no! I don't want this to happen now! No, please, Doug, I can't, not now. When he touched her it was like he touched every part of her body. She didn't know what to say. Was she supposed to be doing something? His face above hers was so calm, his smile unchanging and perfect. My God, didn't he feel it too? Then her eyes asked him to stop and his hand drew back without hurry or hesitation, leaving her once again serene and contented.

"It's okay," he whispered but he didn't understand. She wasn't afraid of what had happened.

He kissed her again but it felt different now. She was *letting* him kiss her, *letting* him slide his hand into her bra and toy with her nipple, still hard and erect. Well, she wanted to let him. But after a few minutes she pushed him away gently and stood up. His face darkened for an instant as he followed her with his eyes.

He stood quickly, placing both hands reassuringly on her shoulders. "Katie, listen," he said.

"No, Doug, I can't. I'm sorry." There was sadness and uncertainty in her face. She lowered her head, shaking it slowly from side to side. Everything had seemed so easy a few minutes ago and now she wasn't sure of anything, least of all Doug. Why couldn't she be more like Marian? she thought in self-reproach. Was there something wrong with her that made it all so complicated?

Doug tipped her head up with his fingers and looked in her eyes. "You're not a child anymore, Katie," he said. "You can't say yes one minute and no the next."

She pulled her head away and stared down into the water, not seeing anything. Her eyes filled with tears. She knew he was right—she hadn't been fair to him. Yet what he was asking was impossible.

"I'm sorry, Doug," she said firmly. "It's just not that easy. Please understand."

Maybe he did because he pulled her close and held her in his arms. She put her head on his shoulder while he tenderly stroked her hair.

"I have to go," she said, stepping back from him and looking at him frankly. "You better go back to the beach."

"I'll walk you the rest of the way to the car."

"No. It's all right. I'd rather go by myself."

His brow furrowed. "Will I see you again?"

She smiled happily, flipping her hair back with a toss of her head. "Yes, it's not that," she said. "I just want a little time to think before I get home."

"I see. What about tonight? Can I call you later? You didn't answer me before."

"No, not tonight. But call me during the week."

She slipped her feet into her shoes. Doug picked up her blanket and tote bag and handed them to her. She clutched them to her chest. He turned and walked away.

"I'll call you," he shouted from a distance.

She nodded vigorously. When she couldn't see him any more she turned in the opposite direction and started to run.

Rose Taliaferro bolted for the telephone and grabbed it on the second ring, but Walter had picked it up already.

"Walt? Is that you?"

"Yeah. What is it, Matt? Hang up, Rose."

Reluctantly, she put the phone back on the cradle, clicking it so they could tell she wasn't still listening. Matt was always calling Walter with problems a good deputy should have handled himself. He had absolutely no self-reliance. The upshot was that Walt often ran to the office on his day off when there was really no need. She never said it to anyone but she secretly suspected that her husband encouraged his deputy's dependence. Over the years he had personally transformed a country-bumpkin outfit into one of the most respected law enforcement agencies of its type in the state and he wasn't about to loosen his grip on any of it. Even in Des Moines they knew who Walt Taliaferro was.

"The thing is this," Matt was explaining in his laconic way. "A boy seems to have disappeared out to the reservoir. The Andreassen kid. You know him?"

"I know the name. What do you mean, disappeared?"

"Well, that's just it. No one's been able to find him. Kastenmeier's already got thirty reports he's been seen thirty places. All false leads so far, the ones we've checked out."

"Right. How long's he been missing?"

"Nobody's sure. Two, two and a half hours."

Walt grimaced. Sometimes there was a tricky current off the point at the reservoir. It wasn't strong but it could panic an inexperienced swimmer. It seemed they had a drowning almost every year out there. When a boy was lost over two hours you had to consider the possibility.

"That's not good," he said. "How many men you got on it?"

"I sent Young. I figured we should have at least two. You want me to send more?"

"Well, he's what?—six years old, Matt. Where are your higher priorities?"

"That's what I figured. I'll pull in the traffic details."

"And start organizing a search. I'll be down as soon as I can." He gave detailed instructions on setting up a command post, recruiting volunteers and assigning them to sweep specific trails. But he knew he'd have to do most of it again when he got there.

"What about dragging the lake?" Matt asked. "You know, we got all that scuba gear last year. It's down at headquarters someplace."

"No. If the boy's drowned we can't do him any good. Let's use our people where they can find him alive."

Walt hung up and shut off the television. He had been lying on the couch in his undershorts watching the Cardinal game. Rose appeared in the doorway, a questioning look on her face.

"Do you have to go?" she asked, but her voice was resigned. "It's not something Matt can handle?"

Walt shook his head apologetically. "I'm sorry, Rosie. A six-year-old boy is missing at the reservoir."

Rose understood. "Do we know the family?" she asked.

"Andreassen?"

The name meant nothing to her. Purely for form's sake she made one last try at keeping him home. "You're not a bloodhound, you know. Matt's been on searches before. Why don't you let him do it?"

"The kid's a year younger than Danny. If it was one of ours, would you want a deputy in charge while the sheriff stayed home watching a ballgame?"

Rose smiled wanly, her eyes misting over. It was characteristic of her husband that he refrained from saying the obvious—that the deputy in this case was Matthew Vollmer, who couldn't lead a search for his own socks in the morning.

"I better shave and get dressed," Walt said, moving toward the door.

Rose put out her arm to stop him and stretched to plant a kiss on his cheek. "You want me to make a sandwich for you to take in the car?"

"Yeah. I'd appreciate it, Sweetheart."

CHAPTER 4

"'Hey, the ball huggers for you?" Jimmy called to his father. He was standing naked behind the car and had just opened the bag with the new bathing suits.

Roger was tinkering with the Coleman stove at the foot of the pier. "Is that what they call them?" he said. "Sure. Why not?" He wondered whether the salesgirl, Alice, called them ball huggers too.

Jimmy bit through the plastic filament that held on the price tag and tried on his suit. It fit pretty well.

"You going for a swim now?" Roger asked. "You want to eat first?"

"No, later."

The boy raced down to the end of the pier and leaped off, tucking his legs up under him. His feet struck the bottom, churning up the thick, mucky silt of the lake bed. He paddled out to where it was deeper, where he hadn't clouded the water. Then he started swimming in earnest, sprinting parallel to the shore.

Roger watched him as he waited for the stove to heat up, amazed at the boy's strength and skill as a swimmer. He looked like an otter or some kind of cunning water animal. When the grill was ready he threw on four frankfurters, neatly slitting them lengthwise with his long-bladed Buck knife as soon as they started to sizzle.

Then he toasted the buns, turned down the fire and nudged Jimmy's to the side to keep warm. He got himself another beer from the car and climbed down the embankment to eat.

The old pier took off from a bank about four feet above the level of the water and ran out no more than ten yards into the lake. At the end of it a ramp descending into the water had mostly rotted away, leaving only the frame and a few broken boards lying across it. Between the embankment at the foot of the pier and the shoreline was a narrow strip of black, gummy beach strewn with rocks and pebbles.

Roger cleared a few of the stones and sat down with his back against the low, earthen wall. The beer was warm by now and not very refreshing. He studied his son frolicking in the water with a curious mixture of pride and detachment. He had the indefatigable energy of a twelve-year-old but he moved through the water with athletic grace. It was hard to realize that boy was his child. Unexpectedly, he thought of Marty, his eldest son, who died in the water.

He passed his hands impatiently in front of his eyes, brushing the image away, and chucked the half-empty beer can into the lake. He watched it bob to the surface and come to rest.

After a while Jimmy toweled off, got his lunch and sat down next to his father to eat. Between bites he chattered enthusiastically about his swimming. He swam fast, didn't he? How many laps would he have done if he were in the pool? But Roger wasn't in an admiring mood anymore. Soon Jimmy realized that his father wasn't interested and stopped talking.

Roger stretched out on his back, cradling his head on his arms. Jimmy picked up a rock and flipped it desultorily toward the pier. It hit one of the pillars with a loud, hollow thump and knocked a chunk of decayed wood into the water. He threw a few more but missed. Then he started getting the range again.

"Cut it out," Roger said sleepily after four in a row had found their target. "It's driving me crazy."

After a few minutes Jimmy got up, looking around for something to do. He went back to the car and peeled off his damp suit, putting on his cut-offs and T-shirt again. Then he cooked himself another hot dog. He carried it down to the beach, taking the Buck knife with him. He sat down near his father and started idly carving a series of trenches in the ground with the knife.

"You sleeping, Dad?" he asked softly after a while.

"No."

"Are we gonna have to go back on Friday so you can pick up your check?"

"Probably. I don't know. It's a long time till Friday."

"If you don't pick it up when you're supposed to, can you get the money later?" The trenches grew rapidly into a set of concentric boxes or moats. He was the king and he lived in this castle surrounded by moats. He planted the knife in the center, point up, and began deepening the lines with his fingers.

"You lose your eligibility for that week," Roger said, "but they add another week on at the end if you still need it. The thing is, if you get a job before the unemployment runs out, then you've lost that money."

Jimmy thought he understood. "Are you gonna get another job pretty soon?"

"I don't know. I suppose I'll have to."

"You gonna go back to the garage?"

"No way," Roger said, sitting up suddenly. There was an odd note of sadness in the way he said it that made Jimmy almost feel sorry for him. Roger stretched out toward his cigarettes. With his body still turned he said, as if he were talking to himself, "Besides, I wouldn't work with that fucking Haller."

He said it so softly that the boy hardly heard him. But Jimmy knew that Haller was the man his parents had been fighting about last night. His mother had called him Glen and that's when Roger had hit her. She screamed, "Glen! Glen! Glen! Glen! Glen!" and he could hear him slapping her each time until she stopped. Then he heard them whispering for a while but couldn't make out the words.

He wanted to say something but couldn't think what. Roger blew out smoke in a long stream. "You know who Haller is, Jim?" he asked.

Jimmy resumed his digging, suddenly feeling his skin heating up. "I think so," he said tentatively. He sensed that his father was waiting for him to say something, that he wanted him to take his side. But the right words didn't come. "Is he why you and Mom were fighting?" he finally said.

Roger snorted sharply through his nose. The question took him unaware. "No," he said after a moment in a strangely subdued voice. "I really don't give a shit what she does. You know that? She's just a cunt like the rest of them."

He sounded hurt, not angry. Jimmy nodded but he didn't know what his father meant. He thought about that funny girl in the ninth grade who all the kids said was mentally retarded but really wasn't. She took off her pants and let the boys look at her pussy for a quarter. Almost everyone knew she did it. Some of the girls even made jokes about her as a way of getting you to stop if you tried to get fresh with them. Anyway, a couple months ago Howie Gerber dared him so he gave this girl a dollar and talked her into letting him stick his finger all the way up. Once he had it in he started pinching and wouldn't let go until she gave him back the dollar. Howie said she could never tell on him because she'd have to admit what she'd been doing.

He felt a tightening in the back of his throat. Mom wasn't like that.

Roger repeated it, this time in acid tones. "She's just a cunt, you know that? You know what that means?"

Jimmy swallowed hard. "No."

"No," Roger mimicked. "No, you don't know what that means." He stared at the boy suspiciously for a full minute, then lay back down looking straight into the sky. Jimmy didn't know what to do. It seemed as if ages had passed until he heard Roger's voice, sounding soft and far away.

"No," he said, referring to what they were talking about earlier. "I think I'll look for a job in Chicago this time."

Jimmy tensed up inside. "Why Chicago?" he asked, trying to sound natural.

"No reason. Change my luck maybe."

Jimmy shrugged his shoulders reflexively. He was afraid of what his father would say if they kept talking about it.

"Yeah," Roger said, drawing the syllable out in a long sign. "You know that song, Jim, 'Goin' to Chicago, sorry but I can't take you'?" He sang the words in a thin, mocking falsetto.

Jimmy sprang to his feet. "I can go with you," he pleaded, his eyes registering the depth of his hurt. What had made him believe that his father really wanted him?

"Bullshit. You'll stay with your mother."

"I'll take care of myself," the boy whined. "Why can't I go?"

"I told you. You'll stay with your mother."

There was nothing to say. Jimmy ran blindly down the beach, his eyes filled with tears. When he reached the point, he wheeled around and screamed, "Fuck you! Fuck you! I don't want to go with you!" Standing there, trembling with a small boy's malignant rage, he heard the words float back to him tauntingly across the water.

Roger didn't look at him. He cupped both hands behind his head in a show of calculated indifference.

Jimmy stopped yelling. He couldn't reach his father by screaming at him. He hopped the bank, no more than a foot high at that point, and ran off into the woods. This wasn't the first time he saw that his father really didn't care about him. He accepted his father's temper—he had learned to accept it—but when he stopped caring it was a different story. It hurt with the kind of pain that would never go away.

Instinctively, the boy reacted with mindless rage. But that only helped for a minute and left him feeling emptied and alone. Soon he'd make himself forget what his father had done but each time it happened was like a permanent scab and each new wound reopened all the others. Somewhere inside him grew the knowledge that his father's coldness was genuine, not an occasional aberration. Now, as calmly as if he were ordering breakfast, he said he'd move to Chicago and leave him behind.

He stopped running. The big jackknife was open in his fist. Deliberately, he plunged the blade as deep as he could drive it into the bark of a tree. As he tried to force it in deeper the downward thrust of his hand pulled it closed, nearly cutting his palm. He didn't care if it did.

He wrenched the knife from the tree and raced on. Maybe he wouldn't come back. Then his father would have to go looking for him. If he got lost and his father found him, it would be just like before.

No. The truth was that his father didn't care about any of them. Not his mother—he had just said so. Not him—he was going to leave him in Arlington when he went away. Not even Marty, though he sometimes pretended he did now that Marty was dead. But Jimmy had been home that night when they had been arguing. Then Marty threw something at his father and ran out of the house. Roger made his mother clean it up and got in his car and went after him. He came back in a couple of hours, unable to find him. Marty had drowned himself. Two days later the police found his body in the river.

Jimmy picked up a large rock and heaved it as hard as he could. *That's* how much he loved Marty! he thought. A family of jays broke from the trees and circled overhead, screeching their alarm. He threw another. *That's* how much he loves Mom! And then a third and a fourth and a fifth.

The last one crashed down through the branches and struck something metal. It sounded like an explosion. Jimmy froze. The silence of the woods after so loud a noise suddenly seemed ominous. Something told him to run but he fought down the impulse. He wanted to see what he had hit.

He stole forward cautiously a few steps, then stopped again. He had caught a glimpse of something dark and shiny through the thick foliage—a car, he thought. What was a car doing out here?

His body tensed involuntarily. A car meant people. Holding his breath, he listened for any sound of movement. He expected the owner to pounce on him at any second. How much damage had he done?

For a full two minutes he held perfectly still. If there's anyone out there, he decided, he isn't moving either.

Or else he was circling around on him noiselessly through the woods.

Staying motionless, the boy was vulnerable to surprise. He still wanted a look at that car. Finally he began creeping forward, angling toward the edge of the clearing, where he could see in all directions.

He was just a few feet from the embankment. There hadn't been a sound from behind him, from the direction of the car. The bright light glinting off the lake stabbed at him in the darkness under the trees, blinding him momentarily. But there was no one in the water.

He took a deep breath and stepped into the clearing.

The sight of the car in the open hit him like an unexpected thunderclap. It was an enormous blue Lincoln sitting preposterously in the middle of the forest. Where his rock had hit it atop the right fender the paint had exploded, leaving a huge, ugly crater the russet color of the primer coat. The dent looked garish and absurd on that highly polished surface, like a moustache painted on a woman's picture.

Inside him, something snapped and all his pent-up feelings burst forth in a cackle of hysterical laughter. He grabbed a stone and flung it impulsively at one of the headlights. It missed, ricocheting off the chrome with the loud ping of a rifle. The next one skipped along the fender, carving a long, deep furrow.

He couldn't stop. He fired stone after stone, his nameless fury spending itself in violent action. He kept it up long after he had smashed both headlights.

After a while it became a game. Eventually he ran out of good-sized rocks. The ones he threw were too large to aim accurately or were clods of hard earth that shattered on impact, forming dark blotches on the grill.

Finally he quit. He plopped down wearily on the ground, then rolled onto his back, his head turned to the car. Its front end was a mess and his arm hurt like crazy. He lay there quietly a minute or so, rubbing his aching shoulder. Then he began chuckling silently. His humor fed on itself, gathering momentum until he pulled his legs up in a ball, rocking deliriously from side to side. Still his voiceless laughter poured out uncontrollably, sounding almost like sobs.

⊄ ⊄ ⊄

Kay Orben strode rapidly along the trail, ducking down sometimes and using her shoulder to ward off the branches. She had told Doug that she needed time to think but thinking, it turned out, was the last thing she wanted to do. It always came back to the same thing—it was wrong to do that with a boy unless you loved him, and you couldn't love a boy you just met. That made sense but it didn't change the fact that those moments by the stream had been—what? Well, had been wonderful. Still, she couldn't shake the notion that she was supposed to feel guilty.

So the argument ran on in circles, always coming back to the same place. The fast girls, she concluded drolly, have it much easier. It would be nice to be able to do what you want without worrying about the rights and wrongs of it. She'd have to see Doug again. Next time she'd keep the brakes on and see what was really going on between them.

She dropped down to the shore and walked along the water's edge where the ground was soft and spongy underfoot. Soon she saw the old wooden pier she had noticed earlier while walking with Doug. She quickened her pace again, knowing she didn't have far to go.

Roger was in the water. He saw her walking toward him a good distance away. Impulsively, he swam under the pier. There was something vaguely titillating about hiding there, watching her when she had no idea she was being observed.

She was tall and her hips turned with a kind of easy, unconscious sensuality as she closed the distance between them. But her slim frame made her look very young, almost like a child. He wondered what she was doing, walking around the lake by herself.

He wrapped an arm around one of the pillars. She was pretty, he saw as she came closer. Her face moved expressively, as if she were thinking to herself. How come she's alone? he thought. A nice piece like that—and what's she so worked up about?

She hadn't seen him yet. With each step she took he felt his body grow more tense.

She paused when she got near the clearing, looking around to see who belonged to the station wagon. There was no one in sight. She frowned for a second, adjusting the tote bag on her shoulder and shifting the blanket under her arm. Now Roger studied her smallish breasts poking gently under her baggy sweatshirt. She had fine hips and long, skinny legs that looked pinkish from the sun. She was no more than fifty yards away. He decided he'd talk to her.

When she drew even with the pier Roger hurled himself into the open with a loud splash. The noise startled Kay. She gasped and pivoted toward him.

He swam two or three strokes on his back, pretending not to notice her. "Oh," he said when he finally turned to the shore, "I didn't know anyone was there."

She laughed, a little embarrasssed. "I didn't know you were there either."

He came out of the water with elongated strides. "I was under the pier," he said, gesturing to the spot. "I like to swim there." They were standing face to face.

Kay nodded noncommittally. His last remark left her nothing to say. She shifted her weight uncomfortably from one foot to the other. There was something strange about the way he looked at her. When he showed no sign of wanting to continue the conversation, she opened her mouth to say good-bye.

"What's your name?" Roger asked quickly, anticipating her.

"Kay. Kay Orben."

"I'm Roger Mapes." He extended his hand.

The formality of the gesture nonplussed her momentarily but she caught herself and shook hands with him. "You must be Jimmy's father," she said.

"Yes. How do you know Jimmy?"

"I don't, really. He goes to school with my brother."

"I see. Are they in the same grade?"

"No. I don't think so. I don't know." Petey had mentioned Jimmy Mapes but she had the impression he was a year or two older. At any rate they weren't good friends.

He kept looking at her. "Is Jimmy with you?" she asked after a few seconds, thankful to have found something to talk about. She didn't know how to break away. He was like a caller who won't let you hang up.

The question seemed to take him by surprise. He swivelled his head around as if he were looking for the answer, looking for the boy in the trees or the water. "No," he said, "I mean, yes, he's around here someplace." He felt lightheaded, like he had no control over what he was doing, but underneath was a strange, catlike sureness. "He went to the refreshment stand awhile ago. You didn't happen to see him, did you?" His eyes looked northward over her shoulder. She had come from the opposite direction.

"No, I didn't," Kay said. "The refreshment stand at the beach?"

"I guess so. It's the only one, isn't it?"

"I came the other way, from down there," she said. She didn't like telling him that. Something in his manner put her on guard, as if he was fencing with her, and she felt instinctively that she was giving him an advantage.

Roger noted her discomfort. Suddenly it rankled him, not knowing what she'd been up to.

"I see," he said, nodding significantly. "What're you doing, camping with your family down there?"

She felt herself blush. It's none of **your** business, she wanted to say. But that would give it away, the same as a confession. "No," she said warily. "I just went to the beach. My car's over there."

"The public beach?"

"I . . . uh . . . I walked the long way around the lake."

Roger smirked, pondering her response. "That's nice," he said. "I like to do that myself sometimes. Take a long walk . . . all by myself."

His gaze had fastened on her eyes. She compressed her lips and nodded slightly. I have to go, she told herself. He has no right to cross-examine me like this.

Don't lie to me! his eyes blazed at her.

She felt that he read what was in her mind. That's what it was that bothered her about him—those eyes, the way they looked right through her.

"There . . . there was someone with me," she murmured, not knowing why she told him.

I'll bet there was! The words exploded in his brain. He saw the whole scene, sharp and clear as a picture taken by lightning. Of course—there was someone with you! So that's your dirty little secret!

". . . But he went back the other way," she went on needlessly.

Roger grinned in triumph. Next she'll be giving me all the details, he thought.

He waited for her, not saying anything. Again, she had a chance to leave but she didn't. He sensed a current passing between them, holding her as firmly as if she were bound. He had to be careful. He wanted a cigarette but he couldn't risk turning away.

His tongue flicked rapidly over his lips. "D'you come down here often?" he asked. "You seem to be pretty familiar with the lake."

"Fairly often. This is the first time this year," she answered warily, as if studying the question for some secret meaning.

"You got a bad sunburn."

Her eyes fell self-consciously to her bare midriff. In her brief bikini pants she felt almost undressed. Why couldn't she just say she was late for dinner or something?

Before she looked up, Jimmy rounded the point about two hundred yards away. He saw his father talking to someone and stopped quickly, thinking at first it might be the owner of the car come to ask questions. But that was impossible.

Kay heard the footsteps and turned. "Oh, it's Jimmy," she said, her relief all too apparent. Now she could finally break away.

Over her shoulder, Roger beckoned Jimmy to come forward. Whatever had been happening between him and the girl, it was over now. He felt dissatisfied. She stood with her face still averted as they watched the boy stride toward them together.

"I guess you have to go," Roger muttered quietly.

She looked at him in surprise. There was a different, almost uncertain note in his voice. "Yes," she said, "I'm late for dinner already."

He nodded curtly.

Again, she didn't know what to say. She wasn't used to feeling ill-at-ease. Finally she just turned on her heels and walked away. All the way down the beach she could feel him watching her.

"Who was that?" Jimmy said appreciatively when he came up to his father. Roger was still staring after the girl, who had not yet vanished around the point.

"A girl. Kay something."

"Petey's sister?"

"Somebody's sister."

Jimmy sucked in noisily through his teeth. "I think it's her car," he said. He told his father briefly what had happened in the clearing.

Roger didn't seem to be listening. "Why'd you do that to a friend's car?" he asked abstractedly when Jimmy finished his story. The boy expected more of a response.

"He's not really a friend," he shrugged. "I didn't recognize it anyway."

Roger kept watching the girl. He seemed lost in thought. A few seconds later she was out of sight. Suddenly he bolted to the station wagon. He paused, momentarily confused, then pulled on his pants over his swim trunks.

Jimmy followed him, his eyebrows raised inquisitively. "What're you gonna do?" he asked.

Roger looked at him oddly. "You'll see," he said. "Let's go. I'm not sure."

He raced up the path they had taken from the highway. Jimmy ran after him. When they had gone about a hundred yards Roger stopped abruptly and looked back to check how far he was from the beach. Satisfied, he took off into the woods, crashing heedlessly through the undergrowth and holding both elbows up in front of his face for protection. Jimmy struggled to keep up. The spiny ferns underfoot scratched his legs painfully. He figured his father was going to do something about the car but he didn't know what.

Suddenly Roger slowed down and began moving stealthily, signaling behind his back for Jimmy to make as little noise as possible. It was like the time they'd gone hunting. They watched where they stepped and eased the branches out of their way without rustling the leaves.

Roger stuck out his arm. "There it is," he whispered. At first Jimmy didn't see the blue Lincoln. Going straight through the woods it was closer than he expected.

They inched forward carefully, circling the clearing. They had gotten there before the girl. Roger put his hand on Jimmy's shoulder.

Kay's first thought when she stepped into the clearing was, How didn't I see that I had scratched the car that badly? Then she saw it wasn't just scratched. There were deep gouges and dents all over the front end and both headlights had been broken. Her heart sunk inside her. How could someone have done this? It had to be deliberate!

It crossed her mine briefly that Jimmy Mapes did it but she didn't pursue the idea. No, it was all her own fault. She had left the car in the woods where there was no one to watch it. Her father would blame her as much as if she had thrown the rocks herself. Why did she have to stay at Lake Barrett if the parking lot was full? Why didn't she just drop off Marian and come home? That boy was the reason. And while they . . . While she was with him someone ruined her father's car.

She began to cry, not because she'd be punished but because it was so vicious and incomprehensible an act. Someone had taken a beautiful car and simply destroyed it.

Anyway, she had to get home. She sighed and laid her blanket and tote bag on the roof to fish out her keys. She unlocked the door and pulled it open slowly.

Roger's arm shot past her shoulder and slammed it back shut. She whirled around and started to scream but he clapped his hand over her mouth, stifling the sound. As she struggled to get free, her eyes bulging with terror, he leaned his body hard against her, pinning her to the car. It was useless trying to squirm away. She dug her nails into his shoulders with all her strength, drawing deep welts down his back, but she couldn't make him let go.

Then Jimmy's face appeared over his father's shoulder, examining her as indifferently as if she were a specimen under a microscope. His eyes were just like his father's. The faintest trace of a smile played on his lips. The horror of his blank expression tore through her like a grisly injury. Her eyes glazed with tears, blurring her vision. Jimmy grabbed her wrists in his young bony fingers and pried her hands from his father's back. Her nails clawed impotently at nothing. The hand over her mouth forced her head backward toward the roof of the car until it was all the way down, pinioned against the sheet metal. The pain in her back was excruciating.

She desperately tried jerking her head from side to side but it took less pressure now to keep it from moving. She was exhausted, drenched with sweat. If only she could get free for a second! If only they would let her say something! They were making a mistake! They had her confused with some other girl!

The boy handed Roger something and then he held the point of a knife between her eyes. "Get something to tie her up," Roger ordered. "Look in the trunk."

Jimmy yanked the car keys out of the door.

"I don't want you to make a sound!" Roger whispered fiercely.

Then he gradually eased off to let her stand up, keeping his hand firmly across her mouth as she rose.

When he let go there wasn't anything she could say. Her lips parted slightly, forming incoherent syllables, but there was no breath behind them. She heard something tear and Jimmy slapped a strip of adhesive tape across her mouth. It startled her and she tossed her head wildly in panic. Roger grabbed her by the jaw and held her still, staring in her eyes. "You don't want to scream," he explained soothingly. "It's for your own protection."

Jimmy put on three more strips of tape, covering her nose too. She couldn't breathe. Did they see that? What if they didn't realize? Her eyes sought out Roger, pleading with him to let her breathe.

"Now relax," he said. "You're going to suffocate." With the point of the blade he punctured the tape over her nostrils and enlarged the holes delicately. She held perfectly still, as if he were removing a speck from her eye.

Roger motioned to Jimmy and yanked her around by the shoulder. Jimmy pulled her hands behind her while Roger held the knife in front of her face as a reminder. The boy bound her hands with adhesive tape, gnarling it in his impatience so that it served more as a rope than a bandage.

The man wasn't holding her now but she didn't have the strength to run away. She knew they'd hurt her if she tried. What did they mean to do?

When Jimmy finished tying her up Roger peered over her shoulder to inspect the bindings. Then he put his hand on her chest, shoved her against the car and stepped back. "It won't do you any good to run," he said.

He severed the hem of her sweatshirt with the knife and ripped it up the front. She felt powerless to resist, as though she were watching a movie. They were doing it to someone else. He cut through the binding at the neck and then slit both arms, removing the garment completely. They were both standing close to her. Jimmy put his hand over her breast, pressing it hard into her ribs until it hurt. She closed her eyes tightly. He let go. Roger neatly severed the band under her bra and it fell apart. He pulled the straps down over her shoulders. Then he hopped up on the hood of the car, sitting beside her, and put his arm around her, resting his hand on her shoulder. She shivered when he touched her. He lay the blade of the knife flat across her throat.

Jimmy fondled her breasts more gently now, flicking her nipples with his fingernails. For the first time a wave of shame swept over her. She kept her eyes closed, hoping only to endure it.

"Go ahead, do it," Roger said evenly.

Jimmy stopped touching her and pulled off his swim trunks.

"Look!" Roger ordered. She didn't realize he was talking to her. "I want you to look. It's not going to hurt you."

She opened her eyes slowly. The man grasped her by the hair and pointed her head toward the boy. She didn't dare close her eyes again but refused to let the image register in her brain.

"What's the matter with you?" Roger snapped at the boy. He pressed the tip of the blade against the edge of Kay's nipple, indenting her breast until a drop of blood popped out. She felt the knife touching her breast but not the piercing of the skin. He wasn't holding her hair any more so she turned her head away.

Roger said, "Are you a virgin?"

Her jaw clenched. She knew it was a question but the meaning of it didn't sink in. He repeated it and she made no answer.

Roger leaned behind her and thrust his hand roughly into her bikini pants. Her body tightened in a spasm. Then he put his hand on her arm and shoved her to the ground. She landed hard on her shoulder and he rolled her onto her back, her wrists digging painfully into her spine. She tried to sit up but he pushed her back down. This time she opened her hands and turned her wrists. It didn't hurt as much.

The boy slid her suit down to her ankles and then his face hovered right over hers as he positioned his body over her. She felt him probing between her legs and clamped her muscles as tight as she could. She wouldn't let him! She poured all her strength into keeping herself tense, forcing herself to stare into his loathsome cold eyes. His hand went down against her, pushing hard. It hurt her unbearably, but she wouldn't relent. Finally he gave up and lowered himself on top of her. He began writhing, rubbing their groins together.

She exhaled deeply, letting her head fall exhaustedly to the side. The man bent over the front of the car, leaning forward with one elbow resting on the hood. He stared as if in a trance out over the trees and his lips were drawn back in a hideous grimace. Suddenly he darted behind the car. Then he was standing over the boy. He grabbed him by the shoulder and pulled him off her. "It doesn't take all day," he hissed.

The boy looked at him questioningly and stood up. He seemed almost relieved. Thank God, she thought, thank God! The tears poured from her eyes. Roger kneeled down beside her and looked in her face. His expression wasn't so cruel anymore.

"Go back to the car," he said to the boy, "and pack up all the stuff. Start the motor. Think you can turn it around? We better get out of here."

Jimmy nodded. He grabbed the first-aid kit he had found in the trunk and the roll of tape—his fingerprints were all over them. His father flipped him the keys to the station wagon. He tugged on his bathing suit and ran off.

Roger bent close to her. Please, please, no! her eyes implored. Have pity on me. He stroked her brow gently, pushing back her matted hair.

"You're never going to tell anyone what happened here," he said softly. "I'm serious about that."

She nodded, closing her eyes.

"All right."

He rolled her over onto her stomach and inserted the knife blade into the maze of tape between her wrists.

"Just lie here a few minutes after I'm gone. Okay?"

She nodded again. Just cut the tape, she thought. I'll never say anything, I promise.

She didn't feel anything as the blade sliced her skin, only something wet and warm against her back. He waited a few seconds and then ran away.

She was too frightened to move. He had told her to wait. When she was sure it was safe, she tried freeing her hands. They were still tied. Oh, Jesus, she thought, what can I do? She struggled to her knees but felt terribly weak. The blood ran down her buttocks and down the insides of her legs. She couldn't stop it. In a panic she got to her feet and started to run. At the beach someone would help her. But her bathing suit caught her ankles and she stumbled to the ground.

In a few minutes she'd try again. First she had to rest and gather her strength.

The door of the car was open when Roger raced up and the engine was running. Panting heavily, he slid behind the wheel and dropped the transmission into low, spinning the wheels on the dirt road as the car lurched into the woods.

Neither he nor Jimmy spoke. Roger stared straight ahead, biting his lip as he sped down the path. His right hand on the steering wheel still held the knife. When he got to the highway he turned south.

"Did you waste her?" Jimmy asked.

Roger's head darted toward him but his expression was fixed. He turned back to the road.

Jimmy slouched down in his seat, smirking complacently. "You had to," he said.

CHAPTER 5

" ' I s e e a l o t of unfamiliar faces," Sheriff Taliaferro said, scanning the crowd of reporters packed into the staff room, "so there's one thing I want to clear up right now. The name's pronounced Tolliver."

The remark helped break the tension. There was a murmur of politely approving laughter, a shifting of feet and scraping of chairs. Walt wanted these men on his side. The press had the power to make his job harder or easier. Which it would be depended on how he treated them and, above all, on how they judged his handling of the investigation. Right now he had little to give them that would appease them on either count. He knew of cops who had developed flamboyant personalities so that they'd make good copy even when they had little information to hand out. But that wasn't his style. He'd be courteous and professional, trusting them to see that he was cooperating as fully as possible.

He began the press conference with a prepared statement deploring the senseless murder of a seventeen-year-old girl and pledging the best efforts of the Sheriff's Department to apprehend her killer. Personally, he offered his condolences to the Orben family. The words sounded hollow and glib to him even as he said them. Then he briefed the press on the current status of the investigation. Hard facts were still meager and a few details had to be withheld so that no one but the killer would know them. It was a standard precaution for weeding out the would-be confessors who are always drawn to such crimes. All in all, he told the reporters nothing they didn't know already. He opened the floor to questions.

"That's not much, Walt."

"I know it."

"Do you have any leads?"

"We have several leads and we're checking them all thoroughly."

"Crank calls?"

"Mostly. But we won't know till we run 'em all down."

"No suspects?"

"No."

"What about the boyfriend? Have you cleared him?"

"No comment. . . . Of course we want to talk to him."

"You haven't yet?"

"Very briefly. And there's no special reason for that either. We'll be talking to him again shortly."

"Would you say this was the act of a maniac?"

"I wouldn't say that. A girl was killed—for no apparent reason. You have to ask yourself what kind of person would do something like that."

"He'd have to be a maniac. Isn't that what you're saying?"

Walt sucked on his unlit pipe. Most reporters tried to do their jobs honestly, just like he tried to do his, but this guy wasn't after a story. Whoever he was, all he wanted was a sensational headline: SHERIFF SAYS MANIAC SLEW KAY. The community was jumpy enough knowing the killer was still on the loose without any inflammatory statements from him.

"You can draw that conclusion," he finally said. "I won't argue with you." He noticed a few of the older reporters smile in grudging respect. Maybe they had him pegged for a small-time sheriff but he knew how to answer a question and still give them nothing they could use.

"Why'd the killer wreck the car?"

"You're asking the wrong person. I'd just be speculating. For that matter, why did he kill her?"

"Are you asking me?"

"Sure—if you can tell me."

The reporters laughed again. It was obvious they weren't going to get much from the sheriff. They'd have to gear their stories to the fact that after two days there was still no break in the Orben case.

"Was rape the motive, Walt?"

"I assume so. The girl's purse—her tote bag—wasn't touched. Right now we're ruling out robbery."

"I understand that. But there are other kinds of sexual abuse."

This time the sheriff paused to light his pipe. Reporters were always on the lookout for just that kind of lurid detail but Walt knew Hilt Greave well enough to guess that he wasn't on a fishing expedition. He had found out something he wasn't supposed to know.

Walt and Hilton had run into each other off and on since they spent the waning days of the Korean war together at Fort Sill, planning the civilian careers that eventually brought them to this room. In a sense, both achieved what they wanted. But for some reason Hilt never left Iowa in spite of all his drive and ambition. He could easily have parlayed his reputation as an investigative reporter into a prestigious job on a big paper, but he evidently preferred to spend his life uncovering those minor, parochial abuses that nobody particularly wanted to see uncovered. Maybe his initial successes came too easily. In any case, sending him down from Des Moines to report on a criminal investigation was like hiring a brilliant surgeon to perform a tonsillectomy. From the moment Walt saw him hanging around yesterday morning, he knew that Hilt would make a nuisance of himself.

Now he knew how. The Department's official release on the killing confined itself to the bare statement that the assailant had tried unsuccessfully to rape the girl, as evidenced by contusions in her pubic area, and that she had resisted fiercely. Small particles of flesh had been found under her fingernails. Naturally, the press had a field day with this material, depicting Kay as a martyr to old-fashioned virtue. It was crassly exploitive, but that didn't bother Walt. He imagined that her family at least drew a small measure of solace from the stories, no matter how cynical the motivation behind them.

But from an investigator's point of view it was a dead end. Police files were full of rapists, virtually any one of whom might, under the right conditions, kill his prey. What intrigued Walt from the outset, however, was the tiny, superficial puncture mark at the edge of the girl's left nipple. It might be some sort of symbolic or ritual wound. He didn't want to get carried away with bizarre theories but whatever the killer's reason for inflicting so unusual an injury, it amounted, quite possibly, to his personal signature. It had to be kept secret. With so little to go on, Walt couldn't afford to let his man know that he had spotted a peculiarity in his M.O. So far it was the only card he held. But Hilt had managed to pry it out of someone—the coroner perhaps, or one of his own deputies.

"I won't have the official coroner's report until tomorrow," Walt hedged in answer to the question. "But as far as I'm concerned, I'd say the attempted rape is the most significant indication of sexual abuse."

" 'Most significant indication,' " Hilt snapped. "What the hell does that mean?" The sheriff wasn't giving him even an oblique confirmation and there was no way to force the issue without sharing his prize with every reporter in the room.

"Well, she was found nude," Walt said blandly. "I'd say that's a sexual abuse." He pointed to someone else immediately, inviting him to ask his question. Hilt glared at him truculently throughout the rest of the press conference.

As the reporters filed out past him, jostling to get through the narrow doorway, Walt gestured to Hilton. "Still remember how to find my office?" he said. "Give me ten minutes."

Walt minced no words. "I'm not gonna let you print that," he said before Hilt even sat down. "You know the reason. You shouldn't have it anyway."

"Sorry, Walt. I wanted a confirmation but I don't need it. My source is reliable."

Walt leaned back in his swivel chair and ran his hand wearily around his face. He was near the point of exhaustion. The call to report to Lake Barrett came less than half an hour after he had wrapped up that foolish Andreassen business. The kid, it turned out, was the only one who hadn't been lost. He had wandered off into the woods to take a leak. Then, instead of returning to his family at the beach, he went straight to the car, plopped down in the back seat and fell asleep. No one thought to look for him there. For over five hours Walt directed search parties, interviewed almost everyone who had seen an unattended child, and did what he could to keep the mother from going off the deep end. They'd probably still be combing the woods for the boy if Walt hadn't finally prevailed on Mr. Andreassen to take her to a nearby motel for a few hours' rest.

It would have been funny except that he wasn't quite home when the choked voice of a deputy came over the radio telling him he'd better get out to Lake Barrett, south of the beach. They had a body.

That was Saturday evening. Since then he'd had only a few hours' sleep. There was a limit to how many nitroglycerine pills he was supposed to take.

"I don't imagine you'll tell me who your source is," he said resignedly, not expecting an answer. "I have a pretty good idea, though. But I'm not gonna box with you, Hilt. You're talking about a story, I'm talking about a killer. There might be a file on him somewhere and we can make him on this breast thing. It could be one of those subconscious acts. Maybe he's asking us to find him. It's happened before."

Hilt seemed unimpressed. "You're guessing," he said.

"I'm hoping. We don't have much else. Just sit on it a couple days. It's not that great an item anyway."

"I'll see. What'll you give me instead?"

Walt pondered. "I got nothing to give you."

"The boyfriend? What do you have on him?"

Walt waved his hand dismissively, his mind moving immediately to another track. Suddenly he didn't mind that Hilt was a reporter, he just wanted to talk to an old and perceptive friend. "Let me tell you what's bothering me—off the record," he said, musing out loud. "I don't even know if I'm thinking straight anymore. Start with the girl. I can understand her struggling. That's only natural. But the tape over her nose was slit very carefully, so she could breathe. The thing is, the knife didn't even nick her. And the cut on her wrist is clean as a whistle. Now how's that consistent with putting up a fight?"

Hilt raised his eyebrows. "Nah," he said cynically. "I wondered the same thing myself. But I got a teen-age daughter. Rape, Walt. You know the kids these days—it's not a fate worse than death anymore. My daughter says she'd resist as long as she thought she could scare him away but after that she'd give in."

"Sure. But she *didn't* give in. She didn't . . ."

There was a tap at the door and a sergeant stepped in without waiting to be invited.

"Here are those reports, Tolly."

"Thanks. Anything there?"

He had asked that the Lake Barrett employees be interrogated to see if they had noticed anything, however trivial, that in retrospect might be helpful. Maybe some man had been hanging around the bathhouse or watching Kay—or any girl—with unusual interest.

"It don't look it," the sergeant said. "Guy had too much beer, got a little loud—manager threw him out, had his buddy drive him home. The parking lot guy says a little kid gave him the finger or something 'cause the lot was full. That kind of thing."

Walt hastily scanned the reports. The usual petty traumas of a busy Saturday at the beach. Four badly typed pages. Officer's name. Subject of interview. Time of interview. Summary of information. Remarks—left blank. Signature. It was all there in correct form—another probe and another dry hole.

He flipped the reports to the corner of his desk. "Well," he said, drawing the word out wearily, "see if you can find the drunk guy's name. It won't help but at least we'll cover our asses when they start saying we haven't done anything."

The sergeant started to say something but just nodded and left.

"She didn't give in," Walt said after a minute, throwing himself back into the discussion with Hilt as though there had been no interruption. "She didn't let him penetrate. That's what's got me going in circles." He lowered his voice. "She wasn't a virgin, Hilt—and don't you dare print that! Still, she fights off a rapist to the point that it costs her her life—but when he actually goes to kill her there's not a sign of a struggle."

"Maybe she's not the reason he couldn't penetrate. Maybe he's impotent."

Walt snorted. So Hilt's source had been Jim Godfrey, the tight-assed little coroner, just as he thought. That fucker—he should have been a veterinarian, not a doctor! If Hilt's information had come from anyone in the Sheriff's Department, he would also have been told about the smear an observant deputy found on the grill of the car. The lab confirmed that it was semen. Obviously Hilt didn't know that or he would have mentioned it now.

Walt wasn't about to tell him. He picked up on Hilt's hypothesis, leaving out the fact that the killer had masturbated. "Sorry, Hilt. Something just crossed my mind. Where were we? When he tries to rape her he can't get it up. He gets so infuriated he kills her in a rage. Is that how it works?"

"Yeah. And smashes the car. A big Lincoln—symbol of virility."

"Beautiful," Walt laughed sarcastically. "Only he didn't kill her in a rage. It was the most cold-blooded and deliberate thing I ever saw. The way he destroyed that car, you'd figure he'd hack her to pieces."

Hilt shrugged disinterestedly. "You're right, it is strange," he said. "He might be a split personality. You know, Jekyll and Hyde."

Walt bit on his knuckles. He felt stymied. "I never heard of that. A man with two personalities—*both* of them murderous, violent—but in different ways."

Hilt seemed to be getting bored with what promised to be an endless round of analysis and speculation. It was an odd thing that

Walt had noticed throughout their conversation. Here was a top investigative reporter but he didn't seem to have any of the cop's instinctive curiosity about people, about what made them do the things they did. He only cared about facts, the details that made up the story.

"Maybe he's got six personalities," Hilt said crankily, "and only two of them are violent. Maybe he once bought a Lincoln and it turned out to be a lemon. How do I know what's in his mind? Now what can you give me on the boyfriend?"

"Yeah. I talked to him yesterday for a couple minutes. He's not the type. Good-looking, decent kid. Well spoken. Should have no problems with girls."

Hilt stood up, reaching behind himself for the door. "Maybe she's the first one who said no to him. Think about it, Walt. It's the ones who aren't the type who are always the type."

Walt smiled. Hilt had a point, and the investigation was certainly getting nowhere following the few other leads. "That's why I'm gonna talk to him again," he said. But he wasn't optimistic.

CHAPTER 6

By late Sunday afternoon the Mapeses had passed St. Louis, angling to the west along the winding channel of the Meramec River. They camped off the road where the bank had been leveled in constructing a bridge. They could get water from the river, which was all they needed. The campsites the state ran offered better facilities but they were always crowded with nature lovers elaborately equipped for life in the wild. Jimmy and Roger intended simply to sleep next to the car on ground still soft and comfortable from spring floods.

But the mosquitoes came after dark as the two of them sat sipping beers that had lost their chill and listening to the tiny, animal sounds of nightfall. Not wanting to leave, they took cover in the back of the station wagon.

In the morning they started driving again, as aimlessly as before. Neither had yet said a word about what happened at Lake Barrett. The car radio was broken and they hadn't seen a newspaper. Nevertheless, the secret was never far from their thoughts. For Roger it was like an unspeakable oath, all the more powerful because it couldn't be mentioned. He had never understood the violence of his own nature. Now that the boy was part of it he watched him warily with a strange, detached curiosity that tempered his usual indifference.

The boy, amazingly, seemed to have no feelings whatsoever. But then he had never looked at the girl with the knowledge that she would die. For Roger, there was this instant—he wasn't sure how long it really was—between the time he cut her wrist and her realization of what he had done. In that moment he was the only person in the world who knew what would happen to her. He couldn't get it out of his mind. The scene was bathed in clear light as though everything suddenly, lucidly, came together. He couldn't remember now what it was he saw, just that he had seen something. It troubled him.

The hot weather seemed to be following them, growing more intense by the day. Before they broke camp Jimmy washed in the shallow, bracing waters under the bridge. The current was surprisingly swift but not very strong. He lathered himself meticulously, even his hair. Feeling clean when they started driving made the heat actually pleasant. He was shirtless and it didn't take long to build up enough sweat so that his back slithered exquisitely against the plastic seat covers whenever he moved.

"How bad you get bit?" Jimmy said. There were about a dozen small red welts on his arms and they were starting to itch.

"Not too bad," Roger said. "Don't scratch 'em."

"I know." A minute later he was scratching unconsciously. "You know what?" he said. "I bet they're not even looking for us."

Roger nodded. "No way they're looking for us. I was thinking about that yesterday. See, there's nothing to connect us with the girl or put us anywhere near that lake."

"Except Fatso at the parking lot."

"But Fatso's gonna say we left hours before." They were both beaming. It couldn't have gone any better if they had planned it. Roger continued talking about how safe they were but Jimmy stopped paying attention. He still didn't know how his father had done it. But he hadn't yet made up his mind to ask. It was fascinating just thinking about it, trying to imagine how it came down.

"What'd you do with the first-aid kit?"

"Huh?"

"The first-aid kit? You throw it in the lake?"

"Yeah." It was where he had gotten the adhesive tape with which he bound the girl. He kept the roll of tape. "What did it feel like?" he asked. Now that they were talking he had to know.

Roger considered the question a minute. It was hard to describe. There was too much involved that he didn't want to get into. "What did what feel like?" he finally said.

Jimmy decided to let it drop for a while but soon his curiosity got the better of him. "How did you do it?" he asked, trying to keep his tone neutral.

"I did it. What difference does it make? You want to write a book about it?"

"Was it exciting?"

No, not really, Roger thought. It was like fucking a woman when you're drunk or tired. You feel it all right but kind of through a screen. There's a screen between you and what it feels like. "I told you, it doesn't matter. It's over and done with. At least I did something. You didn't do anything."

Jimmy flushed. He knew what his father was talking about.

"You didn't get in her, did you?" Roger persisted.

"Sure I did."

"Bullshit. You didn't get in her. She wasn't even cherry."

"Forget it," Jimmy said sharply. He wasn't going to let his father keep taunting him. He could go on endlessly once he got started.

"You brought it up," Roger said, but he had no interest in pursuing it further. "They'll find it, you know. The kit," he said after a while. "Your prints are all over it."

"They're on the car too," Jimmy shrugged.

"It doesn't matter," Roger finally decided. "They don't have anything to match them with."

They ate lunch on the move, just about finishing the groceries Roger had bought in Timmons. There wasn't much money either, twenty dollars or so. Roger didn't stop Saturday night to cash the check. Of course there was nothing to prevent them from going home now. They weren't afraid. But, without discussing it, both sensed that they had cut their ties with Arlington. The money would take care of itself.

The Ozarks changed abruptly from deep, twisting valleys to a region of high, rolling plateaus that looked like the farmland around Arlington. The farms were noticeably poorer though and the towns looked worn and dreary. Apparently there were mines of some kind in the neighborhood. They didn't see any, but there were signs here and there pointing to a mining office and some of the side roads were posted.

They stopped for gas at a Skelly station at the edge of one of the anonymous towns that popped up along the road. Roger bought two Cokes from an ancient machine that held the bottles upright by their necks.

"Your fan belt's shot," the attendant said to Roger, calling him over. He was a stocky man whose brown, heavily lined face gave no clue to his age.

Roger took a look at the belt. When he pushed down on it, cracks opened almost all the way through. "You got one for this car?" he asked.

"Prob'ly."

"Fine. You mind if I borrow some tools?"

"You a mechanic?" the man asked, scratching his neck thoughtfully.

"Yup."

"Makes no diff'ence. I won't charge you none for labor. Might as well have me do it."

Roger didn't know if he was being generous or if he was fussy about lending his tools. "Thanks," he said.

"No point your gettin' your clothes all dirty." The man found an inordinate amount of humor in the observation. His own coveralls, which he wore over a sleeveless undershirt, looked like they were scrubbed regularly but to little effect. He motioned for Roger to follow him out behind the station, where fifteen to twenty cars and trucks lay on the ground in various states of decomposition.

"They'll be six, seven there'll fitcha."

"You don't have a new one?" Roger asked skeptically.

The man didn't answer directly. "They gotta be better'n whatcha got now."

They began opening hoods, where there were hoods, to inspect the fan belts. The mechanic found one that looked pretty good. "Folks around here take care of their cars," he observed, "so ev'ything don't go out at once. Can't get parts off a city car like you can here."

"I'm not from the city," Roger said. The guy seemed to be quizzing him obliquely, out of a general suspicion of outsiders.

The mechanic said the job would take him about forty minutes. Roger and Jimmy walked into town, just to get a closer look. Old men with nothing to do sat in front of stores that had no customers. They noticed the strangers and seemed to pull away without really moving. The place was so depressing it was almost comical. It was like an overdone movie version of hard times with all the details copied too perfectly. When they got back to the garage the mechanic was checking the timing with a strobe. It surprised Roger that he had one.

Jimmy went out back to prowl around among the cars in the yard.

"Car needs a lot of work," the man in the coveralls said. "You a mechanic, you shouldn't let it get like this." In his indirect way he was challenging Roger's description of himself.

"Well, I been out of work. The boss kept my tools." Actually, he hadn't gone to pick them up. The thought flashed briefly through his mind that he'd ask the man for a job, maybe because he'd seen the picture where Johnny Garfield does that on the late show a few weeks ago. He rejected the idea as soon as he formed it—though it might be a kick to live in a town like this for a month or so. In any case, there was no point working for a guy who didn't charge for labor.

"You lookin' for work?" The mechanic stood up, squinting searchingly into Roger's face. "Ever done any mining?"

"No thanks."

"Tha's the way I figger. It's bad work. But I done it sometimes—when I hadn't no choice."

"I wasn't planning on staying around here long. Is that hotel in town open?" Roger wasn't eager to start driving again. The place'd be cheap and he could use a night off from the mosquitoes.

"Yuh. When someone wants to stay. It's clean though."

"Good enough." Roger laughed uncomfortably. "You don't suppose I could find a woman around here?"

"What'sa matter with your'n? The boy got a mother, don't he?"

"It's a long story," Roger said dryly. "You the preacher here on Sundays, is that it?"

The man ignored the remark. "Yeah, we got a house, what they call it. It's way over to Welles though."

"I don't want to pay for it."

The man cocked his head suspiciously. On principle he didn't like the idea of outsiders messing with local women. "Then I'd recommend the roadhouse," he said anyway. "But I can't guarantee nothin'."

"Where's that?"

"The roadhouse? Right past town. When the mines are busy a lot of women got nothing to do. Men work nights, an' it ain't the kind of work as leaves you in the mood."

"The mines busy now?" Roger smiled mischievously.

"Purty busy."

The hotel had been built in an earlier age when people came to use the spas and mineral springs that dotted the area. Now the few that still functioned offered newer accommodations. But the hotel stayed open because the woman who owned it, a widow, had nothing better to do. She still served food and liquor downstairs anyway. The lobby suggested a shabby elegance that was all that remained from the days when you could build a big room almost as cheaply as a small one.

While Jimmy took a nap Roger showered quickly. Although the tin stall had been put in some years ago, you could still see marks on the floor where the feet of an old-fashioned tub had stood. The shower curtain gave off the overpoweringly sweet smell of damp mildew but the room itself was clean, like the man said.

They went downstairs to eat around eight o'clock. The greasy menus listed over twenty dinners but the waitress touted the chicken fried steak. Roger jokingly allowed as how it might be all they really had.

"What time do you close?" he asked the waitress while she cleared the dinner dishes. He figured she'd know what he meant. She was somewhere in her thirties and probably could have made herself pretty if she saw any point. She looked like she had good tits.

She had the mechanic's oblique way of answering a question as if she hadn't heard it. When she had finished wiping the table she said, "Is he your boy? He kind of favors you." It meant either that she wasn't interested in a married man or that she felt uncomfortable making arrangements in front of the boy. He left it up to her to clarify her intentions.

"That's what folks tell me," he said. He had never thought there was much of a physical resemblance. Jimmy was still skinny, with his mother's delicate facial structure. But people said he had his father's eyes.

When the waitress brought their dessert she sighed deeply, shaking her head. "It's been a long day. Been on my feet since two o'clock." She sighed again. "Another hour to go."

"Must be rough in this kind of weather," Roger said casually, half-smiling at what she must have thought was great subtlety.

"It is," she said. She stretched her arms back to dramatize her fatigue, in the process sticking her chest out. In case he hadn't made up his mind. Roger shot a reproachful glance toward Jimmy, who was making no effort to conceal a knowing smirk. "Yup," she said, "as soon as I get off I'm gonna have me a co-o-old beer."

Why drag it out any longer? "How about the roadhouse?" he said.

"Shoot," she drawled sarcastically, laying on her accent with a trowel. "It's two miles to the roadhouse. I'm jes' gonna set me down on the front porch raht here."

Roger left Jimmy at the hotel and drove out to the roadhouse. It was a large, low-ceilinged room surprisingly packed with people. They must have come from miles around. They weren't dressed like farmers. He figured they were connected with the mines. The place was in a constant uproar, the men bellowing at one another above the din of a country-western quartet and the women giggling stridently. When the group played loud enough they sounded pretty good, especially when they did some raunchy, blues-type numbers. It was the kind of music that could make you feel mean. He had a few beers by himself, not trying to strike up any conversations. There were plenty of women but he couldn't tell whether they were available or just flirting. After an hour of watching their lunatic merriment he was fed up with the place. He got in the car and drove back to the hotel.

The waitress was sitting on a rocking chair on the porch, her head tipped back and her fingers wrapped around a bottle of beer on the floor beside her. He thought she was asleep until he noticed she was rocking slowly back and forth. She looked sad and vulnerable. Again Roger had the ludicrous impression that he had stumbled into an old movie.

He pulled another rocker around next to hers and sat down. "Hi," he said. "Looks like it's startin' to cool off."

Jimmy had no intention of sitting cooped up in the room while his father tried to score with the waitress. He left the hotel and wandered listlessly around the town looking for something to do. Roger hadn't offered him any money and he had forgotten to ask. Not that there was anywhere to spend it, even if he had it. The street was quieter than Arlington.

At the movie theater the last show had already started. There were ways to get in without paying. The manager was closing out the ticket booth. Jimmy loitered in front reading the posters, waiting for him to record the final numbers on his report and lock the machine. Then he asked if he could go in.

The manager glared at him contemptuously. He wasn't about to unlock the machine and redo his arithmetic. Wise-ass kid, he thought. He wasn't one of the ones who usually came around though. "You're a smart little prick, aren't you," he said with a sneer. "Waiting for me to finish. All right I'll let you in for fifty cents. It just started ten minutes ago."

"Thanks. Give me a ticket."

"No ticket. Fifty cents."

Around Arlington a lot of the managers let you in free after they stopped selling tickets. "I don't have it," Jimmy said. "Can't you just let me in?"

"You don't have it," the manager mimicked derisively. He closed the booth door and disappeared inside the theater.

Jimmy went around to the side of the building. He rapped on the fire door a few times but no one opened it. In the back he found a flight of cast iron stairs leading to the projection booth. The door was open. He climbed the stairs quietly and looked in.

The projectionist was fiddling with one of the two projectors, the one that wasn't on. Then he lowered the side door and pressed a button that touched off a spark. Through a crack where the door didn't fit properly Jimmy saw a light flickering. The projectionist muttered something to himself and turned a handle frantically. The light blazed to a white intensity. He peered through a scratch in the smoked glass porthole on the side and backed off the carbons until the color tone satisfied him. A bell tinkled briefly on the other machine. The man glanced at Jimmy as he scurried to the other side and knelt down between the machines, looking out toward the screen.

"C'mon in," he said. "Be with you in a minute."

Jimmy had never been in a projection booth before. It was cramped and incredibly stuffy. The man wore only his shoes and a pair of boxer shorts. His shirt and pants were draped over one arm of a tiny, filthy sofa squeezed into the corner.

Jimmy went to a window on the far side of the machine that was on and watched the picture for a few seconds. *The French Connection.* Even in Arlington it had played two years ago. Christ, this place is out of it, he thought.

"See that little black mark up in the corner?" the man said. "The upper right? There'll be another one in a few seconds." He had started the film on the second projector and when the black mark reappeared he threw a switch that sent the picture out from the other machine. On the screen you hardly noticed the change. "Nice changeover, huh? Smooth."

Jimmy watched the movie with little interest. There was no sound in the booth. Two men in the film were arguing heatedly but they looked silly in pantomime. There were only about seven or eight heads scattered randomly through the shoe-box-shaped auditorium, all turned raptly toward the image above them.

The projectionist put the finished reel on the rewind machine and threaded the next one through the head without saying anything. He had a large bland face and a scrawny body but his paunch bulged grotesquely over his shorts. It looked hard as a rock when he moved.

"Sorry to take so long," he said. "You caught me during a changeover."

Jimmy got the impression that the man was expecting him. He came up and stood behind the boy, watching the screen over his shoulder. At close quarters his body smelled rank with old sweat. Jimmy noticed that he was rubbing himself under the armpit. He pulled his head away in revulsion but quickly remembered himself and tried to make it look like he was just glancing around naturally.

"C'mon over here and sit down," the man said, gesturing toward the sofa. Evidently he didn't notice Jimmy's disgust. "Did Rick send you over?"

Jimmy sat down in the corner. "Rick?" he asked.

"Then who sent you?"

"No one. I was just walking around."

The man suddenly got nervous. His eyes darted back and forth between the open door and his clothes on the corner of the sofa. "Why'd you come up here?"

"I didn't have anything to do. Are you expecting someone?"

"No. No. That's okay." The man's voice was urgent but he seemed confused.

"Rick must have sent someone else. I better go," Jimmy volunteered, though he made no move to get up.

"No, you don't understand," the man said hastily. He switched abruptly to a conversational tone. "If you got nothing to do, why don't you stick around. I'll show you how the projectors work if you want. Just let me put my pants on. I got undressed 'cause it's hot. It must be making you uncomfortable."

Suddenly Jimmy understood what was going on. At school they joked about queers but he had never run into one before. He had thought they acted—what was the word?—effeminate.

The thought crossed his mind that the whole town was a little bit crazy. He wondered if the guy was going to try anything. And what. He knew he should leave but he couldn't resist the temptation to stay and see what would happen. He was fascinated by the situation, by the mere fact of being caught up in something mysterious, illicit—something beyond his experience. Besides, the guy seemed harmless. A silly grin half-turned the corners of the boy's mouth. It occurred to him that it was the projectionist who should be scared.

"What's so funny?" The man was reaching for his pants. His wallet had fallen out of the pocket onto the floor. He picked it up and put it on the counter next to the splicing machine. I bet he's got some money, Jimmy thought, at least a few dollars.

"Nothing," Jimmy said. "Don't you ever watch the pictures?"

"Sometimes." The man pulled over a tubular kitchen chair and sat down facing Jimmy, their knees almost touching. When he sat his belly turned into soft rolls of fat on both sides of his tightly cinched belt. He started chatting idly, asking Jimmy meaningless questions about himself.

Jimmy talked vaguely about what had brought him to town. They weren't on vacation or on their way anywhere in particular. Just driving around.

"Well, that's a vacation," the guy said. "It's what my old man used to do. Get us in the car and drive around two weeks every year. Never went anyplace though."

"Yeah, but it's not a vacation," Jimmy said, unable to conceal a teasing smile. The projectionist ignored it. He got up to get ready for the next changeover. Jimmy toyed with the idea of telling him, as matter-of-factly as possible, that he and his father had killed a girl near home and didn't want to go back. The man wouldn't believe him but he wanted to see what he would say. Maybe he'd do it later if the guy kept asking him questions.

Again the projectionist worked in silence as Jimmy watched. In the middle of his chores he ambled over to the outside door and swung it shut. Suddenly it got dark in the corner where Jimmy was sitting. Most of the light had come from that door. Only a single dim bulb burned overhead, the bottom half of it painted black.

For an instant a wave of panic swept over the boy but it passed quickly, leaving his nerves screwed tight with expectation. In a few minutes he'd find out what the guy was going to do. He stood with his back turned, drumming his fingertips on the counter as the rewind whirred faster and faster. The light glinted off his wet bony shoulder. Jimmy wasn't afraid, he had just been surprised by the suddenness of the move. There was a utility knife on the counter among some other equipment, the blade set out only an inch or so. Jimmy thought, I could probably kill him with that but it wouldn't be easy. The girl had been tied up. Again, he tried to imagine how his father had done it. The Buck knife was long enough, he could have stuck it right through her.

The leader slapped noisily against the case. I might want to kill him, Jimmy thought, attaching no particular emotion to the idea. I could take the money. No one knows I came up here. Not the prospect but the knowledge that he could do it began to excite him. The projectionist removed the full reel and dropped it into its numbered bin.

He sat down and started talking again. In a few minutes he had worked the conversation around to the subject of girls. Jimmy readily admitted that he didn't have a girlfriend. It was true but he felt like he was playing a part, nudging the guy along toward some kind of resolution.

"That's all right. Don't worry about it," the man said. "When I was your age I didn't have a girlfriend either. How old are you? Thirteen? Fourteen?"

"Twelve."

"Twelve. Didn't have a girl then. No need, you know what I mean? I've had lots of women. All kinds. You wouldn't believe it, a guy like me. But I've had all kinds. White ones, colored ones. But you don't need 'em, know what I mean?"

The monologue droned on, inching toward a declaration and then sliding away. Jimmy, nodding agreement from time to time, kept his eyes fixed on the man's face, which broke in the semidarkness into jumbled planes of light and shadow. Jimmy wasn't sure what he was hearing. He could pick up the knife while the guy set the projector for the next changeover and stick it in him as he knelt between the machines. He didn't have to kill him. But he wondered what it would feel like just stabbing someone. His father had done it.

"You don't mind my talkin' about sex, do ya?" The pitch of the man's voice had gone up sharply.

"No, it's fine," Jimmy said, the meaning of the question barely registering.

"When I was your age that's all we talked about. Pussy. You do that? A bunch of guys get together, tell stories, y'know? Nothin' wrong with it. Used to measure our dicks too—see whose was biggest. Ever do that?"

"No."

"Nothin' wrong with it." Jimmy thought the man was sweating more now, if that was possible. He laughed nervously between sentences. "Wanna do that? Course mine's gonna be bigger. You're only twelve. But you don't need girls. No reason for 'em. Ya see what I mean? C'mon, ya wanna do it?"

"Wanna do what?" He had completely lost the thread of what the guy was saying.

"Anything. Whatever you want. I'm not gonna hurt ya. You trust me, don'cha?" An unnerving, wheedling tone had crept into his voice.

"Yeah, sure. I guess it's okay." He could loosen the screw and make the blade longer. Do it the second he pressed the changeover button, while his arm was still stretched out. The customers wouldn't know anything happened to him for twenty, twenty-five minutes. He'd take the money, give it to his father. How much could it be? Not much, probably. Everyone must have known he was queer. They'd blame Rick or one of the boys he sent over.

The man stood up. He seemed very agitated, his eyes rolling feverishly. Suddenly he looked like a marionette, a puppet dancing on a string. He didn't know what to do with himself, moving jerkingly toward Jimmy and then toward the seat next to him on the sofa. Jimmy couldn't tell what he was saying—the same thing over and over. It's gonna be good, it's gonna be all right. 'Sgonbe, 'sgonbe fine, fine.

"Isn't that the bell?" Jimmy heard himself saying, faintly, not sure that he had actually heard a bell.

"Ohmigod!" The man lurched toward the projector and threw on the arc switch. By the time the spark caught he had missed the first mark. He started the machine rolling and raced around it to wait for his cue.

As he knelt on the floor Jimmy came up behind him. He held the utility knife in his hand, the point drawn out a full two inches. The projectionist clicked the button and, not moving, watched horror-stricken as the screen went white and the numbered seconds wound through the lens.

"Shit! You made me miss it. I never miss it," he said, turning around, his pasty features tight with failure. Suddenly his facial muscles went slack. "What're you doing with that knife?" he asked bewilderedly.

Jimmy looked down at it. "Nothing. I just picked it up." He didn't know why he was holding it.

"Give it to me. You walk around here with that while I'm runnin' around, someone's gonna get hurt." His voice was firm and commanding. Jimmy handed him the knife in a daze. "You let the blade out? I didn't have it set like that."

"I . . . uh . . . I don't think so. No." He couldn't keep his mind on anything. He thought he was going to black out.

"What you come around here for? What you want here, foolin' with knives?"

Oh, God, just leave me alone!

"Get out of here! You hear me! Don't you come back! You hear me!" He was screaming right into his face. Jimmy staggered toward the door and fell heavily against the .vork counter. The man yanked the door open and he made his way toward the light at the top of the stairs. The cool air rushed toward him, overwhelmingly fresh.

"Don't you come back! You hear me!"

On the street the wailing, bitter voice trailed after him, fading finally in the night.

CHAPTER 7

T UESDAY MORNING at approximately two-thirty a complaint was phoned in to the Arlington police. A woman was playing her radio too loud. When her neighbor called her to ask her to turn it down she hung up on him. He knocked on her door but she refused to answer it. The neighbor thought she might be drunk.

Since the address in question was outside the city limits, the message was routinely forwarded to the Sheriff's Department. The deputy who responded found the radio blaring full blast when he drove up to the house. The woman opened the door for him only after he had identified himself repeatedly as a police officer. She didn't appear to be drunk but her face was puffy and discolored. She explained that she had been having nightmares and was afraid to go back to sleep. She was alone in the house. Her family had left a few days ago and she had no idea when they would return.

The deputy persuaded her to turn down the radio and make herself a pot of coffee if she didn't want to sleep. He warned her that she would be arrested if there were further complaints. As for the nightmares, he thought a sedative might help—but she was probably just scared being alone in the house.

She seemed grateful for his concern and promised to cause no more trouble.

Tuesday morning Kay Orben was buried. It disturbed Walt that he didn't see the Eddy boy at the funeral, but he was sure he'd show up for the interview in the afternoon.

All through the ceremony Walt thought about the call he had received from the district attorney at eight o'clock that morning.

"Walt? Rollins. I'm going for an indictment on the boy."

"You don't have enough to convict, Pete."

"Then get me enough."

That was all.

Around town the news had spread that Doug Eddy had left the beach with Kay, ostensibly to walk her to her car. He was the last person to have seen her alive. They were alone together for a long time—a college boy and an attractive high school girl. Anything could have happened while they were together. But the main thing was that he was an outsider. No one knew anything to say in his defense. *But he's such a nice boy*—words like that carry a lot of weight in a small town. But there was no one to say them.

People Walt talked to around the courthouse admitted that, in the strict legal sense, there wasn't much of a case against the boy. He claimed, apparently, that he hadn't been anywhere near the car. What else could he say? But there wasn't any evidence to support his contention. Just about everybody assumed he had killed the girl. Only the more sophisticated bothered to add that they were a long way from proving it.

Walt knew the pressure was starting to mount. Pressure on him. It was his fault if he couldn't come up with the proof. Of course they blamed the legal system too, with its finicky regard for the rights of the accused and its total indifference to the rights of Kay Orben and her family. But there was nothing they could do about the legal system except complain about it. He was the one they stopped in the streets with their suggestions. He was the one who had to answer their pleas for justice, telling them he was doing the best he could.

Arlington was turning into a lynch mob if ever he had seen one. Oh, no one would storm the jail if they took young Eddy into custody or threaten to string him up from a tree. Doug could walk the streets safely. If he cared to, he could probably still get served in most restaurants in town. The people in Arlington were civilized, law-abiding people. But there are plenty of ways to lynch a man and a fair trial is one of them.

To make it even more frustrating, Walt never believed Doug Eddy was guilty. He had made the point to Rollins as directly as he dared, trying to show him how the facts they had didn't add up to any reasonable hypothesis involving the boy. Where did he get the knife or why did he have it with him? What was his motive? Why would he kill her with almost surgical coldness yet vent his fury on a car?

But he could only raise the questions, then listen silently as Rollins told him it was his job to find the answers. If he pushed too hard on his faith in the boy's innocence they'd say that he hadn't come up with the evidence because he wasn't trying. But he was too good a cop for that. Anyone who watched him at work would swear he was trying to railroad the kid. He'd be damned if he'd miss a single angle, and he didn't let his men slacken off either. It was just that he had this gut feeling that with Doug Eddy they were barking up the wrong tree.

What he needed was another tree.

"I'm acting as a friend of the family, Sheriff, not as the boy's legal counsel. I wouldn't think he needs counsel. But before you talk to him I just want to get straight on where we stand."

Walt cut him off right there. Doug, though badly shaken the first time Walt talked to him, had seemed more than willing to cooperate. He consented readily to being checked over by the medical examiner—for scratches, it turned out, though Walt avoided telling him the reason. At the end of their talk the young man even suggested a second interview later in the week when he'd be thinking more coherently. Now his lawyer showed up.

"Did the boy ask you to represent him?" Walt said.

"I'm not representing him. But no, he didn't. His parents were very upset after he called them Sunday. They asked me if I could come out and take a look at the situation—as a friend. I'm not on a retainer."

"Did the parents come with you?"

"No, they . . . uh . . . they thought . . . "

"I see."

"You're jumping to a conclusion, Sheriff. There are medical reasons for them not being here you know nothing about. They're very fine people." His manner was extremely subdued, as if a penchant for understatement were rooted in his character rather than in any sense of tactical advantage.

"All right," Walt said, a little abashed. "Now what can I do for you?"

"As I said, the question is, Where do we stand? I've been in town less than two days but I get the distinct impression that Doug is suspected of . . . of murder. Is he a suspect?"

"He was the last person to have seen her alive, Mr. Emmonds. Naturally, . . . "

"Is he a suspect? I understand the dead girl scratched her assailant pretty badly . . . "

"Not necessarily, sir. We found fragments of skin and dried blood under her nails but they might just as well have been her own. We couldn't run a type. She tried to tear off the bindings on her wrists and her hands were covered with blood anyway."

Emmonds' features hardened momentarily. It violated his sense of fair play that the boy had been induced to subject himself to an examination, the ground rules of which stipulated that he well might fail but couldn't possibly pass. But that was water under the bridge right now. He didn't want to antagonize the sheriff needlessly.

"Be that as it may," he said evenly, "you've been making inquiries about Doug's family and about his record at school. Yet he tells me you haven't apprised him of his rights."

"We're not quite as formal in Iowa as you are back east. But we have no intention of violating anyone's rights," Walt said coldly, making an effort to match Emmonds' reserve. He resented the lawyer's interference though he sympathized with the motive that had brought him out here. Yet the fact remained that the boy's having an attorney only made the sheriff's position all the more difficult.

Officially, of course, he was an arm of the state, an arm of the prosecution. That's how Emmonds saw him. But in his heart he was on Doug's side—until he found reason to think otherwise. He wanted to tell Emmonds that he was the best friend Doug had. He still hoped the boy would talk freely, would volunteer some reasonable explanation for not having walked Kay all the way to her car. Without that, Walt had no grounds to ask the D.A. to hold off. Yet that was their only chance. Once Rollins got his indictment, Doug ran the risk of being swept to a conviction despite the flimsiness of the evidence. At best he faced the agony of a trial. And, naturally, the investigation into other areas would be severely curtailed.

But confiding in Emmonds was out of the question. It was unprofessional. Moreover, there were serious risks in openly aligning himself with the defense. Emmonds was a gentleman, but if it was to his client's advantage he wouldn't hesitate to use such an admission for all it was worth. To be of any help at all, Walt had to hold his cards close to his vest.

Emmonds said, "I'm sure you don't mean to violate his rights. But you have to understand our position. Unfortunately, Doug didn't accompany the girl to her car. If he had, she might still be alive. But that's the extent of his responsibility. I don't see how he can tell you anything more that bears on the crime." He paused. "Of course if he's still a suspect it's a different story. In that case I think I should be present when you interview him."

Walt shook his head dejectedly. That was exactly what he was afraid of. Emmonds was forcing them to be adversaries.

"I believe you're not a criminal lawyer, Mr. Emmonds," Walt said softly. "You'll just make matters worse by interfering." That was as far as he could go.

"I doubt that very much, Sheriff."

Walt wheeled peevishly toward the intercom on his desk and pressed down hard on the button. "Jerry?" he snapped. "Is the Eddy boy out there? Read him his rights."

"His what?"

"His rights! Don't you ever watch television!"

*

The interview was a complete disaster. Although Emmonds did not prohibit his client from answering questions, he did everything in his power to keep the atmosphere formal and tense, to make it harder for the sheriff to break through the boy's reticence.

Initially, Walt proposed that they drive out to Lake Barrett to retrace the path Doug had taken with Kay and then back to the beach. But Emmonds hemmed and hawed until Walt withdrew the suggestion. He guessed that the lawyer was not simply objecting for the sake of objection. Kay had led the way. She was familiar with the woods. If Doug got disoriented and went past the rivulet where he said they had stopped, it would create the impression that he had been lying about leaving her. It was a valid concern, though Emmonds knew enough not to express it directly.

"Doug," Walt said, trying to be as delicate as possible, "I'm not asking you this because I blame you for what happened. But I have to know. Why didn't you walk Kay all the way to her car?"

Doug shook his head sadly without answering for a while. "She didn't want me to. I suppose I could have insisted. I never thought . . . " His voice trailed off. He shrugged his shoulders when he realized he didn't know how to finish the sentence.

Walt nodded understandingly. He saw the burden of guilt the boy carried, but he'd bet anything it wasn't the guilt of a murderer. "Okay," he said, accepting the boy's answer and then pausing a moment. "But why didn't she want you to go the rest of the way? Did you have an argument or something? A misunderstanding?"

"This was more than two miles from the car, Sheriff," Emmonds broke in. "It was a long way from where the girl was killed."

Doug winced.

"I realize that," Walt said.

"No, it wasn't an argument. Nothing like that," Doug interrupted. He hesitated, unwilling to go on without further prompting.

"You'd been talking? What were you talking about?"

"Well, we seemed to like each other. Y'know, you can tell sometimes. We sat down by this stream for a while. I guess we were kind of wondering about the future. She asked me to call her again."

They were getting somewhere. He said they "liked each other" and they paused for a while in a romantic spot. It was easy enough to imagine what happened. Walt wanted to believe Doug was reluctant to be more specific out of respect for the girl, not because he had anything to hide. But he needed details, a plausible accounting of the time they spent together. He decided to take it slowly.

"All right. So you sat down. And talked. Do you have any idea how long you were there?"

"It's hard to say . . . "

"I don't see the point, Sheriff," Emmonds interjected. "Doug admits he was gone about two hours. The fact is, neither of them was in much of a hurry. They're kids. Under the circumstances it would be strange if there were any signs of haste."

You fool! Walt thought. Can't you see I'm not trying to hurt the boy? It was obvious that Emmonds wasn't worried about the time thing. He was simply trying to prevent Doug from admitting any sexual contact with the girl, however inconsequential. The prosecution, he feared, might use such an admission to depict the boy as a frustrated sex fiend, trying to put the make on a girl the first day they met and going berserk when she said no.

But Emmonds' cautiousness exposed his client to an even greater danger. Sooner or later Doug would have to tell his story. If he held anything back, if he let Rollins drag the truth from him on the stand, a few innocent kisses on a summer afternoon would look suspicious indeed. No, he had to tell Walt what happened—spontaneously, candidly, and from the beginning. He couldn't afford to wait till he was cornered.

But when Walt tried to resume the questioning the moment had passed. Doug's natural, even commendable reluctance to discuss his relations with Kay had been buttressed by the lawyer's interruptions. He was extremely vague about what led up to their separation. He could reconstruct very little of their conversation. Finally Walt asked him, as tactfully as he knew how, if they had done any petting.

Doug turned to Emmonds, a beseeching look on his face. "You're completely out of line," Emmonds said icily. "Certainly the girl's character isn't in question."

Walt's patience snapped. He ground his fingers into his leg below the desk, barely suppressing an urge to lash back. Emmonds didn't want his client to talk too freely. Fair enough. But it was hitting below the belt to suggest that Walt was merely interested in lurid gossip. "It's Doug's character I'm talking about," he finally articulated, the words barely escaping through his lips.

"You don't have to answer the question," Emmonds said flatly.

Doug lowered his head. He was obviously confused, not knowing what was the right thing to do. "We didn't really do that much anyway," he muttered.

Now that Walt had his admission it didn't do him any good. Rollins would love to know that the suspect had reluctantly confessed to having had some sort of sexual dealings with the victim—dealings which his lawyer had been unwilling to let him discuss. He'd see it in the same light as Emmonds—because Emmonds hadn't trusted the boy to talk openly.

Walt stood up and walked slowly to the window to get himself a cup of coffee. He poured in cream and sugar, which he had stopped taking years ago, to give himself a little more time to calm down. When he returned to his desk he took out a pipe and packed it carefully to the brim. He had to face facts. Maybe everyone else was right about Eddy and he was wrong. He thought he understood exactly what had been happening but it could be that the boy was guilty and that he and the lawyer had been outmaneuvering him all along.

No. He had been wrong before but never that wrong. He didn't care how it looked, the boy wasn't the killer.

But the faint glimmerings of doubt made it easier to ask his next question. "Doug, you know how she was killed, don't you?"

"With a knife."

"That's right. Do you own a knife? A hunting knife or a jackknife?" For some reason Emmonds didn't object.

"I have a jackknife. It's in the dorm somewhere."

"Do you ever carry it with you?"

"No. I think it's in a box of stuff that I brought from home."

"What kind of knife is it?"

"A regular jackknife."

"We'd like to see it. I'll arrange to have someone pick it up. Is Mr. Emmonds driving you back to Iowa City?"

"No, sir, I'm taking the bus."

Walt stood up again, signaling the end of the interview. "Then I'll have a deputy give you a ride. You'll give it to him, okay?"

He offered Doug his hand over the desk and immediately faulted himself for the gesture. Here was the last person to see Kay alive and he still hadn't really leaned on him the way he should. But he just couldn't think of the kid as a suspect. Maybe he was letting his feelings get in the way. Shit—a cop had to go with his feelings or there'd be nothing to fall back on when it got rough.

Doug took his hand gratefully. He felt he hadn't been as forthcoming as he would have liked and now he had to demur once again. "If I can find it," he said sheepishly. "It might still be at home. There's a lot of that stuff I didn't take with me."

"If you can find it," Walt said. He walked them out to the parking lot, stopping first at the front desk to arrange for an officer to drive Doug back to school. Then the three of them stood awkwardly beside the cruiser while they waited for the driver. They couldn't think of anything to say to each other.

There was no one in the room when Jimmy woke up. He didn't know the time but something told him he had slept late. For a few minutes he lay on the bed trying to remember what happened last night. Something at the theater, about trying to sneak in. No, after that. And there was something else when he got back to the hotel too.

He turned on the shower and stepped in without waiting for the hot water. The humidity must have been near one hundred percent and it felt good to get out of the stickiness. The cold brought him awake. He kept the temperature down even after the hot water came in.

Slowly, the pieces fell together. Absurd. Why had he done those things?

What the hell, he wasn't going to worry about it. He thrust his head defiantly under the nozzle and let the cold water stream down his face.

When he got out he left the shower running in hopes it would cool off the room. As he toweled off he heard a key turn in the door.

Roger stood outside the bathroom holding a small bag of groceries. "What the fuck happened to you last night?" he said accusingly.

"Why? How'd you find out about it?"

"Find out? You came in here like you just heard the world ended. Phyllis thought you saw a ghost."

Jimmy rubbed his hair vigorously with the towel. "No. This queer tried to put the make on me. It didn't amount to anything," he said as he ran the towel over his face, hoping it would hide his dissimulation. His father usually could tell when he was lying.

Roger let it pass. "It wasn't your night, I guess." He walked away to put down his bundle on the lamp table by the window. With his back to the room he said quietly, "You want any breakfast? Phyllis let me have a few things."

Jimmy thought that was pretty funny. His father was embarrassed at taking food from a woman. "Yeah, I'm starved," he said, coming up to see what his father had brought. "She must've thought you were terrific."

"The greatest thing since sliced bread," Roger grinned. He tapped the boy playfully on the end of his penis. "Take good care of it, son, and it'll take good care of you."

Some of the food would have to wait until they got back to their campstove but there was half a loaf of bread, a jar of peanut butter and a can of some kind of sausage that needed no cooking. Having no utensils in the room, they used the sausage links to scoop out the peanut butter and then wrapped them in slices of bread. It wasn't half bad.

While they were eating Roger said, "I told Phyllis you were a virgin. After the other day, I figured you needed a few lessons."

He said it so off-handedly Jimmy didn't realize what he meant at first.

Then he blushed. "What'd she say?"

Roger shrugged his shoulders and stuffed his mouth with sausage. "Last night she'da said yes to the Marines. 'Course you're not the Marines," he mumbled through the food. "But I don't know now. You kind of shook her up the way you acted last night."

"It's no big deal," Jimmy said with affected nonchalance.

"No, not when you got queers falling all over you."

They finished their meal in silence. Jimmy enjoyed the new relationship that seemed to be developing with his father. Roger still teased him constantly but it didn't have the same edge of cruelty to it. They were more equal—well, not equal, but more like a father and son.

Roger said, "Y'know, Jim, after I pay for this room we won't have much money left."

"Do you want to go home?"

"No."

They looked into each other's eyes a few seconds. It was that simple. Both understood that a choice had been made between Arlington and stealing money somehow.

Roger considered the risk for a moment. If they got caught, no matter how petty the job, Jimmy's prints would connect them with Lake Barrett. Still, it was better to make a break once and for all than to let yourself fall back into the same old trap. When he put it that way his doubts evaporated. An odd phrase floated unbidden to mind: I'll come out the same place in the long run. It puzzled him, what the words meant. He took them to mean he had nothing to lose. Which was true, but he felt he had to say something to Jimmy, to make sure he understood.

"You know, we can't afford to get caught," he said.

Jimmy smiled enigmatically. "Fine with me," he said.

They talked about it some more as they drove out to Phyllis's house. She lived in a rundown trailer court located halfway to the next town. About thirty old trailers had been set up as a sort of instant housing development, the units rented by the month to the families of men who drifted from one marginal mining job to another. The pits around there were mainly shoestring operations that hired extra men when they got a big order and laid them off when they filled it. Still, the women who moved into the court always made a point of telling everyone that such accommodations didn't really suit them—but they'd do till they found something permanent. Phyllis had seemed awed by their bravado, their boundless capacity to learn nothing from experience. The jobs never lasted more than a few months, a year or year and a half at most. The last time Phyllis's husband got laid off she told him she wasn't going with him any more. She had her job as a waitress so she'd keep the trailer and make what life for herself she could. He left without trying to argue with her. When she told Roger the story she didn't say whether it happened in the last few months or years ago.

By the time they pulled into the yard Jimmy and Roger were in an exuberant mood. They hadn't made any definite plans but the main thing for Jimmy was that they were embarking on a mysterious adventure. Roger wasn't so sure, but the boy's high spirits were infectious.

Phyllis fixed a pot of coffee that was half chickory and they sat around the table in her tiny kitchenette, talking and laughing unreasonably at each other's stories. Jimmy had wondered why his father had promised to stop by again before leaving but now he wasn't sorry they came. She was different from what he expected, especially after his father had told him she'd been willing to give him his sexual initiation. Of course, that could have been something his father just said. In any case, he was glad the subject never came up. He liked the feeling of sitting idly at the table and hearing her laughter. She was warm and impulsively generous, and she didn't patronize him the way most grown-ups did.

"Hey, Phyllis, do you want to come with us?" he blurted when she went to the stove to get more coffee.

Roger lowered his eyes and shook his head slightly.

She shut off the range and turned to Roger, a quirky smile on her face. The question gratified her but it had to come from Roger too.

"I thought you were going home?" she said to him.

Roger took a long drag on his cigarette. "No. Sooner or later, I guess."

Her eyes narrowed doubtfully. "What're you guys gonna do?"

Roger opened his hand in an indeterminate gesture. He didn't know how much to tell her. Beyond that, he wasn't ready to commit himself to another woman. "Nothing special," he said. "See what happens for a while."

She turned to the boy. "All right, Jim. Why the shit-eating grin?"

He didn't answer her. He liked the way his father put it, that was all. See what happens.

It was obvious Roger wasn't going to say anything else. That hurt a little though it didn't surprise her. "Half me says yes," she said almost wistfully, as if the boy's invitation needed some kind of answer. "God only knows why. But not this time. I'd get tired of moving in a couple days anyway. You guys want more coffee or do you have to be going?"

Roger stood up. "We better go."

She looked at the pot in her hand as if she wasn't sure what to do with it. "Well, listen," she said, her face flushed in girlish confusion, "you need any more food? I got plenty here, really, if there's something you need."

"Thanks. No. I don't think so."

She nodded and found a place for the coffeepot on the counter. Leaning back against the refrigerator she pointed a finger at Jimmy. "Take care of yourself, okay? I want to say good-bye to your father."

Jimmy went outside to wait by the car. A baby and a small dog were sitting in a patch of shade behind the tailgate. It was a good thing he saw them. He picked up the kid and carried him over to his mother, who was sunning herself in the next yard. "Oh, my Lord, he crawl off again?" she said. "I swear I'm gonna hafta chain 'im to the house."

Phyllis waited for Roger to put his arms around her. "I'm not usually like this," she said, finally turning away from his kiss. "If you go back to wherever it is and it doesn't work out . . . I'll prob'ly still be here."

"Arlington. No, I don't think I'll go back." He twined his fingers in her hair and pulled her head down to his shoulder. "You wouldn't want me back here either," he said softly.

"No, maybe not." She held him tightly, her hands reaching under his jersey to caress his bare back. Soon her fingers found the hard scabs that ran from his shoulders in parallel lines down almost to the middle of his back. She traced them lightly over and over, not thinking what she was doing.

"It doesn't hurt?" she murmured after a minute or so.

"No."

Slowly he felt her drawing away from him. Last night she had asked him about those scratches and he put her off with a joke. But now he had told her he was from Arlington. The killing must have been in all the papers. Maybe she was putting two and two together.

She stood at arm's length, searching his eyes. Finally he had to look away. She reached out and touched him on the cheek, a gesture in lieu of a thousand questions. "Roger. Be careful," she said.

He returned her thin smile. "Sure," he said. "You too."

CHAPTER 8

''THIS IS STUPID,'' Jimmy said. "Nobody's gonna see us."

"I don't care if it's stupid. Get me the knife."

Jimmy grunted and climbed over the back seat. "I can't see a fuckin' thing," he said. "Put on the light."

Roger switched on the dome light. "Found it?" he asked impatiently after a few seconds. The less light the better.

"Yeah."

It went dark immediately. Jimmy crawled back with the knife.

"Why don't they just put 'em in boxes?" Roger muttered more or less to himself. He was having trouble figuring out how to open the package.

Jimmy clicked his tongue in derision. "Christ, what'd you have to get pantyhose for?" he said querulously. "Stockings are dumb enough."

"They don't sell stockings in drugstores," Roger said. He finally got the pantyhose out of their container and spread the two legs. Jimmy cut them apart at the crotch. "Since you're so finicky, you be in charge of lingerie from now on." He handed one of the legs to Jimmy. "Two more minutes," he said, checking his watch. "And don't forget to put it on."

It was an extra precaution. If everything went right no one would see them.

From where they were parked they could see the front of the house. No lights had gone on. It had been dark since the first time they cruised the neighborhood, around dusk.

Roger had pointed it out. "That's the one," he decided immediately. "The layout looks perfect." It was a smallish, two-story bungalow set back on a large lot. Since this was the last street in the development, the woods came up to the backyard. A hedge on each side marked the property line, running all the way to the sidewalk. Already, with twilight still falling, it held pockets of deep shadows. Once they made the front yard their flank would be covered.

Jimmy had wanted to go in immediately, as soon as it got dark at the latest. Roger said no. There were none of the obvious signs of people on vacation—newspapers or mail piled up, curtains all drawn—but something told him the house had been shut up. "It's the grass," he finally decided. "See?" The lawn had been mowed fairly recently but compared to the others on the block it looked slightly unkempt. It didn't have the same, perfect nap.

"Let's not take chances," he argued. "Wait till the neighborhood's asleep."

Despite his impatience, Jimmy had to agree. With their luck running so good they'd be foolish to take chances. Roger drove back to the highway and found an inconspicuous place where they could park and make plans.

Roger said they'd drive by the house again at eleven to make sure it was still dark and to double-check the layout. Around two they'd park on that other street, the one that dead-ended about three doors down from the target. Jimmy would go first. Roger would follow him three minutes later. In the meantime he'd watch for trouble. If he saw anything he'd turn on the parking lights. Jimmy had to hide near the hedge and watch for the danger signal. When the three minutes were up he was to start moving to the first cellar window. "Just lie there and wait for me," Roger said. "Put on your mask. Don't do anything yourself. Same when we get inside. I'll decide which window to try."

On and on he went, with set procedures, variations and contingency plans for everything. Jimmy was amazed at how much he had noticed in one trip through the neighborhood. It was a side of his father he had never seen before. He rehashed the same points over and over, sometimes quizzing the boy on the most petty details. Jimmy had figured they'd just get there and do it. It wasn't like they were hitting Fort Knox. As long as they didn't make noise or turn on any lights they'd be okay.

He thought maybe his father was psyching himself up. It was as if he had to keep talking. My God, the boy thought, am I going to have to listen to this for the next three hours?

"Do you think there's much money?" he blurted the first chance he got. "What if they keep it in a safe?"

"Nah. They're not rich enough to have a safe."

"How much do you suppose there'll be?" Jimmy persisted. "A couple hundred dollars?"

"Maybe. A lot of people keep that much in the house. Don't worry about it. What we get we get."

Who's worrying? Jimmy thought. He's the one with the stocking masks and rubber gloves.

At eleven-fifteen the house was still dark.

At five minutes to two Roger coasted up to the intersection with his headlights out and shut the engine. All the houses in the neighborhood were dark now. They waited a few minutes to make sure no one heard them drive up. It was then that Roger opened the stockings and Jimmy got the knife and cut them apart.

Jimmy holstered the knife and a screwdriver in his belt under his T-shirt. Roger checked the flashlight, pointing the beam toward the floor. They both had their gloves on.

He nodded to Jimmy. The boy opened the door quietly and stepped out, closing it behind him just far enough to turn off the dome light. Roger slid over to go out the same door. Jimmy strolled calmly across the intersection and turned left. It was over a hundred yards to the hedge and he didn't want to act suspicious. Besides, no one except his father was watching him anyway. It was kind of a trip, walking down the street just like any neighborhood kid on his way home. He didn't even bother walking on the strip of grass between the sidewalk and the street like his father told him. His sneakers were quiet enough.

When he got to the hedge he looked around quickly and darted into the yard. About thirty feet back he knelt down close to the oushes. In the deep shadows he couldn't be seen from the street. The only trouble was the hedgerow blocked his view of the car. The genius hadn't thought of that! Even if he put on the fucking parking lights he'd never see them.

Not that it mattered. There wasn't going to be any signal. Nothing had gone wrong. Nevertheless, it vexed him enormously. Fucking, half-assed plans!

Three minutes was a long time to wait. It seemed like half an hour and still no sign of his father. He felt his heart pounding. This was the exciting part, when you didn't really know what was going to happen.

He was about to creep forward to see what was keeping his father when Roger came racing around the corner in a low crouch and flung himself to the ground. He rolled over a few times until he was hidden in the shrubbery, just like in a war movie.

"Anyone see you?" Jimmy mouthed anxiously.

Roger shook his head.

Jimmy waited for him to get up before heading toward the back of the house. When he had gone far enough he stopped.

Roger tapped him once on the shoulder and he ran to the first cellar window and lay flat on the ground. A second later his father was right beside him. He shined the flashlight around the window frame, trying to see if it was alarmed. Jimmy pressed his face against the glass and peered inside. He couldn't see much—a few tires propped against a partition.

"Can't tell," Roger whispered.

Jimmy pulled the screwdriver from his belt. Turning to give it to his father, he was startled into an explosive guffaw, only partially stifled. Roger already had on his stocking mask. His nose was twisted to one side and his hair, held down by the mesh, looked painted on like a ventriloquist's dummy's. Jimmy clapped his hand over his mouth and tried to think about something else. Roger glared at him but the expression made him look even funnier. Jimmy was sure no one had heard him.

Roger motioned for him to wait while he crept down to check out the other windows. Dutifully, Jimmy got out his mask. Putting it on was harder than he thought. He really had to stretch it to get it over his face. Once in place, it wasn't uncomfortable except that his eyelashes brushed against the fabric whenever he blinked. He tried to see what he looked like in the window but it was too dark to get a reflection.

Roger came back. "This one," he whispered almost inaudibly. He took the screwdriver in exchange for the flashlight. Jimmy shone it on the window latch. Suddenly from the back of the cellar their images came floating toward him. He recoiled involuntarily. In the smudgy glass it was as if they had undergone some hideous transformation—as if their faces had melted. For a few seconds he stared into the mirror, unable to conquer its weird fascination.

He shook his head rapidly, forcing himself back to the business at hand. The window was hinged at the top and locked by a fastener at the bottom that pivoted into a groove in the sill. Roger probed toward the fastener with the point of the screwdriver, breaking off pieces of wood as he twisted it in. Finally he jammed the shaft all the way through. It was wedged in tightly but, jerking it back and forth, he managed to inch it slowly toward the tongue of the lock. Jimmy saw the upper half start to turn and then Roger, his arm aching from the strain, let go of the screwdriver and blew out a mouthful of air.

"Here goes," he panted. "You hear anything—run." He pushed open the window. Jimmy held his breath, waiting for the electric howl of the alarm. It never came. They grinned at each other like kids in a candy store. It was so quiet Jimmy thought he heard his T-shirt scraping against the ground as he slithered forward to hold up the window.

Roger ran his fingers carefully around the inside of the casement, feeling for contacts for a silent alarm. He shook his head and backed off to give Jimmy room to get in.

"No. Hold it up," Jimmy mouthed.

Stretching awkwardly, Roger propped up the window on his fingertips.

The boy wriggled halfway in but then had nowhere to go. It was too far to lower himself head first to the floor. "Shit!" he whispered, his voice sounding hollow from inside the building. He'd have to go in feet first.

Roger saw that he was having trouble backing out. He grabbed his shoulder and pulled. As the boy slid backward the window came down, the edge of the frame catching him hard on the neck.

"Watch it!" Jimmy whispered fiercely.

"Sorry."

It was easy the other way. When his hips were in Roger shone the light on the basement floor for him to see what was down there. Nothing. He let himself fall, landing flat-footed on the concrete floor. He was in.

Roger handed him the flashlight and poked his head inside.

"Feet first," Jimmy reminded him.

"Yeah. I want to see if I can fit."

It was obvious that he couldn't. He tried it in different positions but his shoulders were too wide.

"Wait a minute," Jimmy said. "There's gotta be a back door."

The door wasn't in the plan. "All right," Roger conceded. "It's over there. Hurry it up."

Using the flashlight sparingly, Jimmy groped his way to the cellar stairs. At the top he found himself in a hallway leading to the kitchen. A back door gave onto a small porch. He opened it a few inches and Roger sidled in, shutting it quickly behind him.

There was enough light from outside to see fairly well. As long as they didn't parade by the front windows there was no danger of being seen.

Roger said, "Okay. Let's not waste time."

"Let's not rush," Jimmy said simultaneously.

Roger smiled. That was equally reasonable. He led the way upstairs, where there were four rooms and a bath. The master bedroom faced front. "Keep down," he said.

They made their way to either side of the big dresser. Sitting on the floor, they pulled out the drawers one by one and rummaged through them.

"What're we looking for?" Jimmy said.

"Anything valuable."

"You think they keep the money here?"

"How the fuck would I know?"

The way they whispered voicelessly back and forth, inclining their heads toward one another, reminded Jimmy of kids talking in class. The teachers called it "visiting." Any minute he expected to see Mr. Carner stick his head in the door. "Jimmy! Roger! Stop that visiting!" He had to laugh.

Roger looked at him quizzically but didn't say anything.

The dresser was full of women's clothes. In the fourth drawer Jimmy found a jewelry case. He looked inside, then slid it across the carpet to his father. "Here."

Roger turned the flashlight on the contents. "I think it's junk," he said.

"You sure?" His voice registered his disappointment.

" 'Course not." Roger examined the stuff again more carefully. "Not junk but not expensive."

"Yeah, but there's a lot of it."

"Nothing we can do with it." He picked out an old-fashioned watch and flipped it to Jimmy. "This might be worth something."

Jimmy stuck it in his pocket. "You're gonna leave the rest?"

"Yes. Don't be a baby. We're not here for souvenirs."

There was nothing else in the dresser that interested them. Pantyhose—but Jimmy was in no mood for joking.

They slid over to the companion piece, which belonged to the husband. More clothes. "Y'know what?" Roger whispered. "People probably don't leave money around when they go on vacation."

"Great," Jimmy said sarcastically, a little too loudly. "Why didn't you think of that before?"

"Why didn't you, big shot?"

Roger decided he might as well take some of the man's socks. He had brought only a few pair from home and he couldn't wash them as often as he liked. Then he reopened a drawer they had gone through before and picked out the short-sleeved shirts. The collars were half a size too small but it wouldn't matter if he wore them open. When they finished with the dressers he sent Jimmy downstairs to find a bag to put the stuff in. While the boy was gone he searched the end table and the closet. There were a lot of shoe boxes but they were either empty or had shoes in them.

The other bedroom belonged to a child, a boy around seven or eight, if they had to guess. Jimmy found a small transistor radio in the back of the closet. It didn't work, but it might just need batteries. He decided to take it.

Roger went into the guest room by himself, sending Jimmy to search the kid's playroom. Each got little more than a cursory glance. They were finished upstairs.

Jimmy dumped what they were taking into a large green wastebasket liner and carried it down to the living room. Except for the fact that he moved in darkness, the house was losing its sense of strangeness. It was amazing how quickly it stopped being exciting. But that was good in a way. It meant they weren't playing a game.

Roger had found the breakfront where the good china and silver were stored. It looked like they had full service for twelve. The china, whatever its value, was useless to them but the silver was worth taking. The handles said sterling.

From the doorway Jimmy watched him remove the cases from the drawer. "Silverware?" he whispered incredulously.

"Sure. Only I don't know how to fence it. But you can get good money for it—when I find out."

I'd rather get something we can use now, Jimmy thought. After the experience of breaking in, the robbery itself was turning into a bummer. He had already given up on the idea that these people had money in the house.

Still, Roger insisted that they search every remaining closet, drawer and kitchen canister. Jimmy got disgusted after twenty minutes and gave up. They hadn't found anything. He stretched out on the thick carpet in the den, his head cradled despondently on his hands.

Roger didn't have the heart to order him back to work. But he persisted in opening drawers, idiotically shining the light inside like he expected to find diamonds. Eventually, the fruitlessness of his efforts got to him too. "I'm gonna see what's in the cellar," he said, not even bothering to whisper.

Jimmy didn't move. He was trying to figure out where this fiasco had left them. His father had clean socks and half a dozen drip-dry shirts. He had a radio that didn't work. Plus a lot of valuable silver that they apparently couldn't sell. He wondered why anyone would want to be a burglar. They were successful at it and they were still broke. They'd probably wind up going home after this. He found himself half-wishing the owners of the house would show up. Then the shit would really hit the fan.

He chuckled to himself ironically. They thought they were so smart when they figured out that the house was deserted. But people carried their money with them—obviously. If they walked in right now it wouldn't be like with that faggot in the theater, you could bet on that. This time he'd be ready.

Roger yanked him back to reality. "Jim? Let's go. We might as well take some food."

Jimmy pulled himself to his feet and headed sullenly for the kitchen. Roger had opened the overhead cupboards and was standing on the counter tops so he could reach in easily.

"I'll toss 'em down to you," he said.

The shelves were well stocked with items they could use. Two large canned hams. A variety of soups. Tuna, ketchup, peanut butter, boned chicken. Roger flipped him the cans and he read the labels and lined them up on the floor. They didn't even have this kind of stuff at home. There was crabmeat and Spam and shrimp cocktails in jars. Then came the desserts—applesauce, cling peach halves, four cans of chocolate pudding, mixed fruit cocktail.

"You like pineapple? No? Neither do I. Hey, salted peanuts! How about that!" The food kept coming faster and faster. "Brown mustard or gray mustard? C'mon, you don't have all day."

Roger tried his hook shot with a can of instant coffee. Jimmy reached out and speared it deftly. More cans flew through the air, too fast to keep track of them. Jimmy gave up trying to arrange them or even see what they were. They rained down on him from all angles as Roger remembered all his old trick shots. He was having a ball. Whistling "Sweet Georgia Brown" softly through his teeth, he pantomimed an elaborate windup and forgot to release the can.

His silliness was contagious. Once Jimmy started laughing he wasn't able to catch very well. The wilder throws bounced off his hands, thudding softly against the carpet tile. The supply of groceries seemed endless.

Suddenly a can of baked beans clanged violently on top of the stove. The sound reverberated through the house. Jimmy froze. He watched in horror as the can caromed off the dials and rolled clattering toward the edge. The second it hit the floor the room was perfectly quiet. Neither of them moved.

"Hey, we're getting too loud," Roger finally said. His voice seemed to come from far away. He lowered himself gingerly from the counter, landing silently on his toes.

Jimmy came to his senses immediately. Without saying a word he tiptoed into the living room to see if they woke anyone across the street. The houses were pitch dark, just like before. Nothing stirred at the windows. But now the stillness out there made his flesh crawl. It seemed ominous and deathlike. He returned quickly to the kitchen.

His father was gone, probably checking the side windows. It was hard to see anything through the hedge but there were no traces of light. Their nerves were on edge, Roger decided. The noise hadn't been as loud as they thought.

He found Jimmy waiting in the kitchen. Through their grotesque masks they nodded solemnly at one another.

Jimmy got another wastebasket liner and started gathering up the cans. Some had rolled across the room. He didn't bother with them. Roger watched him for a minute. If he tried to help he'd only get in the way. Having nothing to do, he opened the refrigerator. It had been cleaned out but the freezer was packed. He found four steaks and handed them to Jimmy, who took them without looking up and slipped them into his bag. They'd have two tonight when they made camp and two more for breakfast tomorrow. Any more would spoil.

In a few minutes they were ready to go. Roger held the groceries, Jimmy the lighter bag with the silver and clothes. At the back door Roger revised the escape plan. Instead of having Jimmy wait at the hedge with the stuff while he brought the car around, they'd go directly to the car together. They'd be out in the open longer but they could drive off as soon as the engine started.

Jimmy agreed.

Roger closed the door behind them, holding the knob so the bolt wouldn't click in the latch. They stood motionless on the porch, listening. Not even a bird chirped. Then through the eerie silence came the faint whine of a truck shifting gears in the distance. The sound reassured them, reminding them of the road.

CHAPTER 9

OVER BREAKFAST Friday morning Rose said, "Helen called while you were in the shower. She wondered if you'd seen the paper."

"Yeah. What about it?"

"The Des Moines paper? Hilt Greave has a story about the case."

Walt drew his lips back with a loud sucking noise. The story must have meant trouble if it had activated the distant early warning system of Helen by way of Rose. He pretended to be unconcerned but as soon as he finished eating he excused himself from the table, mumbling something about taking a short walk. Rose knew he was going to Herriot's for the paper.

It was easy to see why Helen got upset. The article implied that Walt was single-handedly blocking a speedy resolution of the Orben case. The way Hilt painted it, Pete Rollins, the Arlington County D.A., was ready to make an arrest and go before the grand jury, but he was held back by opposition from the sheriff in charge of the investigation.

Anonymous friends of Rollins' were quoted as saying the D.A. was confident an indictment would be handed down eventually, "as soon as the whole team is on board." He felt he had a strong, albeit largely circumstantial case. These friends also speculated that the sheriff "was working on some theory of his own right now" but would finally come around.

Rollins himself refused to comment directly on rumors that he and Sheriff Taliaferro had reached an impasse. All he would say was that they were in the process of evaluating the case. But he lent some credence to the reports when he remarked that law enforcement people often disagreed about the worth of circumstantial evidence.

Toward the end of the article Hilt touched briefly on Walt's reasons for arguing against an arrest at this point. (The suspect was never mentioned by name but you had to be living in a tree not to know it was Doug Eddy.) Here he brought in the item he got from the coroner—at least he buried it at the bottom of the article, Walt thought—but he explained it so perfunctorily it seemed as if it was Walt and not the killer who had the breast fixation. Anyone reading the piece would have assumed that Walt just sat around his office all day waiting for a known breast-stabber to turn up.

Hilt never referred to Walt's real reason for fighting against an indictment, though he knew it perfectly well—that he was afraid Rollins might succeed in railroading the Eddy kid for a crime he didn't commit.

As soon as Walt finished reading the paper he slammed it down and phoned Hilt's hotel. But while the operator was looking up the room number he realized he was about to make a fool of himself. Hilt'd be ready for him with his well-rehearsed platitudes. *Gee, Walt, a reporter can't let personal feelings interfere with a story.* Besides, he'd be yelling at the wrong guy anyway. He hung up.

It was clear that Rollins had orchestrated the whole thing. Hilt was only his messenger boy. Pete must be shitting in his pants right now, Walt thought, waiting for me to call. I won't give him the satisfaction.

But that didn't solve anything if Rollins wanted a showdown.

Walt respected Pete Rollins for what he used to think was his single-mindedness. Now for the first time he saw what it looked like from the other side of the table. You had to hand it to him—he knew how to attack without putting his own ass on the line. Nothing wrong with telling a reporter they were "evaluating the case." The zingers came from his "friends."

Sure they did. He personally told Walt ten times if he told him once that he needed "the whole team on board." No one else used those Watergate phrases. In fact he must have made damn sure that Hilt used exactly those words in his article. They were his private signal to the sheriff that he meant business, that he'd go public if he had to. Let Walt explain to the voters why he didn't want a grand jury hearing the evidence against Kay Orben's killer.

The more Walt thought about it the angrier he got. Which one of these "friends" had the gall to say the sheriff had "some theory of his own"? In twenty-five years of police work he'd never been patronized like that!

And fucking Hilt Greave just gobbled it up.

Some theory of his own! That was precisely the problem, wasn't it?—that he *didn't* have a theory. Unless you called it a theory that Doug Eddy was innocent.

There were only two choices. Either the killer was Doug Eddy or it was someone else. When you put it that way it sounded ridiculous, but that was how he'd been approaching the case. He had let the ball play him instead of him playing the ball. Why had he wasted so much energy trying to exonerate young Eddy? He had already answered that question to his own satisfaction. And the worst thing was that in concentrating on Eddy he had fallen right into Rollins' trap. You can't put "someone else" on trial. He had to forget that Doug Eddy existed.

He stalked out of the house, neglecting in his agitation to kiss Rose good-bye.

The goddam article was right. He *had* been sitting back, waiting for the evidence to tell him which way to turn. He'd have to be more aggressive—more mentally aggressive. He'd go over every detail again . . . and again . . . until he forced it into some semblance of sense. He had been too leery of jumping to a conclusion. That was his mistake.

Christ, he'd jump to a hundred of them if that's what it took to come up with the right one.

Walt brewed a fresh pot of coffee and cleared the top of his desk. Then he asked Matt Vollmer to bring him every scrap of material connected with the Orben case. As soon as Matt deposited the stuff and bustled off, he locked the door and spread it all out in front of him, arranging it in piles according to the sort of information contained. Lab reports went into one stack, field interviews in another, returns from other jurisdictions on his various requests for assistance in a third. He put the material related to Doug Eddy on the far corner of the desk. The drawer of physical evidence stayed right in front of him. When he was finally ready to get down to work there was barely enough space for his coffee mug, ashtray and legal pad.

He picked up the coroner's report and re-read it a few times, always pausing at the box where the cause of death was listed. *Exsanguination.* Such an odd, formal word—it meant that someone had slashed the wrists of a young girl, already helplessly bound, and let her bleed slowly to death. Given the fact that she hadn't been able to run very far—given the fact that she was lying down most of the time—Jim Godfrey had estimated that it would have taken a girl of her age and general health about twenty minutes to die. (That wasn't in the report. Walt had asked him a few days ago.) He wondered if the killer had stayed around to watch.

Then he noticed for the first time that the report didn't say when the girl's breast had been pierced. The omission could have been an oversight on Godfrey's part. Hadn't Jim nodded that night when he said it looked like a postmortem wound? Maybe he'd changed his mind. He made a note to ask him if she could have been alive when it was inflicted. The killer might have done it simply to intimidate her.

But with what?

He reached for Doug Eddy's knife in the evidence drawer, then caught himself quickly. He wasn't going to start up on that again.

No, there was someone else by the lake that day. A camper— someone on a hike. These back-to-nature types always had knives—better than Doug's old jackknife too. But the path around the lake didn't connect with any of the excellent hiking trails in the area. A casual hiker wouldn't find himself at Lake Barrett. It had to be someone looking for an isolated spot.

Or someone who had driven down one of the abandoned access roads.

He leafed through the daily logs for the week prior to the murder. A few of his more zealous deputies liked to go down to the lake at night to hassle the kids they found necking there. Occasionally they rousted someone camping illegally. He wanted to know if they had run into anyone that week, especially Friday night.

Nothing. Of course such an encounter might not show up in the logs. The men knew he thought their forays into the woods were a waste of time so they generally didn't mention them in their reports. He'd ask them specifically the first chance he got.

He pored over the photographs taken at the murder scene, trying to construct a scenario in his mind. Was the guy waiting at the car for Kay, or had she run across him when she was walking by herself? More than likely he would have been at one of the four clearings between her car and where she split up from Doug. Each was at the end of one of the access roads.

He leaned back in his swivel chair, rubbing his hand hard across his mouth. God, if only he had one clue to tell him someone had been in those clearings recently!

Kastenmeier and Grissom had searched the two clearings closest to the car for the murder weapon before he pulled them off for another assignment. There was no chance the guy dropped his knife in the open if he took the trouble to throw the first-aid kit into the water. In any case, the results of their search were somewhere in the drawer—two plastic bags containing bits of nondescript litter and a truly astonishing number of contraceptives. Bringing them in was their way of ribbing him about his objections to their teeny-bopper vice raids. He held up the bags, peering inside to see if there was anything to suggest the clearing had been visited shortly before the murder. Almost everything looked like it had been through quite a bit of weather. There was a garment tag that was considerably fresher but it turned out to be clipped off a kid's bathing suit. Judging by the size Danny wore, the suit was for a boy about eleven or twelve years old. If the kid had been there Saturday, he might have seen someone. But it was a manufacturer's tag and a common brand at that. Without the store name it would be useless trying to trace the suit.

Search other clearings, he wrote on his pad, making a mental note to tell the guys to leave the rubbers where they found them.

He got himself another cup of coffee and returned to the desk. He didn't sit there for long.

The missing piece to the puzzle was why the guy had killed her *and* vandalized her car. He paced back and forth the length of the office. The answer wasn't anywhere in the piles of data collected so far.

In a way, the assault on the car gave him a better line on the guy than the killing itself. It was quirky. Routine checks on every known rapist in the area hadn't even turned up a possible. He leaned over his desk and buzzed the sergeant on duty outside on the intercom. "Jerry? Have Matt get me everything in the last couple months on auto felony—burglary, theft and vandalism. See what the city police have too."

It was a shot in the dark but it certainly couldn't hurt to check. Maybe the car was the catalyst, not the girl. Let's say she caught him in the act of doing something to the car. Then he pulls a knife on her. At some point he gets the adhesive tape from the first-aid kit in the car . . . before he undresses her because her sleeves had to be slit . . .

Matt tried the door knob, jiggling it loudly when it didn't turn immediately. Walt let him in.

"What you want this auto stuff for, Walt? How come the door's locked?"

Walt waved off the questions. "Listen to this, Matt. I'm thinking out loud. The guy's trying to steal the car, or break into it, and Kay catches him. He pulls a knife . . . "

Matt shook his head. "No sign of tampering—locks or ignition. It's in one of them reports."

Walt bit his lip. "Yeah. All right. Let's say he was just starting . . . "

"What makes you think he was already at the car?"

"It's a hypothesis. That's all."

"Well, if the guy hadn't done anything to the car yet, what makes you think he wasn't just admiring it. It's a gorgeous machine."

Walt's eyes fell to the sheaf of papers his deputy was still holding. For a dumb guy Matt sometimes made a surprising amount of sense. Without evidence of tampering he didn't have a car thief any more, just someone hanging around a big new Lincoln.

"Try this then. He's a vandal. When she walks up he's throwing rocks at the car."

"Not with all that racket. A girl, by herself—she'd be too scared to get near the place."

This was getting embarrassing. "Maybe he had finished the vandalizing before she got near enough to hear." He laughed. "Then why does he stick around, right? See, I'm trying to figure an angle that brings in the car as well as the killing. How's this sound? Pulls the knife, ties her up, undresses her. Tries to rape her. Can't. He has some kind of hang-up. Okay? So what does he do? He jerks off against the front of the car. Then he's so ashamed that he picks up a rock . . . "

It was easy to get carried away with this kind of psychological speculation. Matt listened impassively. "Wait a minute, back up a minute," Walt caught himself. "I'm forgetting something. The lab says he masturbated *after* the car was smashed. When he can't rape her he gets so frustrated—frustrated, not ashamed—that he smashes the car. Then . . . "

"When does he kill her?" Matt interrupted.

"When?" He wasn't ready for the question. "After the rape attempt?"

"I don't like it," Matt said decisively.

Walt threw his arms out in exasperation. "I don't care if you *like* it," he said, his voice rising in pitch. "Does it make any sense?"

"Not to me, Walt. It's too complicated."

"Look," Walt explained with exaggerated patience, "it doesn't have to make sense to you, it just has to make sense to the killer. He's a psychopath. His mind doesn't function like ours."

Matt gazed at him blankly.

The answer has to be complicated, Walt thought defensively. What was it Hilt said—that we were dealing with a Jekyll and Hyde type? Yes, and I said it was different because this guy had two violent personalities—a cool one that slit her wrists and a hot-tempered one that smashed the car. God, it was incredible to think there could be so much hatred in a man that it needed two ways to express itself.

Maybe it was two people. He had never thought of that before. For the better part of a week now he'd been insisting it's not Doug Eddy, it's someone else. Some*one* else. But why just one? Two men opened a whole range of possibilities, all of them disturbing. Somehow it was easier to accept the idea of a single deranged man lashing out at the world than of a pair of killers egging one another on. His upper lip curled in disgust. Sure, there were plenty of cases—Leopold and Loeb, for instance—but the idea of men killing together, not for money or gain, men killing in packs . . . it was somehow subhuman. It did violence to his deepest instincts about how people dealt with one another.

He shook his head and took a deep breath. "All right," he said aloud. "Why don't you sit down, Matt? Let's run through the whole thing again—only this time we've got a team of assailants."

A low, unnatural sound, begun some time ago, gradually trickled down through the layers of sleep, forcing him to take notice. He squirmed uncomfortably, resisting the impulse to wake up. Suddenly it stopped. Jimmy Mapes lifted his head, wholly alert in an instant. He peered into the darkness, seeming to sniff the air like an animal sensing danger.

What was it? He tried to remember how it sounded but there was nothing now. His father lay on the ground not far away with his head almost under the rear bumper. His pants, which he had rolled up to use as a pillow, had been shoved to the side. He tossed restlessly, his body jerking in uneasy spasms. Maybe he heard it too but he didn't wake up. When he rolled onto his side Jimmy saw his back streaked with dirt. Earlier they had been caught by the edge of a very brief thunderstorm, just enough to settle the dust. And in the warm and clammy night air anything that touched adhered to the skin.

In a few minutes Jimmy lowered his head, trying to put the sound out of his mind. Whatever it was, he wouldn't hear it again. But his eyes wouldn't close. He didn't feel like sleeping anymore. The other night he and his father had sat up late talking. Around three in the morning the far-off howling began.

Roger said, "Coyotes."

"Really? Around here?" Jimmy asked, his voice rising in momentary excitement. It was hard to think of coyotes within a few days' drive of home.

"Yeah. Anyway it's some kind of wild dog." They kept up their wailing an hour or so and then moved on.

This sound tonight had been more human—a low, guttural moan. Jimmy couldn't tell how far away. Maybe it was a dream, suggested by the dogs. The notion upset him. It was better if it came from out there.

He stood up, brushing the congealed dust from his body where he could reach, and set out toward the live oak that stood by itself at the foot of a gentle declivity about half a mile away. He crossed a field left fallow for the year. Old furrows made the ground uneven and treacherous. He had to step carefully to avoid turning an ankle. A quarter moon hung poised above the tree. As he walked down the slope it seemed to rise higher in the sky. Its light, glinting palely off the short, dead stubble of last year's harvest, made the land look inhospitable.

He sat down at the base of the tree, gazing back toward the car silhouetted on the crest of the knoll. A faint breeze stirred the air but it felt unpleasant on his bare skin, clogged with a long day's sweat and grime. One day the weather would have to break and it would come down in torrents. It would clear the air—at least for a while. He was sick of this constant stickiness.

On his left he heard the rustle of a jackrabbit bounding an erratic course. His head wheeled instinctively but wherever it was, he didn't see it. The other, tiny sounds were probably field mice. You had to be still for a good while before you could hear them.

He thought, I'll stay here till morning. Maybe I'll sleep. But he felt awake now, too awake to lie down. He didn't know how long he'd have to wait before dawn. Cloistered under the twisting branches of the live oak, he realized he was listening attentively. That eerie sound still bothered him. Gradually, he persuaded himself that it hadn't been a nightmare. As long as it wasn't just in his mind, he wasn't really afraid of its coming back. Maybe the next time he could tell what it was.

No, there was something besides a strange noise in the middle of the night. He felt depressed—and lonely—though he couldn't put his finger on a reason. Traveling with his father, his days were full—interesting if not always exciting. They were getting along better than at any time in the past, except of course for that odd, tranquil period right after Marty died. Roger's sullenness, his quickness to take offense, had all but left him. Still, something was missing. The last few days the boy had felt more and more cut off from reality. He loved the car, the idea of driving nowhere with his father and of camping wherever they stopped. But the feeling grew that it wasn't enough. Sooner or later he'd want to reach out in some other direction.

Then it started again. At first it was a series of sharp, anguished gasps coming from the direction of the knoll. They weren't loud but the sound carried well on the still night air. It was his father, moaning in his sleep.

Jimmy leaped to his feet, pausing as if suspended for a moment to listen before starting to run. He thought he heard words but they were slurred and jumbled together, the voice that uttered them rising and falling at random. It was like some primitive incantation, its logic buried to the mind. He raced across the open field, stumbling a few times but managing to keep his balance. He told himself to shorten his stride, to match it to the width of the furrows, but he couldn't make himself slow down. The dead stalks pricked the soles of his bare feet and poked cuttingly between his toes.

Several times he heard the same cry, two words stretched out in a ragged glissando of pain. *It's not?* he thought. Is that what he's saying? *Oh no?* As he got closer the voice seemed to be coming from everywhere. It confused him but he kept running toward his father.

"Dad! Dad!" he panted, sprinting the last thirty yards. His father was muttering feverishly—words that had no meaning—his lips seeming to form different syllables than the ones Jimmy heard. He writhed on the ground, his eyes open but unseeing.

The boy stopped short a few steps away. He felt helpless, not knowing how to bring his father out of the nightmare. The sweat poured from Roger's face, forming rivulets with each contortion of his features. Despite himself, Jimmy continued to hang back in awed fascination.

Finally he stepped forward, placing his hand gently on his father's shoulder. Roger sat bolt upright, his eyes staring blankly straight past the boy.

"Dad? You all right?" Jimmy asked softly. His father looked terrified. He breathed shallowly, sucking air in rapid gulps. Slowly he began to awaken.

Jimmy touched him lightly on the shoulder again.

Roger turned to him, utterly bewildered. "Jim?" he said, his voice hoarse with exhaustion. "Wow."

"Are you gonna be all right?"

"Yeah." He reached his arm out, resting it heavily across the boy's neck. Jimmy sat back on his haunches, letting his father transfer as much weight to him as he could. Roger's head hung down. He was still breathing hard, not yet over the panic of waking up. Drops of sweat formed on the tip of his nose, growing larger until they fell of their own weight. He seemed to be watching them as they formed a small puddle between his thighs. After a few minutes he shook his head like a wet dog.

"Wow," he said again softly, not yet wanting to comprehend what had happened. "I was having a nightmare."

CHAPTER 10

S H E I L A   M A P E S   S T O O D in line at the Unemployment Office for over an hour. She had thrown on a faded blue house-dress and a kerchief to cover her hair. Roger had picked up his last check the day before he left but he hadn't given her any of the money. Since then she had scraped by, spending next to nothing herself and always expecting him to return any moment. She used her own paycheck Wednesday evening to pay bills just as she normally did, not thinking that she might need the money herself. Actually, it was a superstitious gesture, as if reducing herself to penury would force him to come back. She was getting more and more worried. Thursday she wrote a check for thirty-five dollars—it was the highest round figure their balance allowed—but had to use most of it to buy food and a few items from the drugstore.

The more she thought about it, the less confident she was that he'd ever come back. Oh, he'd gone away lots of times, once even taking the boys with him. But this time seemed different. Things between them had reached a point where there was really nothing to come back to. There wasn't a relationship any more. Maybe there never had been but it was more obvious now. And it wasn't just that, it was a little bit of everything—his job and Marty dead and nothing down the road to make the future look any brighter. Yes, this time he wasn't coming back. In the long run she was better off without him. They'd both be better off.

But the long run wasn't going to help her get through the next two weeks until she got paid again. And by then more bills would have piled up. Friday morning she called in sick, too upset to face the prospect of eight hours answering a phone. Roger'd have to come by the house to pick up his booklet before going down to the Unemployment Office. By noon she couldn't sit still any longer. She had smoked a pack and a half of cigarettes. The damn thing was she didn't really know what she wanted to happen.

She debated going down to the Unemployment Office herself. It was pointless. She knew they wouldn't give her the money.

Finally she got dressed and went anyway. Maybe if she told them a good story they'd let her have the check and she could forge his signature on it. The checks were there, already printed. At least they'd have to listen to her. She had to get out of the house.

For over an hour she waited in line. A couple of times people said something to her but she was in no mood for small talk. Her perfunctory responses discouraged them from trying again.

When the clerk finally motioned for her to step forward she handed him Roger's packet without saying anything. He glanced at her and at the name on the booklet a few times. She wore the same look of sullen defiance as most of the people who came to his window.

"This isn't your booklet," he said. "Your name isn't Roger Mapes?"

"It's my husband's. I'm supposed to pick up his check for him." She wanted to say something else, to tell him the story she had worked out, but she just couldn't bring herself to go through with the charade. Inside, she seethed with anger and resentment— against Roger, and the clerk, and the long line, and herself.

"Sorry. Checks can only be given to the person whose name is on the booklet. Your husband will have to come down here and get it himself." He handed her back the booklet.

She took it but didn't move aside.

"Ma'am? Did you hear what I said? Is there any reason your

husband can't get down here today?" He was a kid in his early twenties with a thick brown moustache.

"Why can't you give it to me? I'm his wife. It's not like I'm trying to steal his money." Her voice was flat and toneless, more weary than stubborn.

"Those are the rules," the clerk said softly, as if they were talking in a library. "A recipient has to be able to work. If he can work he can come down for his check. I'm sure your husband knows that. Now there are other people waiting in line . . ."

"*I* waited in line," Sheila mumbled, feeling hurt but not really understanding what she was saying. They couldn't shunt her aside just like that. "I waited over an hour," she whined. "Please, I'm entitled to that money."

The clerk sucked in his cheeks. He was losing his patience with her. "I'm sorry, ma'am. There's nothing I can do."

A man behind her tapped her on the shoulder. "Look, lady, I've been standing here . . ."

She whirled on him angrily. "Look yourself!" she snarled. "You wait your turn until I'm finished." She continued to glare at him, her lips twisted in a hateful sneer.

"Lady. Lady!" the clerk said. "Take it easy. You want to talk to the administrator? Huh? Explain to him what the problem is?"

"I want my goddam money, that's the problem! You got it right there in that drawer." She was talking louder now, almost shouting. She couldn't stop though she wanted to desperately.

Behind the counter, typewriters stopped clicking. Everyone turned toward the scene at the front window.

"Look, lady . . . Mrs. Mapes, I can't . . ."

She leaned across the counter, reaching for the file drawer with the checks. The clerk drew back as if her touch might kill him. "C'mon, cut it out!" he said, raising his voice too.

"Calm down, lady," a voice said behind her.

"Hey, get mine too, willya, lady?"

"What the hell is going on here?"

"Please, lady, you can't . . ."

"I think she's crazy."

"I want my goddam money! I don't have a fucking cent, do you know that! Do any of you know that!" She was screaming hysterically while around her everyone else jabbered at once. In back of the counter clerks scurried over from all directions. Behind her the line of recipients broke and surged forward to get a better look. She was trapped, penned in on all sides by leering, curious faces and bodies pressed against her.

"Somebody get a hold of her," one of the voices said, more commanding than the rest.

"I need that money! Can't you see that! Goddam you, I'm entitled to it!" She had lost control of herself completely, her voice choking in sobs and rage. At her back a man jostled against her. She swung her elbow hard against his ribs, knocking him backward for a second. He flung his arms around her, pinning hers to her side. Others reached out, pawing, helping him subdue her.

"Take your fucking hands off me! Leave me alone!"

Behind the counter a man in a tie pointed to an interview room off in a corner. Three men held onto her, trying to carry her away. The crowd backed off gradually, clearing a path. They were almost silent now, listening in amazement to her incoherent, heart-rending shrieks. But once they got her behind the counter she seemed suddenly spent. They let her walk the rest of the way.

She remained calm after that. The administrator, the man in the tie, spent forty-five minutes listening to her story, which, she said, made her feel much better. He was sympathetic but at the end there wasn't much he could suggest to help her through her financial crisis. He was sure, however, her husband and son would be back pretty soon. In the meantime, maybe her boss or someone in her family would lend her money, or was there someone she could stay with until things got back to normal?

She stood up, regarding him with a bitter half-smile. "No," she said. "But thank you. You've been very kind."

From the Unemployment Office she walked to the Mayflower Coffee Shop, where she usually ate lunch. At two-thirty in the afternoon the place was deserted. She asked for a grilled cheese sandwich and coffee.

Paula wrote down the order. "You not workin' today?"

"No. I took the day off."

"Heard anything from Roger yet?"

She shook her head.

Paula nodded understandingly. "Between you and me, kid, maybe it's just as well if you don't."

When Sheila finished her coffee she asked Paula if it was all right if she paid her tomorrow.

"Sure. Next time you're in."

It was too late to go to the bank. It didn't matter. She knew what they'd tell her anyway. Since it wasn't a joint savings account she couldn't withdraw the money without her husband's signature. She wondered though—if he deserted me and he doesn't claim the money, how long will I have to wait to get it? She'd have to find out, first thing Monday morning.

⊂╞   ⊂╞   ⊂╞

As if pulled by an invisible string, one end of which was anchored in Arlington, Roger and Jimmy swung north before they left Kansas. They had to be able to camp near fresh water. Their course took them up through Iowa, cutting obliquely across the Missiouri watershed, past rivers splayed neatly as the fingers on a hand.

Ever since that horrible nightmare their days had settled into a narcotic sameness. Whatever exhilaration Jimmy had once found in aimless drifting seemed to have vanished beyond recall. They weren't on the run—because no one was after them—but they weren't going anywhere either. Jimmy felt the lack of purpose. With next to no money and food soon to run short, there were decisions that had to be made. Otherwise, they'd find themselves back in Arlington, taking up where they left off as if nothing had happened.

Jimmy half-suspected that was what his father wanted. It made a certain amount of sense, not drawing attention to themselves by disappearing forever on the day of the murder.

But that was exactly the point. They had killed a girl, after all—or at least Roger had killed her. Were they supposed to go home after that, go back to school or their friends as if they were no different from anyone else?

Yet Roger refused to discuss their alternatives. If he just said, Yes, we're going back—because it's safest, or because I'm tired of living in a car like some fucking itinerant—Jimmy had decided that he could accept it. But Roger wouldn't make a decision one way or the other. He seemed to be waiting until their circumstances made it for him. One morning they'd wake up broke and hungry and within an hour or two of their house. And they'd go home. They didn't even have the guts to admit that that's what they were doing.

It pissed Jimmy off. Every time he tried to force the issue his father wormed out of it with one excuse or another. He never lost his temper but maybe it would have been better if he did. He spoke only when necessary and then in as few words as possible. The rest of the time he seemed oblivious to the boy.

Jimmy kept his resentment inside. He remembered how frightened his father had been and now he saw him just sitting back passively, letting their fate slip out of their hands. It was a kind of betrayal, even worse than the outbursts of hostility he more or less took for granted. He sensed that his father was still scared—he didn't know about what—but there was no sympathy accompanying the intuition. His disillusionment felt like an empty space growing inside him. He didn't know how to deal with it. He blamed Roger for his weakness, his sudden paralysis. If that's how he wants it, he fumed, recalling how forceful his father could be when it suited him—if that's how he wants it. . . . But he never completed the idea. He spent hours staring doggedly out the side window.

For most of three days they drove in silence, each making what accommodation he could with the heat and the boredom and the filthiness of his body.

The evenings, however, were considerably better. On Friday and again on Sunday it sprinkled for a few minutes shortly before dusk. The air hardly cooled off at all but at least the humidity, so brutal and enervating during the day, loosened its hold until the next morning. It was a pleasure to breathe deeply. After a swim and some supper they slipped into an uneasy cameraderie. As night approached Roger seemed to find his son's presence reassuring. Just doing something—moving around outside the car—helped both of them unwind.

They talked vaguely about the future. Roger was still reluctant to commit himself to a plan but Jimmy wheedled him into promising that they wouldn't go home. Of course his promises didn't mean much as a rule. Nevertheless, Jimmy found some measure of satisfaction in knowing that his father wasn't determined to drag them back to Arlington.

Late Sunday night Roger surprised Jimmy by suggesting that they get themselves fishing rods. They had just finished the last of the canned hams so it was only natural to think about their dwindling food supply. But Jimmy knew they didn't have enough money to buy even the crummiest gear. Roger usually steered away from discussing their desperate finances.

The boy hesitated, wondering if this was really an invitation to make plans. If it was, he didn't want to say the wrong thing.

"What do you think we could catch?" he asked, stalling for time to see how the wind blew.

"I don't know exactly. Carp. Smallmouth. Catfish, I'm pretty sure."

"We'd have to buy the rods, wouldn't we?"

"You know any other way?"

"Do we have the money?"

Roger shook his head. "What do you think about pulling off another job?" he asked matter-of-factly.

Jimmy couldn't suppress a triumphant grin but his father wasn't looking. He was staring intently at the end of his cigarette. Then he blew on the ash to make it glow a bright orange.

"Sure. How?" Jimmy said.

Roger shrugged his shoulders as though, having posed the idea, he had suddenly lost interest in it. He laughed quietly under his breath. "It won't be the same as last time, I can tell you that."

They talked for a while about the different ways they might do it. Sitting together in the darkness and quiet, it was hard sometimes to remember that they were actually planning a crime. It didn't seem real. But gradually, amid all the fantasy and idle speculation, a few points became clear.

Certainly they weren't going to break into any more empty buildings. The payoff didn't justify the risk. Whatever they decided on, it would have to involve people.

Armed robbery was out of the question, and they couldn't just walk up to a house with a knife in their hands. Then Roger said that most women would open their door without thinking for a father and son who told a plausible story.

Jimmy liked the idea immediately—as soon as he realized his father was serious. Once they got inside they'd just have to pull a knife on the woman and she'd give them whatever she had in the house. It sounded incredibly easy.

Besides, the house would protect them, Roger said. It would give them a margin for error.

Jimmy didn't understand what he meant by that. Why were they even talking about errors? But he made no comment. The beauty of the scheme was that it was so simple nothing could go wrong. He couldn't get over it. "You mean we just ring the bell and ask if we can come in?" he said excitedly, not so much questioning the plan as voicing his admiration.

"Something like that," Roger said diffidently. "We give her a reason. I'll handle that. If she says no, we just go someplace else."

"Oh, she wouldn't do that," Jimmy said, raising his eyebrows in a mock leer.

Roger smirked. "No. But she might ask me to come back later without the kid."

So they had adopted a strategy. But beyond that point they went around in circles, unable to decide how to put it in action. The slightest detail gave rise to an argument. Most of the time Jimmy gave in pretty quickly. But he kept coming back to the fact that Roger insisted on doing it in the afternoon, when they were more likely to find the woman alone. There was nothing wrong with that except her husband undoubtedly carried more money.

Finally Jimmy said, "Why can't we tie her up or something until he comes home? He's not going to do anything if we got her?"

Roger shook his head. "No. We'll get enough money from her. There's no point in sticking around any longer than we have to."

"Yeah. But what if we don't get enough? What if she's only got a few dollars?"

Roger's eyes narrowed. "You can't have it both ways," he said adamantly, his voice firm but controlled. "We get in and get out."

This time Jimmy didn't let it pass. It wasn't only the money. It struck him his father had reasons he wouldn't discuss.

Still, Roger kept saying no, but he didn't stop Jimmy from pursuing the argument. That wasn't like him. But the reiterated and unexplained denials were too much for the boy's patience.

"Look," he said sharply, "gimme one good reason. That's all I want—one good reason."

"I just don't like it, that's the reason!" Roger snapped back. But even as spoke, he seemed to realize that that wouldn't be the last word. In a softer voice, he added, "Let's see how it goes. We'll get enough money from her. Don't you worry about it."

Jimmy thought, Sure. And there were supposed to be hundreds of dollars in that house in Missouri. But his father had left the door open, at least a little. The boy stood up and wandered around to the other side of the car. He didn't understand what was bothering his father—what was making him behave so uncharacteristically. "You know what?" he said tentatively. "Either way we're gonna have to kill them . . . 'cause they could identify us easy."

Roger nodded, so slightly the boy wasn't sure there was any movement at all. He kept waiting for a response.

Jimmy's right, Roger was thinking. If they went into a house it would have to come to that anyway, no matter what they said now. He could picture them doing it once they were caught up in the situation. But planning it in advance—he didn't like the sound of it when it was laid out so logically, didn't want to think that many steps ahead.

There were things the boy didn't understand—that moment in the clearing when it suddenly came to him that the girl would be dead in a few minutes. She was as good as dead. It was the strangest feeling, as if there was an imaginary line you crossed without even realizing it. It seemed that nothing very important had happened, but he saw that she was going to die. If the knife blade had been pointing up it would have sliced the adhesive tape . . . but he had pointed it down. Then he stood right there above her and she crossed that line and the moment should have been obvious but it wasn't. Looking at her, he couldn't see any change at all. It was a subtle thing, too trivial to remember. Like who, watching that scene, could have told you whether his wrist turned up or down?

That was what he had seen as he stood by the girl, that the difference between alive and dead was less than he had imagined. When Marty died everything flew apart, exploded on him just when he thought he had a hold on it. But when the girl died nothing happened.

Jimmy still waited for his answer. He couldn't see why a man who had killed someone before was so reluctant to talk about doing it again. It never occurred to him that that might be the reason. But he didn't mind waiting.

Finally Roger said, "I was thinking the same thing myself." It was almost a commitment. He didn't turn to look at the boy and his voice sounded hollow and remote.

"It's up to you," Jimmy said meekly. There was something eerie in his father's tone that made him suddenly afraid to push any harder.

There was another long silence. Roger stared straight ahead into the darkness of the woods. He stretched his arms over his head and yawned wearily as if resigning himself to something inevitable. "All right," he said. "But let's not do it tomorrow. I . . . uh . . . let's hold off a day or two."

Sheriff Taliaferro, who had been sitting with his swivel chair tipped back off the floor, suddenly leaned forward and spread his arms on the desk. The clatter of the casters on the brittle linoleum distracted the woman. She stopped talking abruptly in mid-sentence.

"Excuse me," Walt said. "Please go on, Mrs. Mapes."

The truth was he hadn't really been listening the past several minutes. She had told him a couple times that her husband had been missing for more than a week but it didn't click right away that he had left home on Saturday, the day the Orben girl had been murdered. As soon as he realized it he seized on the coincidence like a dog with a bone.

Normally, he was able to brush these random notions aside or at least file them away mentally if they seemed at all promising—as this one obviously didn't. Mapes apparently had a history of running out on his wife—small wonder, now that he had talked to her—and there wasn't a shred of evidence to connect him with the killing or to put him anywhere near Lake Barrett that day. In fact she said he left early in the morning so he would have been long gone by four or five in the afternoon. Besides, his latest theory had him looking for two men anyway.

Still . . . he tried to picture this Roger Mapes to himself while Mrs. Mapes droned on in the background. When their son had committed suicide a year or so ago, Walt had handled the investigation. It was perfectly routine, but there was something about Mapes that stuck in his mind. Now for the life of him he couldn't remember what it was. It was nothing concrete, just a vague impression he had at the time that Mapes was an odd one, that he didn't act quite the way you expected him to. Though how a man is supposed to act when his son kills himself is a good question.

Shit, Walt thought self-reproachfully, what's the matter with me? Here I've got this woman in my office and I'm not even listening. Sure, the Orben case had top priority but he had let it become an obsession. It had reached the point where he started looking at anyone without an alibi for the afternoon of May 10 as a suspect. That was paranoia, not police work.

He forced himself to snap out of his reverie. Fortunately, the woman was too preoccupied with herself to notice that he hadn't been paying attention. But when he leaned forward unexpectedly and looked in her eyes, the sudden movement brought her monologue to a halt.

He asked her to continue.

"Where was I?" she said. "I just don't know what I'm going to do. I tried every place—the Unemployment, the bank. They all say they're sorry but there's nothing they can do. It's not their problem."

The sheriff winced visibly. With her thin, nasal whine, her voice catching occasionally in her throat, she projected her unhappiness like an accusation. Everyone refused to help her, not because they couldn't but because they didn't want to. Now was he going to do anything, or did he have some excuse too?

"Mrs. Mapes," he said deliberately, "you said your husband's gone away several times before. Don't you think, if you just wait, he'll be back pretty soon?"

He saw the tears well up in the corners of her eyes. "No, he won't come back this time," she said, starting to cry. "I know he won't. And do you think I'd be any better off if he did? You have no idea what it's been like."

Walt lowered his eyes to his desk top. Her logic didn't make sense but he understood the desperation that had brought her to his office. As terrified as she was of resuming her wretched marriage, she needed her husband back. Maybe she still loved him—whatever that meant in a case of this sort. It made no difference one way or the other. The fact remained that she was broke—the small amount of money they had was all tied up in his name. And she wasn't the type of person who could cope with life on her own.

So she came to the sheriff. Whether she wanted him to find her husband for her or simply take legal cognizance of the fact that he was missing, he didn't know. He guessed it would be to her benefit if it could be established that Mapes had deserted her.

In either case his hands were tied. As a matter of law, with no reason to suspect foul play, he couldn't even accept a missing person report, much less act on it, until the party had been gone fourteen days.

He explained the situation as carefully as he could, suggesting delicately that she come back the next Monday if Roger still hadn't returned. She said she didn't understand a law like that but she accepted his position with the same dumb fatalism she had used so tellingly to reproach all the others who had been unable to help her.

She made Walt feel impotent. The interview was obviously at an end but she didn't get up to leave. She was going to make him send her away.

He clucked his tongue in frustration, not relishing the prospect. "Your son is with him?" he said, thinking the fact offered a glimmer of hope.

She brightened perceptibly. "Yes. Does that make a difference? I have a right to my son. Can't you do anything about it? Isn't it kidnapping or something?"

Walt tried not to smile. It wasn't what he had in mind. "Not if he's the legal father," he said. "I was just wondering—would your husband take the boy with him if he didn't intend to come back? Most men in that situation don't want the responsibility."

Sheila snorted contemptuously. If she saw his point, she refused to accept its implication. No mere conjecture could stand against her self-pity. "If he wanted responsibility," she said with devastating irrelevance, "I wouldn't be here right now."

As soon as she left, Walt began girding himself for his showdown with D.A. Pete Rollins. The first thing in the morning Pete's secretary had called. Would it be convenient for the sheriff to be in the district attorney's office at four-thirty that afternoon?

Not as convenient as for him to be in mine, Walt thought. But he didn't argue the point. It was just like Rollins, who had always dealt with him directly in the past, to send the invitation through formal channels. Walt, of course, answered his own phone. So Pete was calling attention to the difference in their positions. If Walt didn't like the arrangement, he'd have to hash it out with an underling.

Well, he didn't like it but he'd be damned if he'd get involved in this one-upsmanship bullshit. He'd let Pete have his symbolic victories but he wasn't going to yield an inch when it came to Doug Eddy.

The D.A.'s office was on the third floor of the old county courthouse. It was once an elegant building, spacious enough to accommodate all the W.P.A. gimcrackery. Though it had been allowed to deteriorate since the new facility had been built at Meade River, Walt was still partial to its old-fashioned dignity. Its dingy, paneled corridors suggested the mystical power of order and law in a way that the new building, with its featureless halls and functional, acoustically tiled offices, could never approximate. It would be a shame when Pete finally gave in and moved out there.

Laboriously, he mounted the stairs. By the top he was puffing like a whale. He took off his cap and mopped his damp brow. His angina—that was another reason Pete should have come to see him.

No, don't start thinking like that, he told himself stubbornly. He didn't want favors, to be treated like an invalid.

If he was out of breath it was his own fault. He knew better than to start up with cigarettes again. Still, he needed one right now.

His hand trembled slightly as he fished the pack from his pocket. He lit one. He'd be over it in a minute. Leaning against the banister, he drew in the smoke deeply, letting its warmth and its flavor relax him. When he finished it he was ready to go in.

Pete ushered him into his office and then made him wait a few minutes while he conferred with his secretary outside. When he returned his manner was coldly professional.

"Thanks for coming, Walt. I wanted you to know I'm going for the indictment."

"You could have told me that over the phone."

"I thought you'd want to discuss the case. You're still in charge of the investigation."

That's right, Walt thought, bristling at the veiled threat implied by the "still." And I'll be in charge of investigations around here long after the voters have thrown you out on your ass. Rollins didn't worry him though. He didn't have the nerve to try to get him bumped from the case.

But he didn't say anything. He wanted to see just how hard a line Rollins was going to take.

The D.A. sat down behind his massive oak desk and took a deep breath. "Listen, Walt," he said grimly, "there's no reason we have to be at loggerheads over this thing. I got a solid case to give the grand jury. I'm not concerned about it. So I'm not trying to rush you into anything. Believe me, I'm not. But there's an incredible amount of pressure to wrap this thing up. I'm sure you're getting it too."

"Get to the point. You don't have to tell me about pressure."

"The point is, I'm going to move on this. I want you along. I can't wait till you're satisfied you've got an airtight case—if that's what's hanging you up. I've held off on your account as long as I could. Now I think it's your turn to bend a little."

"Pete, we're not talking about doing little favors for each other . . ."

"I know we're not. We're talking about the fact that the chief law enforcement officer is supposed to present the evidence to the grand jury. You'll have to testify at the trial so you might as well do it now."

Walt reached across the desk for one of Pete's cigarettes. "Let me ask you a question," he said, not meaning to sound flippant. "Are you sure the kid's guilty?"

"I got a good case, Walt. A damned good case."

"That's not what I asked."

"You want my opinion? Then yes. He's guilty as hell."

Walt wasn't taken in by Rollins' air of assurance. "Then what do you need me for?" he said. "You can get your indictment without me holding your hand."

"Don't play games with me, Walt," Pete snapped, his jowls trembling. "I'm not worried about the grand jury and you know it. But what happens after that? This is the biggest fucking case this county's ever seen. How's it going to look if the sheriff decides to sit on the sidelines?"

"Look to who, Pete? You're not worried about my image all of a sudden."

"You know what I mean!"

"I know exactly what you mean," Walt said, pleased that he was managing to keep his voice down. He wanted Pete to be the one who seemed overanxious. "You're afraid this thing's gonna blow up in your face and you don't want to be out there alone when it happens."

"That's a pile of crap!"

"Is it? Look what you've got. Two witnesses who can place Eddy two miles from the scene of the crime an hour and a half before it happened. He left the beach with her—-that's all. The rest is conjecture. You've got nothing whatsoever to connect him with the killing."

"I got opportunity. I got motive."

"What motive?"

"What motive?" Pete spluttered. "What do you suppose they were doing in the woods? He put the make on her and she turned him down."

Walt sat back in his chair. "If the kid doesn't take the stand," he said coolly, "you can't even talk about that. His lawyer'd have to be crazy to let him testify."

Pete eyed him levelly, the corners of his mouth turned up in a vindictive sneer. "Then unless he's crazy," he said, calling Walt's bluff, "the kid is dead. The jury's got to think he walked the girl to her car. That means nobody else could possibly have killed her."

Walt knew he had made a mistake, starting with an argument Rollins had no trouble demolishing. It put him on the defensive. "That's not the point," he said, snuffing out his half-finished cigarette. "So he testifies. He kissed the girl. What does that prove? Where's your violent intent? It's not even suspicious behavior."

Pete shook his head. "Walt," he said condescendingly, "you're being awfully naive. How's it going to look when he says he goes into the woods with her, they stop for a little hanky-panky, and then she doesn't want him around anymore? They had a fight, huh? Looks pretty bad, doesn't it?"

"The question is, How does it look to *you*, Pete?" Walt said, drumming emphatically with his finger on the arm of his chair. He saw what Rollins was doing and he was getting worked up. "The kid's got no history of being mentally unstable. He's good-looking, popular with girls. You can't believe for a minute he turned into a rapist and murderer just because some girl didn't put out for him the first day they met!"

Pete merely grinned. "That's another thing," he said. "I've got people checking into his background. You watch—he's not going to be the angel you think he is."

"I checked him out already, Pete. I never said he's an angel. He's *normal*—can't you understand that? Try and remember when you were nineteen. You got what you could off a girl and that was the end of it. You didn't go crazy every time one said no." He spoke heatedly, his finger now jabbing the air to punctuate each phrase. "That's where you lose me, Pete, and that's where you ought to stand back and take a good look at yourself. Because it's a terrific jump from petting to murder. You got no evidence for making that jump. Everything we know about the kid argues against it. I know what you're trying to do. You can get your goddam indictment whenever you want it. And maybe you can get a conviction— if the kid's got no one but his lawyer raising these questions. That's what you need me for. You'll twist that kid inside out on the stand and I'll be there to help you stampede the jury—*but the boy isn't guilty!* Go ahead if you want, Pete, but you'll have to do it without me."

Pete remained silent during the sheriff's tirade. When it was over he took a cigarette from his case and tapped it nervously on his desk before lighting it. "I can tell you this much," he said bitterly. "I'm not going to let you blow me out of the water. If you want out, I'll see that you're out."

Walt stared at him incredulously a long time without saying anything. He found Rollins' cynicism almost physically revolting. First the D.A. tried to railroad a kid he wasn't sure was guilty and now he threatened the man who tried to stand in his way. "Forget it," Walt finally said softly, not hiding his disgust.

Pete turned his head away. "I'm sorry, Walt," he said feebly. "I didn't mean that the way it sounded. Maybe you're right. How'll it be if I hold off a while—another week or so? It'll give us both time to see where we stand."

Walt started to say something but changed his mind. Pete had hedged his concession but it was good enough for now. "Yeah, fine," the sheriff said. "I told you the other day, we're looking for two guys, not one. Doug Eddy had nothing to do with it." His voice was suddenly thick with fatigue. He wanted to be out of there but he didn't have the energy to get up.

Pete smiled woodenly. "You told me. But do you have any

leads?'' He felt better now that they had switched to an area where the sheriff's own performance left room for improvement.

"Not yet. But things keep coming in.'' It was an effort to remember what he was trying to say. . . . There was some point he wanted to make. . . . "Do you remember Roger Mapes?''

Pete mulled over the name. "I don't think so.''

"His son committed suicide last year? His wife was in my office. Mapes disappeared a while ago. May 10, in fact. They had a fight and he walked out.''

"Do you think he might be the guy? You know where he is?''

"No. The pieces don't fit.'' He shrugged his shoulders confusedly. "He left too early. He had his little boy with him.''

"Then what are you telling me this for?''

Walt looked blankly at Rollins across the desk a few seconds. What was he telling him that for? He wasn't sure. He knew he was floundering. He felt so incredibly tired all of a sudden.

"I don't know. Maybe I was just . . .''

"Are you all right, Walt? Do you need a pill or something?'' There was genuine concern in Rollins' voice.

"I'm fine. Really.'' He struggled to get hold of himself, to make the connection that was there in his mind. There was some reason he kept thinking about Mapes—about him, or was it his wife? "It's just . . . everything comes out sooner or later. Somehow, we find out. Like Mapes's wife coming in today. Somebody's got to know the killer. You see? Sooner or later, we got to get a break.''

Pete wasn't sure he saw the point, or that Walt saw it either. But that wasn't important now. He came around the desk and put his hand on Walt's shoulder. The sheriff's eyes were closed and his forehead rested lightly against his fingers.

"Well, I hope it's sooner,'' Pete said, almost in a whisper, "for your sake.''

CHAPTER 11

I T W A S J U S T a farmhouse flanked by two outbuildings. Perched on the slope of a bare brown field, it looked from the highway like a toy that had been set down temporarily and then forgotten.

There was no special reason they picked it. Like all the others they saw around there, it was rather isolated from its neighbors to the north and south but within good shouting distance of a similar house almost directly across the road.

Roger eased the car onto the shoulder, pulling all the way over until the wheels on Jimmy's side were practically in the drainage ditch. He shut the engine. They had said four o'clock and it was a quarter past.

Jimmy looked around. There were actually four houses they could walk to with no trouble but the one up ahead seemed closest.

"That one?" he asked.

Roger shrugged. "It makes no difference to me," he said. "Let's get going."

The Dutch Reform settlers were among the first to farm the northwest corner of Iowa. They came from places like Buffalo and Cincinnati around the middle of the nineteenth century, answering a vaguer form of the same impulse that led other, more fanatical sects to found utopian communities or that drove them as far west as Utah and Oregon. But the Storm Lake Dutch were fired by no visionary schemes. Skeptical of ambition and terrified of worldly pride, they were content to lay claim to the first good land they came upon. They took only as much as they needed and left the rest to whoever came later.

Their descendants kept their modest farms intact, neither increasing them nor letting them diminish by as much as a rod. They live where they always lived, forming pockets of solid, if no longer fervent, Calvinism in a region now dominated by different persuasions.

Georgia Heynen was one of these people. This afternoon she sat in her den chatting idly with Joyce Miller. It was an ideal day to have company. Jack and Alan had run into Omaha on errands and wouldn't be back until late. They promised to pick up cold cuts at the German market on the way home. Then Caroline, with her interminable rehearsals, announced as she ran out the door that she couldn't be counted on for supper again today either. She must be making a pest of herself, Georgia thought, bumming meals with the kids who lived closer to school.

Well, you only worried about such things if you were looking for something to worry about. Everyone gone made it an odd, lazy day. No chores especially demanded her attention. No meals had to be prepared—except, of course, for Jonathan, who was never a problem. And even he seemed determined to give her a few hours to herself. Despite the heat, he had been playing in the yard almost all afternoon.

Not used to having so much time on her hands, she had been more or less at loose ends until Joyce dropped in around one. They had lunch together and then settled down in the den. She always got a kick out of being with Joyce, who was, by local standards at least, an unusual person. She wasn't quite so "Dutch" as everyone else. And Georgia had two kids who were older than Joyce, one just a year younger. There was a special piquancy to a friendship with a woman more than twenty years her junior.

Helped by coffee and the air conditioner, the hours slipped by unnoticed. Finally Joyce glanced at her watch.

"Oh, my God!" she said, jumping to her feet. "Will you look at the time!"

Georgia held up her hand. "Please don't run on my account," she said. "My family's scattered to the four winds today. Sit a while, if Howard won't mind."

Joyce accepted the invitation readily. "Don't worry about that," she said with an impish grin. "He's very independent. He can look after himself till I get home."

Georgia chuckled appreciatively but there was a hint of wistfulness in her eyes. "You want to hear something funny?" she said. "Before I got married, that was going to be my big personal crusade—not to have to put dinner on the table the minute my husband walked in the door. I haven't thought about it in years. I don't know why, but your saying Howard would wait reminded me."

Joyce couldn't tell whether she was serious or not. "I wouldn't think it's that important," she said, "what time you eat."

"On the contrary, it's terribly important. When I was a girl I thought the only people in the world besides us who ate right away were coal miners. Really. Miners and farmers. 'Cause in the movies they always did something else first. I don't know what—they read the paper or something." She spoke with her head cocked to one side. Though the words were meant to be amusing she had lapsed, despite herself, into an oddly reflective mood.

Joyce waited a moment for her to go on. Georgia was usually pretty tight-lipped about personal feelings, but now she seemed on the verge of letting her hair down.

"So what happened?" Joyce finally had to ask.

Georgia smiled wryly and furrowed her brow. "What happened? Nothing, I suppose. The first year we were married, I tried to get Jack to change. There were other things too. You know how it is. When you're seventeen you think, I'm never going to marry a farmer. I'll move to the city and be . . . God-only-knows-what. Then when you get married you swear you'll never become like your parents. We're such a—what?—*limited* people, y'know. Our world ends at the horizon. My mother only got to Chicago once in her life. I was positive I'd never be like that. But . . . " She shrugged and let the sentence trail off.

No, that wasn't at all what she had meant to say. Joyce would get the impression she was complaining. Really, she wasn't. A part of her still subscribed to the old-fashioned Dutch notion that dissatisfaction was sinful. Besides, she couldn't honestly say she had anything to complain about. It was just that a combination of things had started her thinking—the empty house, the kids, except for Jonathan, gone or away so much of the time, Joyce's incredible youth.

She tossed her head back, thinking maybe she didn't have to say anything else. Joyce would understand what she'd been trying to say.

"Oh, listen," Joyce said, "we all bend to the prevailing wind. Only with me, I promised myself I'd never ask another woman what she used on her floors. Now, I swear, I sometimes think it's all I ever talk about."

Georgia laughed. That was it exactly. You discovered in little ways you weren't quite the person you once intended to be.

She stood up. "You want some more coffee?" she asked. "I just have to plug it in. I don't know what's gotten into me today. Not having anything to do, I guess."

When they came back from the kitchen, Georgia's introspective mood had completely worn off. They gossiped about the usual things. But for Georgia, who could never say to her husband what she had said earlier, the sense of shared intimacy lent a special feeling to the afternoon. It had a texture, a richness she could almost rub up against. In the pauses in their conversation she heard the quiet droning of the air conditioner in the basement. She began to feel languid. Slowly, she raised her coffee cup to her lips. Its aroma was sweet and refreshingly pungent.

Jimmy was out of the car in a second, striding rapidly toward the driveway that led to the Heynens'.

Roger got out and slammed his door. Jimmy turned. "Wait a minute," his father hissed angrily. He walked down the road to make sure he had parked far enough on the shoulder to conceal the license plate.

"We don't have to sweat the car," the boy said when his father caught up to him. "Nobody's gonna remember seeing it."

"We better sweat the car," Roger said testily.

They turned up the driveway, a narrow strip of macadam that curved back to the garage, then looped around it to the barn and equipment shed beyond. A flower bed ran along the edge of the pavement starting just a few steps from the highway. It was planted in tulips and pale yellow daffodils. They walked single file, Roger leading the way with his eyes on the ground directly ahead of him.

"Who are you?" a small voice startled them on their right.

Roger spun around on his heels, his arms jerking up reflexively. Jimmy wondered why he was so jumpy. A boy of about five or six had come up to the driveway from the field. His face and his clothes were splattered with mud. He must have been playing near one of the irrigation pumps.

Roger composed his face into a smile. "I'm Roger. Who are you?"

"Jonathan."

"Hi, Jonathan. Is your Daddy at home?" He stooped down to the boy's level.

Jonathan demurred, momentarily shy. "He went with Alan," he finally said.

"But Mommy's home?"

Jonathan nodded.

"C'mon, let's go see Mommy." Roger reached out to lift the boy over the flower bed. He drew away, turning his shoulder. "You don't want to see Mommy?"

Jonathan shook his head sullenly. It was too early to have to go in.

Roger hesitated, then stood up and continued toward the house, leaving the child standing by the driveway. Somehow he hadn't considered that small children might be involved. His upper lip curled under his teeth. Well, it's too fucking bad, he decided. It doesn't change anything.

Jimmy was waiting for him not far from the garage. "They got company," he said, meaning the car in the driveway directly behind the one inside. The second bay was empty.

"So what?"

Roger mounted the few steps to the back door and rang the bell. Jimmy fell into place at the bottom of the stairs. Thst was one of his father's ideas, that he was supposed to act like a kid just tagging along. She had to see him but not get the feeling that she was being confronted by two people.

"Ring it again," the boy said after a minute or so. "If she doesn't let us in, I'm gonna grab the kid."

"Take it easy," Roger said. "The thing is, just take it easy."

Sure, Jimmy thought, like you're doing. He was nervous too, but the tension didn't seem to affect him like it did his father. Ever since they had decided that this would be the day, Roger had been acting more and more strangely. At times he spoke with a clipped precision, as if he knew exactly what he was doing, but at other times it seemed almost as if he was walking in his sleep. He'll be all right, Jimmy kept telling himself, but the possibility of something going wrong suggested itself vaguely in the back of his mind.

A woman opened the door. She peered timidly at the two strangers through the mesh of the closed screen. "Yes?" she said.

"I'm sorry to bother you, ma'am," Roger said, "but we had a little car trouble over here . . . " He left the sentence unfinished, inviting a response.

Georgia frowned doubtfully. "My husband's not home," she apologized. "I'm sure he could help you . . . "

Roger interrupted her with a disarming grin. "Actually, I'm pretty sure I know what the problem is. I was wondering if we could borrow some tools—a couple screwdrivers and some pliers."

Jimmy felt his spirits starting to rise. His father was good at this kind of bullshit, he thought with amusement. He'd give him credit for that.

Georgia grinned, feeling slightly foolish. "Of course." She

looked at the boy, now almost hidden behind his father. He was a nice-looking kid, skinny and with a pleasant smile. "Please, won't you come in? The tools are in the cellar."

In the kitchen another woman was leaning against the counter. She had one hip thrust out and gazed at them curiously. Who's she? Roger wondered, returning her look. Was she Jonathan's mother? She was more the right age but she didn't seem to be the woman of the house.

Georgia paused awkwardly as she showed them the way. Again, she seemed mildly flustered, unsure of what explanations or introductions were in order.

"Our car broke down," Roger announced as if to the room at large, taking advantage of Georgia's momentary confusion. He was stalling for time before going down to the cellar. He wanted to talk to them first, to size up the situation. "I think I can fix it but I need to borrow a screwdriver."

Joyce smiled politely. "Then it's nothing serious?"

"I hope not."

Georgia stopped and came back to the middle of the room. "I'm afraid I'm not being very hospitable," she said graciously. She offered them drinks and something to eat. "How about a cold glass of milk?" she asked Jimmy.

Oh, shit, he thought, we're going to get stuck here in the kitchen. What did his father have to start up with them for? They'd be down in the cellar already if Roger had only kept his damn mouth shut.

But there was nothing he could do now without arousing suspicion. The four of them sat down around the kitchen table while Georgia bustled about serving refreshments. It galled the boy. A minute ago he had been marveling at how easily they had gotten into the house. He had to make an effort to keep his elation from showing. But now he saw the other side of the coin. At least when you break into a house no one expects you to be sociable.

Yeah, it was turning into a joke but he was in no mood to appreciate the humor of the situation. His father seemed to be having the time of his life though. While Jimmy sullenly polished off a piece of cake to go with his milk, Roger had a beer and told all kinds of stories. He told them they were headed for Algona, where his wife had been visiting a sister who just had a baby.

It was dumb. As far as Jimmy knew, Algona was just a name his father had seen on a road sign. If either of these women knew anything about the place, they could find out he was lying without even trying.

After a few minutes Jimmy tuned out the conversation. He was getting fidgety just sitting around. A couple times, glancing at Joyce, it struck him that she wasn't talking either. She was almost staring at Roger, watching him with an expression of mixed curiosity and disdain. Maybe she suspects something, he thought, but it didn't seem likely. She was probably just uptight around strangers—or she thought his father was an asshole, that was all.

Finally, even the older woman, who seemed every bit as gabby as Roger, decided it was time to break up the party. Jimmy, lost in some private fantasy, heard the scrape of her chair as she pushed back from the table. "Well—you're probably anxious to get going," she said to Roger. "Let me show you what my husband has downstairs."

Jimmy gulped down the rest of his milk and hurried after them, leaving Joyce alone in the kitchen. As he reached the door to the stairway, he hesitated a moment. He thought he could feel Joyce looking at him from the kitchen, her eyes boring into the back of his head. But he didn't let himself turn around.

There was no light on the stairwell and what came from behind him, from the hall, was quite dim. The cellar, however, was brightly lit. Poised at the top of the stairs, he watched Georgia leading his father down. She moved slowly, one step at a time. They looked like divers going over the side of a ship, descending gradually toward that pool of bright yellow light.

He had that same weird feeling he had that night in the projection booth. It was like time had slowed down everywhere else but it raced faster and faster inside his brain. The scene broke into images of amazing clarity and then whizzed by him too fast for him to get a good look at them. He started to feel giddy.

He shut his eyes a few seconds, trying to get a grip on himself. The Buck knife was in his pocket. Down in the cellar they'd be alone with the woman. He'd wait for a signal from his father or else he'd know the right time to pull it out on his own. They could do it exactly the way they planned. His fingers traced the rough bone handle through his pants pocket. As soon as Roger grabbed her he'd be ready. He'd show her the blade and she'd stop struggling. She wouldn't dare scream.

He didn't know how long he stood there. Not long. When he opened his eyes his father and the woman were gone. They had reached the floor and had passed out of the narrow rectangle of his vision toward the far corner of the house. Nothing moved down there. He felt calm.

When he came up behind them they were rummaging through an assortment of hardware at the workbench. They took no notice of him immediately. Then Roger turned and glanced at his son over his shoulder.

"Hi," he said casually, holding up a small electrical clamp. "I don't know if he has the size we need here."

Jimmy darted his eyes questioningly in the direction of the woman, who hadn't looked up yet. Are we going to do it now? the gesture meant. What are we waiting for?

Roger didn't seem to understand him. His neutral expression remained unchanged. It flashed through Jimmy's mind that one of them must be crazy. Had they really come down here because something was wrong with the car? If his father was just going on with the pretense that got them into the house, he was doing a hell of an acting job.

The woman turned to the boy, smiling asymmetrically in feminine bewilderment. "I never understood why they made these things so complicated," she said. "There ought to be one little dingus that takes care of everything."

Jimmy muttered something in acknowledgment of the remark. Off to her side, his father lowered his head once in a single, curt nod. Then he went back to poking around all the junk on the workbench. When he spoke, it was in the same natural tone as a moment ago. "That's probably what we're going to have to do," he said. "Bend one of these to get it to fit."

I'm sure he nodded, Jimmy thought to himself, getting more and more confused. That was the signal but it could have meant anything.

Roger said, "Would one of you please hand me those pliers—the little ones on the end?"

The woman had to do it. She was in Jimmy's way. He felt himself tense involuntarily as she stretched across the work table to where a set of matched tools hung from a pegboard. It seemed they'd never have a chance like the one they had now. Still, he didn't know what his father expected him to do.

He slid his hand into his pocket and slowly drew out the knife. He glanced down at it surreptitiously as he held it close to his side. It would take less than a second to snap out the blade. He cupped his left hand over his right to conceal the handle, which was too long to be covered by his palm, and practiced the movement of opening it in his mind.

"These?" Georgia asked Roger.

"Yeah. Fine."

Jimmy watched in fascination as she handed him the pliers. Their fingers touched briefly, sending a shiver down his spine. Then he heard the tiny, sharp click of the blade locking in place.

He didn't realize what the sound was at first. He hadn't opened the knife intentionally. He just wanted to be ready.

Roger heard it too and must have known what it was. He turned completely around and looked straight at the boy, his eyes hard and suddenly wrathful. Jimmy shook his head frantically as if to deny what he had done.

Georgia looked uncertainly from one to the other, a puzzled frown on her face. Either she hadn't seen the knife or its meaning didn't register. She opened her mouth to say something, to ask what had happened to get them both so upset.

Suddenly she froze. Slowly the muscles in her face went slack, her mouth gaping wider and wider.

"Oh," she gasped, a soft, voiceless whimper of belated surprise.

For what seemed an eternity, none of them moved. Jimmy still held the knife in both hands down by his belt. He didn't menace her with it. He seemed hardly aware that he even had it, let alone that it was what she was staring at.

Then she started sidling away from them, the small of her back pressed hard against the workbench. Her hand inched out ahead of her, her fingers groping their way along the stainless steel surface as if they were trusted to lead her to safety.

There was no reason to go after her. Soon her hand felt the wall at the far end of the workbench. For a few seconds she probed tentatively at the obstruction, refusing to believe her way had been blocked. She had fled less than three agonizing feet. With nowhere to go, she wedged herself tightly into the corner.

She seemed to shrivel up inside herself, growing smaller and smaller. Her body slid down the wall until she was sitting on the floor with her knees pulled up in front of her. She cowered behind them, staring with wide, frightened eyes at the blade of the knife.

Roger extended his hand placatingly and took a single, cautious step forward. He wanted to soothe her. But she wasn't watching him and only saw his approach in the corner of her eye. A wave of black panic crashed down on her, sweeping away her last frail defenses. She closed her eyes like a baby and started to scream. The sound tore through the room like the screech of a siren, raucous, inhuman, incredibly sustained.

For a moment it seemed to paralyze Roger and Jimmy. Neither made any move to quiet her down. Under the piercing, long-drawn-out note of her shrieking, they heard the sounds of footsteps running toward them upstairs. Roger touched Jimmy on the shoulder and the boy, responding automatically, gave him the knife.

Abruptly, Georgia stopped screaming. She gasped for air, each breath rasping painfully against her raw throat. Tears poured from her eyes, now clenched shut less tightly.

They heard Joyce open the cellar door and race down the stairs. She stumbled near the bottom but kept moving forward. As she reached the workroom she staggered against the door jamb and held onto it for support. Her eyes searched desperately for Georgia, whom she heard whimpering faintly somewhere in front of her.

It took her a second or two to locate the sound. Her friend was huddled in the corner, her head partly in shadow beneath the work table. A man knelt beside her holding a knife blade poised at her throat.

"Don't move and don't make a sound," he commanded in a voice so low Joyce had to strain to understand him.

Roger sat slouched in an armchair with his ankles crossed out in front of him. He had made the women lie on their stomachs and ordered Jimmy to tie their hands securely behind their backs. Their legs and their mouths weren't taped. He wasn't afraid they would try to run and, with all the windows shut because of the air conditioner, they could scream all they wanted without being heard.

His manner throughout this was deliberate, even professional, though occasionally, in a word or gesture to his son, his prisoners caught a glimpse of the anger seething inside him. The boy took his cue how to act from his father. He said little and did as he was told.

As soon as the women were bound, Roger sent Jimmy to drive the car behind the garage.

It was Joyce's first inkling that these men weren't simply going to rob them and leave as quickly as possible. All the time Roger had been leading them up from the cellar and made them lie down and submit to being tied, he had assured them that no one would be hurt if they didn't cause trouble. She believed him. To do otherwise was unthinkable.

But now she got scared. "Do you want money?" she blurted before Jimmy could get to the door. "We'll give you money. Just get out of here before anyone comes." Despite the urgency of her plea, her voice was amazingly cool and authoritative. She had no idea what Georgia expected would happen but she didn't want to alarm her with her new-found suspicions.

Jimmy stopped to hear what she had to say about the money.

Roger smiled sardonically. "I'll worry about someone coming," he said. Then he told Jimmy to get going again.

"All right, now what time does your husband get home?" he asked Georgia.

"I don't know," she blubbered. "Late. He's in Omaha." Following Joyce's example, she was trying to control her emotions. It wasn't easy.

That's too convenient, Roger thought. Maybe she wanted to discourage him from waiting—or to lower his guard if her husband was due any minute. "Where's Alan?" he said unexpectedly, figuring her answer would show if she was telling the truth.

She started whimpering hysterically all over again. Somehow the mention of the name made her think Alan was also his prisoner. How else did he know about him?

"He's with her husband. He's her son," Joyce volunteered to spare Georgia from answering.

"I didn't ask you."

"Well, that's where he is."

Roger wagged two fingers at her. "You better watch your attitude," he warned ominously. "You're a wise-ass, you know that?"

"Yes, sir," she said sheepishly. There was a hint of mocking condescension in her voice.

If he noticed it he let it pass. He got down on the floor and took Georgia's face in his hand. Gently at first, he made her tell him the names of her children and where they were at the time. Then he began asking questions about them, gradually picking up the tempo until he was grilling her mercilessly.

"What's Sylvia's phone number?"

"Who's Evelyn's husband?"

"What's Caroline doing?"

"Sylvia's children—quick—give me their names."

"Where's Alan right now?"

After nearly five minutes he stopped. He hadn't tripped her up once. "Okay," he said, taking his hand off her and going back to his chair. "I just don't want any surprises walking in that door, that's all."

Georgia smiled feebly. His relentless cross-examination had exhausted her physically but in a strange way it bolstered her spirits. It forced her to concentrate on her children and grandchildren.

Joyce said, "You've got a remarkable memory if you kept track of all those names."

The compliment pleased Roger. "You want to quiz me?" he said.

"No, I'll take your word for it."

When Jimmy came back, they went off in a corner and conferred in whispers about what they would do. Lying on the floor, Joyce strained to overhear them but couldn't make out more than an occasional, meaningless word.

"Can I ask you something?" Joyce said as soon as their discussion broke up.

"No."

"I just wanted to know if you'd let us sit up . . . if you're going to be here awhile. It's painful, lying on your face like this."

Roger smirked knowingly. "We're going to be here awhile," he said. That was really what she was asking.

Joyce swallowed hard. It was difficult enough having her fears confirmed, but on top of it came the discouraging realization that he always seemed to be one step ahead of her. "Then can we sit up?" she asked anyway, sounding a little abashed for the first time that afternoon.

"Yeah. You can lean against the wall."

Once they were settled, Roger and Jimmy got down to business. Georgia told them where to find money and her jewelry collection. There was over fifty dollars in their two purses and forty-three more in a desk drawer in the study. The only thing in the jewel case that seemed worth taking was a simple pearl necklace.

Then each took a turn guarding the hostages—Roger with the Buck knife, Jimmy with a carving knife he found in the kitchen—while the other roamed through the house looking for anything else that caught his fancy. Roger found a twelve-gauge shotgun in the basement but there weren't any shells. There was also a floor safe back in the corner.

"What's the combination to that safe?" he asked Georgia the next time he relieved Jimmy.

"My husband knows. I don't. But there's no money in it. It's just for records."

"I thought farmers always had money in the house."

"Some of the older ones still do. But we pay everything by check."

"Then maybe we came to the wrong house."

Georgia couldn't help smiling at the deliberate irony of the remark. By the odd psychology that applied to their situation, they all seemed to be growing comfortable in their roles. It suddenly struck her that she would never have thought it possible that he could make jokes and she could laugh at them. Maybe that explained the whole mystery of how some human beings could treat others like animals. You just got used to it, like she got used so quickly to being a hostage.

He had asked her something but she didn't catch it. "I'm sorry," she said. "I didn't hear you."

"Your husband must have the combination written down somewhere."

"Yes, but it's in our safety deposit box."

"If I got a look in that safe we might leave," Roger said. "We wouldn't have to wait for your husband to open it."

"I realize that."

"Good. Now do you know where your husband keeps the shells for his shotgun?"

"In the safe. He doesn't want the children to get them."

When Jimmy came back from his foray the long period of waiting began. It was twenty minutes to six. They all sat in silence in the living room, the women bound on the floor with their heads below the level of the front window, Roger stretched out in the armchair. Jimmy got up from time to time and paced around nervously. It wasn't the boredom that bothered him, it was the sense of not knowing when something would happen. Finally his father told him to sit down and keep still.

He tried it for a few minutes. He didn't know why the rest of them weren't saying anything. He didn't feel like talking himself but it would help pass the time if he could listen.

"Can I go watch television?" he asked after a while. "We might be here all night."

"No. I want to be able to hear when someone drives up."

"I'll turn the sound off. I just want to watch."

Roger considered the idea. "Okay. But stay alert."

The boy jumped up from the sofa and ran down the hall to the den, carrying the carving knife with him. There was no harm in having a lookout posted on the opposite side of the house.

"How old is he?" Joyce said acidly as soon as Jimmy was out of hearing. "Twelve? Thirteen? Why'd you have to get him involved in this kind of thing?"

Roger took a deep drag on his cigarette and held the smoke in his lungs. Then he exhaled slowly, watching the smoke tumble across the room until it got sucked into the exhaust of the air conditioner. He didn't say anything to answer her. That was his answer.

It was a good question though.

Jimmy sat down in front of the television and flipped the dial a few times to see if he could find anything to watch. But it was past six already and most of the channels had on the news or something equally boring. Finally he found one on the UHF band that was still showing cartoons. He lay flat on the floor and stared disinterestedly at the screen, his chin resting on his hand.

A character he didn't recognize was trying to escape from a dinosaur by scurrying behind a rock. Every time the dinosaur took a step the picture shook. It was stupid but he had nothing better to do.

Georgia studied Roger's face a long time, trying to decide how to phrase what she was going to say.

"Excuse me," she began timidly, then waited to be sure she had his attention. "Your boy . . . do you have any other children?"

Roger hesitated before answering. There was something so earnest in her tone that made it impossible to ignore her.

"I have another son."

"Older or younger?"

"Older."

"I see. I don't mean to pry. . . . You talked to Jonathan in the yard, didn't you? That's how you knew Alan was with his father?"

"Uh-huh."

"I was wondering—he's going to be coming in pretty soon, for his supper. He usually doesn't stay out much past six-thirty. I . . . would there be any harm if I sent him to a neighbor's? I could telephone her and ask her to give him supper and watch him till I call for him later. Do you see what I'm asking? You could listen in when I call. I wouldn't say anything to put you in jeopardy. Believe me, she'd never suspect. I'm just thinking of my boy."

She spoke slowly in so hushed a voice that Roger, against his will, was caught up in the mood of intimacy she created. He had wanted to interrupt her, to cut her off as soon as he realized what she was getting at. But he didn't do it. Now it was harder.

He shook his head. "It's impossible," he said, almost as if the decision was beyond his control. He had reasons but she didn't want to hear them.

"He's just a boy."

"It's impossible."

Strangely, she seemed to understand. "Then will you promise me something?" she said. "You won't hurt him."

"I told you before. If you don't make trouble, nobody's gonna get hurt," he said, the hard edge partly returning to his voice.

Georgia's heart sank in her breast. Had he exempted Jonathan specifically from whatever he planned as the last act of this . . . this tragedy, she would have been satisfied. But at some point, obscurely, she had stopped putting faith in his general assurances. Without even realizing it, she had somehow accepted the fact that she would probably die.

Now that Jonathan's life lay under the same shadow as hers, she couldn't accept it. She wanted to plead with this man, to beg crying on her knees for his pity—if not for herself then at least for her baby. But she couldn't approach him. She had tried, appealing to his warped fatherhood, but inside him there was nothing to touch, nothing to reach out to. Nothing, except the chilling litany of no-one-gets-hurt.

She looked over to Joyce, her eyes sorrowful and apologetic. She never doubted for a second that Joyce would understand her necessity. Joyce smiled at her bravely.

The clock said six-thirty. In the den, Jimmy changed channels. He stopped at a game show. The contestants jumped up and down, mutely clapping their hands. Sometimes they pouted and grimaced excessively. He started giggling. Without the sound on, it was a terrific show.

At twenty minutes to seven Georgia heard the soft click of the back door opening.

"Mommy?"

Roger sat up.

"Jonathan. . . . Listen to me. Run! Run away—as hard as you can! Do you hear me! Run!"

"Run, Jonathan! To the highway! Run to the highway!"

For a split second the child's confused face appeared at the end of the hallway. He saw the terror in his mother's eyes as she screamed at him. The strange man and Auntie Joyce sprang into motion. In sheer panic he turned and raced out the back door.

"Get the fucking kid, will you!" Roger bellowed at Jimmy as he ran in from the den.

"What?" The living room was a chaos of shouting and movement. The women were up, still yelling at Jonathan as they started to run. Roger spun wildly in the center of the maelstrom, a crazy machine gone out of control. He slashed the air desperately with his knife, trying to keep his prisoners from escaping.

"The kid! Out the back door!"

Suddenly Jimmy understood. As he turned, Joyce flung her body into him. He fell heavily to the floor, the blade of his carving knife within an inch of his face. She wriggled on top of him, pinning him down with her weight.

Roger clamped his powerful hand over her face and pulled her backward enough for Jimmy to squirm free. As he scrambled to his feet Georgia rushed toward the doorway where their three bodies were tangled. Roger, stooped over and still holding Joyce, hulked in her path but she bore on regardless. She lowered her shoulder and smashed into his side.

Jimmy hesitated less than a second. Her momentum sent her sliding headlong across Roger's back as he fell to the floor. Somehow the Buck knife had slashed through her blouse. Instantly, the torn fabric turned bright red along a line that ran from her shoulder to her elbow. The boy spun around and ran through the kitchen toward the back door.

For a while the two women were more than Roger could handle. With their hands tied behind their backs, they thrashed their legs wildly, flopping like fish. Finally Roger managed to grab Georgia by the chin and drag her back into the middle of the living room.

Joyce, too exhausted to run, got to her feet nevertheless, but then fell back against the cupboard in the hall. Her slacks were soaked with blood from dozens of cuts on her hips and legs. Painfully, she righted herself and stumbled past the doorway toward the kitchen.

"That's enough!" Roger barked. His chest heaved with rapid panting. Kneeling on the carpet, he held Georgia's spent body motionless, her back arched brutally across his thighs. He lay the blade of the knife against the taut skin of her throat.

Joyce saw it as she crossed the doorway. She stopped and came back.

"Hey, you! Come back here!" Jimmy shouted from the head of the driveway.

Jonathan heard him but he didn't look back. He was almost halfway to the road but now someone was chasing him. He pushed himself even faster. His tiny legs churned desperately, knees flying outward in his wobbly gait.

Jimmy lowered his head and took off at a gallop. He had a lot of ground to make up. After thirty paces he felt his thighs begin to loosen and stretch. He lengthened his stride and lifted his head. He was sprinting easily now, his arms close to his sides. The knife, which threw him off-balance at first, swung effortlessly in his hand like a relay racer's baton.

Jonathan was still a good way in front but each step narrowed the gap. Down the long sweep of the driveway Jimmy followed the boy. For a few yards they ran straight into the reddening sun. A car, silhouetted atop the highway embankment, hissed by in a second. Perhaps its driver noticed two boys racing frantically toward him, but if he did he thought nothing of it.

Soon Jonathan was moving slower and slower. Frightened, he looked back for his pursuer every few steps and saw how fast he was gaining. Finally the pavement leveled off for the last short stretch before it rose to meet the highway. Jonathan kept running as hard as he could. He hit the incline ten yards in front, his legs aching horribly and his chest about to explode.

Suddenly he knew he'd never make it. He veered sharply to the side, trampling through the flower bed as he entered the field. Open as it was, it was his territory. He played in these fields in the spring before the crops were in and in the fall after they were harvested. In his panic, he felt safer there. He stumbled onward in agony, driven by instincts stronger than pain.

Jimmy picked up the turn and slackened his pace. The kid had nowhere to go and he could run all day if he had to. His body exulted in its prowess. Even at a lope he closed rapidly on his prey. Then he reached out his hand and touched Jonathan's shirt.

Jonathan fell to the ground. Jimmy glided past, then swung around and walked back to him.

"C'mon," he panted, gesturing with his head in the direction of the house.

Jonathan, lying on his side, shook his head wildly. He wouldn't get up. Jimmy grabbed his arm and jerked him to his feet. As soon as he let go the boy slumped back to the ground.

"Shit," Jimmy said, "I ran as far as you did. If I give you a minute will you walk back to the house?"

Again Jonathan shook his head stubbornly, his terrified eyes riveted on Jimmy's face.

"You want me to use this?" Jimmy said, brandishing the knife.

The threat meant nothing to the child after the reality of being caught. He could still hear his mother yelling at him to run. No matter what happened, he wasn't going back to the house.

"All right," Jimmy said. "Have it your way." He stooped down behind the boy and wrapped his left arm around his chest. He had no trouble lifting the boy but walking was going to be difficult. He had to do it though. He had to get back to the house. God knew what was happening there.

"You little fucker!" He said after a few steps. "Are you gonna walk or aren't you?"

Jonathan had started squirming to resist being carried. He wouldn't give up. He flung his legs out trying to wriggle free. His fingers pried at the arm that imprisoned him but found no purchase on the slippery skin.

Jimmy reeled backward, almost losing his balance. As the boy's legs swung back they sometimes struck him in the shins. "Cut it out!" he hollered. "I'm not gonna let go!" He held out the knife in front of the kid's face.

But his yelling only made Jonathan struggle more desperately. He dug his fingernails into Jimmy's forearm. His legs stopped flailing randomly as he slammed his heels deliberately into his captor again and again.

Bellowing incoherently, Jimmy refused to let go. He tried to twist the boy in his arm to escape from his kicking. His face turned crimson with rage.

And then the knife thrust downward, the heel of the blade brushing his arm. It entered the boy's body as if nothing were there.

Jonathan stopped moving instantly. His blood spurted out across Jimmy's hand. His head fell forward.

Jimmy dropped him quickly and stepped back. He knew he was dead. His quiet, sweat-covered face glowed reddishly in the deepening twilight. The knife, incongruously, lay on his stomach, where it had fallen when Jimmy released it a fraction of a second after letting go of the boy.

Jimmy shivered and picked it up by the handle. He threw it as hard as he could across the highway, watching to make sure it cleared the far side. Then he took Jonathan by the hands and dragged him a few yards into the drainage ditch.

Jimmy rinsed the blood off his arms with the garden hose. He didn't seem to have blood anywhere else. When he came into the house he found his father sitting on the floor leaning back wearily against the front door. He had a quart of beer in one hand and a cigarette in the other. He flicked the ashes on the carpet beside him. He looked like he had been through a wringer.

Jimmy threw himself full length on the sofa.

"Did you get him?" Roger asked after a few seconds.

"Yeah."

"Where is he?"

Jimmy motioned vaguely outside.

Roger raised his eyebrows curiously but he didn't say anything. He assumed Jonathan was dead.

Several minutes passed. Roger ground out his cigarette in the rug and lit another. Jimmy, lying on his stomach, lifted his head.

"What'd you do with them?" he said. It hadn't registered before that the women weren't in the room.

"One's over there," Roger said. He pointed through the double doors to the dining room.

Jimmy leaned out from the sofa and peered over to see. Joyce lay on the floor curled up in the fetal position. Roger had tied her legs together with drapery cord and lashed her arms behind her to one of the legs of the table. He had also taped over her mouth. She stared back at the boy with mournful, unblinking eyes.

"The other one's in the bedroom," Roger said.

Jimmy came over and sat down next to his father. He took a few swallows of the beer but it hardly dented his thirst. "Are we gonna wait for the old man to come home?" he asked softly.

"No. No way."

Jimmy nodded. He had lost interest in sticking around any longer himself. They had over ninety dollars and that was fine with him. "Then we better get going," he said.

Slowly they pulled themselves to their feet. Roger seemed lost. He stood by the door gazing blankly around the room as if in a daze. Jimmy waited for him to give orders but it didn't take long to realize that his father wasn't thinking coherently.

"Hey, Dad, c'mon," he pleaded, trying to snap him out of his trance. It upset him, seeing his father like that.

"Yeah. All right. Let's go. You know what you have to do?" Roger finally mumbled. His voice sounded fuzzy like he was just waking up.

"Uh-huh. This one here."

Roger looked at him oddly as if he didn't quite understand. Then he bent down and picked up the Buck knife lying next to the beer bottle. He walked slowly, like a very old man, down the hall to the bedroom and pulled the door closed behind him.

Jimmy stood over Joyce. His head was cocked to one side and his lips were parted slightly, giving him a somewhat sneering appearance. Well—he couldn't do it like that, not with her looking right at him, her eyes so calm and defiant.

Quickly, he yanked off the tablecloth and threw it down over her. A pair of pewter candlesticks rolled across the floor. Joyce started tossing convulsively, trying to shake off the cover.

In the kitchen he found another sharp knife. It was much smaller. When he came back she had made half a circle around the table leg and dragged the heavy table almost two inches, judging by the indentation in the carpet. The white linen cloth lay crumpled over her throat.

She was bucking like a wild animal, her eyes now ablaze. He knelt down on top of her, straddling her hips to prevent her from turning. Then he ripped open her shirt. He flipped one end of the tablecloth over her face and used the other end to wipe off the knife handle. Gripping the knife through the fabric, he positioned the point on the band of her bra directly below her left breast. With his free hand he arranged the cloth over her chest. She kept writhing so violently the knife slipped from its place.

He repositioned it carefully, trying to follow her movements. Then he closed his eyes and leaned forward.

She lay still. He straightened up and watched for a second as the red stain spread through the tablecloth.

He found Roger sitting on the corner of the bed, his fingers stroking the blade of his knife. The boy felt something snap inside him, like the clean cracking of a twig.

"Jesus Christ!" he shouted. "Are you gonna do it or aren't you?"

Roger looked at him stupidly. "Yeah, I'll do it," he said.

"Then do it!" Jimmy stomped out of the room, slamming the door behind him.

He paced back and forth the length of the living room, unable to gain control of his rage. His head pounded fiercely in pulsing waves that felt like they were searing his brain. At that moment in the bedroom if he had a knife he would have plunged it into his father. Furious, he pulled over a small bookcase that stood by the wall.

Roger came out of the bedroom. The first thing Jimmy saw was the blood covering his shirt.

"Better take it off," he said sharply.

Roger looked down at his chest. "It's okay," he said. "Let's go."

"It's not okay. What if someone sees us?"

Obediently, Roger unbuttoned his shirt and let it slip to the floor. Jimmy ran into one of the boys' rooms and came back with a dark-colored T-shirt. His father pulled it on.

Outside, it was pitch dark. A full moon, visible in the early evening, had disappeared behind a thick cover of clouds. The temperature had fallen dramatically.

"Are you okay?" Jimmy asked with unexpected solicitude.

"Sure."

"Then let's hurry it up. We're up shit creek if someone comes now."

CHAPTER 12

WHEN WALT CAME HOME Monday evening after the meeting with Pete Rollins, Rose took one look at him and told him to get into bed. He didn't give her an argument, which showed her as clearly as anything just how terrible he felt. His face was the color of a newspaper.

He swore he didn't have any chest pains. He was tired, that was all.

Maybe that was it, Rose tried to persuade herself. She didn't like to think about his heart. Of course he never told her when he had pains, but it could be just tiredness. She'd see how he felt in the morning and take it from there.

She helped him get undressed and crawl into bed. Then she went downstairs and fixed him a cup of hot soup and a tunafish sandwich.

That damned case, she thought—it was simply unfair. In big cities there are men who are homicide detectives. They dealt with that sort of thing on a day-to-day basis. Not that they were necessarily better investigators than Walter—though maybe they were—but at least they were used to running into stone walls. Hundreds of murders went unsolved every year. Even she knew that. Everyone knew it. But in Walt's entire career there were probably no more than two or three times that he actually had to track down a killer.

155

No wonder he couldn't keep it in perspective. He let it prey on his mind.

When she brought the food upstairs he was lying on his back staring straight at the ceiling. She put the dishes on the nightstand. "Walt," she said, "Honey, look what you're doing to yourself. And what for? Can you bring the girl back to life?"

He turned his head away. "Please, Rose, I'm just a little tired, that's all."

She smiled resignedly, shaking her head. "Okay, then get some rest. Do you want anything to drink?"

"No. I'm not really hungry either."

"Well, I'll leave it there in case you change your mind."

A few hours later Hilt Greave called from Des Moines. Rose answered the phone. They chatted a few minutes and she was surprised to find out that he had left Arlington.

"Yeah," he said, "the paper called me back over the weekend. There didn't seem to be anything happening on the case you got there." He paused, momentarily embarrassed. "I'm sorry, Rose. No reflection on Walt."

"Please, Hilt, you don't have to apologize. It's no one's fault that the killer hasn't been caught yet." Now it was her turn to regret a remark. She was defending her husband's performance when it didn't need her defense.

"No, of course not," Hilt said. "But listen. Is Walt home? Can I talk to him?"

"Well, he's home but he's resting. Is it anything that can wait?"

Hilt considered a moment. A man in his forties knows that "resting" is a euphemism. "It might be important," he said. "I don't know what happened at that showdown with Rollins."

Rose didn't know anything about any showdown. Walt never told her these things. Rather than confessing her ignorance, she said, "Can't you tell me what this is about? I'll tell Walt when he gets up."

"Okay. I just found out that there was this double murder tonight out at Storm Lake. Two women were stabbed to death."

"And it's connected with the case here? How come the Department hasn't called?"

"Well, it's just my hunch that it might be connected. I don't have many details yet. The Department hasn't called because they probably don't know about it. I found out 'cause one of our stringers in Storm Lake phoned the paper. The police out there are probably still too confused to think about calling Arlington—if it even occurs to them. That's another reason I wanted to tell Walt. He shouldn't have to read about it in the paper."

"*Another* reason?" What was the first one?

"Sure. If my guess is right, it lets Doug Eddy off the hook." He laughed. "Unless he happened to be dating a girl in Storm Lake last night."

When Rose hung up she debated waking Walt to tell him the news. Obviously, he was going to be mad when he found out if she didn't. But so far it was only Hilt's suspicion that these new killings had anything to do with the Orben case. (Wasn't it odd, by the way, how men looked at these things? "It lets Doug Eddy off the hook"—as if those poor women had done him a favor.) It would be a different story if the Department had called.

Besides, there was nothing Walt could do right away in any case. Even if he tried calling Storm Lake, it would be morning before he could get the full picture. She knew what it was like in police departments when something important happened. Only one or two people knew the whole story and they were too busy to tell anyone else. They'd probably give him the runaround for a while. In his condition that was the last thing he needed.

She made up her mind. She'd let him get a good night's rest. If this awful business at Storm Lake had nothing to do with him, she'd save him needless hours of aggravation till he could know that for sure. And if it opened new leads he'd need all his strength for the job awaiting him. But it bothered her, taking such decisions on herself. It made her feel sneaky.

She put on the television. The news was more than half over and they didn't mention the killings. Either they didn't have the story yet or they had already covered it. On the radio there was a short bulletin that wasn't any clearer about the facts than Hilt had been.

Around eleven-thirty she went to bed. She didn't put on the light so as not to disturb Walt, but as soon as she got settled she could tell that he wasn't sleeping. He didn't move or say anything but she sensed his watchfulness like an intruder in the room.

"Walt?" she said softly. "Is anything the matter?"

"No. I just can't seem to close my eyes."

"Do you have any pain?"

"Not really. I took a couple of pills."

His "not reallys" came at a point when most men would be calling the doctor. But she knew him well enough to understand that his physical symptoms tonight were only the outermost sign of some deeper distress.

"Do you want to talk about it? Did something happen between you and Pete?"

He didn't remember telling her how much trouble he was having with the D.A. "No," he said, "we got that straightened out. I was just thinking about the case. You don't really want to hear about it." They spoke in whispers as they always did in bed.

"If you want to tell me, I do."

He hesitated, searching for the words to express himself. "Not the case so much. It's me, Rose. I'm only a county sheriff. You want six deputies to direct traffic after the football game, I'll figure out a way to do the same job with five. But I'm no Kojak. I'm a good administrator, that's all."

Rose gave an obligatory laugh. "What brought this on all of a sudden? Self-pity's not like you."

"It's not self-pity. It's realism. Sometimes I don't even know what it is I'm supposed to be doing. This whole business has got me tied up in knots."

The words went through Rose like a chill. Walt wasn't the least bit egotistical but he always had confidence in himself. Now his doubts corresponded with something she had found herself thinking the last several days. In the middle of telling him something she'd suddenly realize he wasn't paying attention. He was thinking about the case. And she wondered what he hoped to accomplish with this constant preoccupation. There were only so many facts, after all. You analyzed them once . . . twice . . . three times. What was the good in doing it again? If the answer wasn't there, mere stubbornness wasn't going to help you to find it.

"Maybe you're trying too hard," she said, wanting to encourage him but not by pretending the problem didn't exist. "I'm sure you've done everything possible. Sometimes you have to accept the fact that it isn't enough. You can't keep running in the same circle forever."

"Is that what it looks like—that I'm going in circles?" he said after a minute. He sounded like a man whose spirit was gone. "The trouble with me is that I see all the pieces but I just can't put them together. I focus on one thing at a time. First it was the breast wound and then it was Doug Eddy, and two men not one, and today something else. A real detective keeps his mind open. He's got all the information right up here. When he sees something, he knows where it fits. You know, Rosie, I keep thinking—if I weren't so stupid I could figure this thing out . . . "

Rose snapped on the light. "Now listen to me," she said. There were tears in her eyes. "You're not stupid. I see what this case is doing to you and I'm not going to sit here and listen to you belittle yourself. This isn't the first crime in Arlington county and it isn't the first one you haven't been able to solve. Those things happen sometimes. You look at the pieces, but maybe some of them aren't there. You can't blame yourself for that."

He reached out to her and placed his fingers gently on her lips. She tried to protect him like a mother cat with her kittens—protect him even from himself. That was Rosie all over. But right now her kindness was not what he wanted.

Rose covered his hand with hers and pressed it hard against her lips. She slid down and rested her head on his shoulder. He supported her with his arm. Finally he stretched up to switch off the light. "How come you can never argue with me in the dark?" he said, teasing her affectionately.

She snuggled up tighter to him and closed her eyes.

Walt still couldn't sleep but inside himself he felt stronger, refreshed. Just talking to her was a balm, it was like a break in a fever. It was good holding her in his arms.

She was right, too. When something became an obsession you lost your sense of proportion. Running in circles seemed better than not running at all. But it was time to stop for a minute and take a hard look at himself. He wasn't the Walt Taliaferro anymore he had always known. This afternoon a woman had come to see him and he had sent her away. She was alone in the world . . . frightened . . . penniless—and he hadn't given so much as a thought to helping her. He became fixated with her husband. All day long he kept thinking about Roger Mapes. When Rose came to bed that's what he'd been thinking about. Roger Mapes. Who was he anyway? A guy who left his wife on May 10, that was all. A guy who was out of work and had a tough life—a suicide in the family—and an unhappy marriage . . . and finally got fed up enough to throw his kid in the car and take off for a while. It was the kind of thing that happened every day. It was sad, really.

So she came to him for help. But he wasn't interested in her problems. He wanted her to solve his. She was just a nobody and he had this big case. Make her husband the murderer. Make her son the accomplice. Sure. Why not? He's only eleven or twelve—but wasn't there something he saw somewhere about a young kid?

No, it wasn't the kind of day he was proud of. When things got to that point he had better slow down and find his bearings again.

⊂╪   ⊂╪   ⊂╪

Half an hour after Roger started driving the rain came down. Streaks of ragged lightning surrounded the car, illuminating their faces so they seemed to jump toward one another like a bizarre funhouse illusion.

"Wow! D'you see that one!" Jimmy exclaimed. A bolt of lightning touched the crest of a hill right past Roger's shoulder. Its afterglow flickered palely a second or two before fading. The thunder, a single deafening blast, placed it less than half a mile from the car.

Roger concentrated on the road but his face seemed relaxed, his eyes bright and alive. He had started to loosen up a few miles from the farmhouse. Jimmy wasn't surprised. The same thing had happened at Lake Barrett.

He had slowed down to twenty. The rain came down in slanting sheets that rippled over the pavement, driven by sudden gusts of wind. Except in the lightning he could barely make out the white line. But he loved driving in the rain, hearing the hiss of the tires on the road and the steady slap of the wipers. Between each pass of the blades the rain built up so thick on the windshield that it was like looking through lenses that made everything shimmer and wave.

Up ahead a pair of taillights flashed sequentially on the shoulder. Roger touched the brake lightly and coasted in behind them. He started to open his door.

"Where are you going?" Jimmy asked.

"To establish an alibi," Roger said with a wink as he got out of the car.

He walked casually up to the other car and tapped lightly on the driver's window to get his attention. A well-dressed couple in their sixties were sitting as far apart as possible, each staring sullenly out the front window.

"George!" the woman gasped. Her voice came muffled to Roger through the tightly sealed car.

George turned his head and looked aghast at the stranger, drenched to his skin, who stooped down and held his face less than two inches from his.

"I saw you stopped," Roger said. "I wondered if anything was wrong."

George fumbled for a button and his window slid down three-quarters of an inch. In the wind, a light mist drizzled in his face. He winced but he didn't pull back. If this man came out in a downpour, it was the least he could do. "No. No problem," he said. "Just waiting out the storm."

"That's probably wisest. It shouldn't last too much longer," Roger said. "A lot of people drive through puddles too fast—get water in their engines. I thought . . . "

"No. No problem."

"Glad to hear it. When you start up again, pump your brakes a few times. It helps dry them out."

"I will. Thank you. And thank you very much for stopping, young man."

"Yes, thank you," George's wife said, leaning over from her side.

"It's all right." He straightened up and waved pleasantly to them and trotted back to his car.

When he got in, Jimmy was laughing. His father's hair was soaked, hanging down over his face, and his clothes were as wet as if he'd gone swimming in them.

"You're the asshole of all time," the boy informed him immediately. "What kind of alibi is that? You just proved we were near here."

Roger grinned back at him. "No, I just proved I'm a terrific guy. Your average triple murderer wouldn't go out of his way to help someone in a thunderstorm, would he?"

"No. Unless he was trying to prove he was a terrific guy."

Roger took a playful swing at the side of the boy's head. Jimmy ducked and grabbed his arm and they tussled a few seconds across the front seat. They were both laughing but they were too tired to keep it up very long.

Roger put the car in gear and pulled out slowly around the big sedan. Through the rear view mirror he saw the old couple smiling at him and waving as he drove off.

"Bye-bye, George. Bye-bye, Mrs. George. Take care of yourselves now, y'hear," he lisped with saccharine mockery.

"Good ol' Roger," Jimmy said. "Makes friends wherever he goes."

"That's right, Killer. Just like you."

The rain slackened off, just as Roger predicted. The storm moved rapidly east. The lightning gathered in one quarter of the sky up ahead and the thunder rumbled in long sonorous rolls. Above them the sky grew lighter and the moon glowed faintly through the clouds.

Roger said, "Let's stop at a motel in a little while, before it gets late. I could use a hot shower. Have dinner out too."

"Great."

He drove another twenty minutes or so, through a deserted small town where the light from the street lamps formed dark yellow splotches on the glistening asphalt. The rain had stopped completely but no one had come back on the street yet. The only place open was a run-down cafe with a plate glass window. It had hand-lettered specials Scotch-taped all over it. There was no one visible inside, not even a counterman.

Right past the town three enormous grain elevators hulked in the darkness, their concrete sides blackened by the rain. A hundred yards further was an old-fashioned auto court. Each unit was a separate bungalow.

Roger parked in front of the office and went in to register. "How much for a room with two beds for me and my son?" he asked the woman who finally emerged from the back to wait on him. She was incredibly skinny and sallow-looking. Her dress hung limply from her shoulders, as if she had just gotten over an illness and lost a great deal of weight.

Whatever her problem was, it hadn't ruined her disposition. She was friendly and helpful in a terse sort of way. "It's seven dollars," she said, "but I can let you have if for six if you use only one of the beds. There's just the two of you?"

"Yeah. We'll use both beds."

"Then it's seven dollars." She looked at him curiously yet with a certain solicitude. With his hair and his clothes still soaking wet, he looked like something the cat had dragged in.

"Fine." She handed him a pen and a card to fill out. "Does the shower work?"

"I'll let you have number four. It's got the best shower."

"Thanks. And is there anyplace we could get something to eat around here?"

"A couple, if you're not too fussy. There's Ralph's back in town and a truck stop a couple miles down the road. It's open all night."

"I saw Ralph's. What's the truck stop like?"

" 'Bout the same. Get a lot for your money, both places."

He pulled a bunch of crumpled bills from his pocket and found her a five and two ones. She put the money in the drawer and turned to get him his key from the board.

"That's number four, I said? Quite a storm we had there for a while, wasn't it? Looks like you got caught in it."

"Yeah. A branch blew down in the road. This trucker got it

caught in his axle. Almost caused an accident. He needed a hand getting it out. It was all wrapped about around the axle there. Whew!'' He glanced down at his arms, which were covered with abrasions and a grid of fine scratches.

Her eyes followed his. She had noticed his arms too and wondered about it. "Well, you'll get a good hot shower in four, you'll feel a lot better," she said, shaking her head sympathetically as she handed him the key. "That's an awful fine thing to do—give a fella a hand in weather like this."

Roger grinned at her broadly. "Yeah. I thought so myself."

They ate at the truck stop. After nearly a week of making do with what they had in the car, it was a treat just reading the menu and making a choice. Roger had a steak, Jimmy the roast turkey dinner. There were rolls and soup, potato, salad and pie.

Afterward, back in the cabin, Jimmy lay on the bed thinking while his father undressed. He had killed two people that day but he couldn't really say what it felt like. The whole experience had blurred in his mind. He didn't think about the people who were dead, just about the act of killing them itself. It wasn't the big deal he thought it would be. Still, he had done it. He wouldn't mind doing it again. He fell asleep as soon as his father turned out the light.

CHAPTER 13

WHEN WALT CAME DOWNSTAIRS in the morning it seemed to Rose that he looked considerably better. The color had returned to his face. She told him about Hilt's phone call.

He was obviously quite angry but he said only half a sentence about it and then let it drop. She knew how he felt and he didn't like yelling at her in front of the boys.

Besides, he was eager to get started making phone calls. Since he hadn't heard anything from the Department yet, he figured he ought to talk to Hilt first. He tried him at home.

"You just caught me in time," Hilt said. "I'm on my way to Storm Lake. Would you believe they're turning me into a crime reporter after all these years?"

"It won't do you any harm. Rose told me you called. What can you give me on it?"

Hilt filled him in quickly on the latest developments. During the night a third body—Jonathan's—had been found near the road. Also stabbed. If there were any suspects, the local authorities weren't talking about it. It looked like robbery was the motive.

"Shit," Walt said, "what'd you have to tell me that for? Was there any sex angle at least?"

"Sorry. Not so far as I've heard. But they might be hushing it up. There are cops who do that, you know."

165

Walt got the inference. "So I've been told. What makes you think it's the same guys as here? It is more than one, isn't it?"

"Seems to be. Nothing much, really. The fact that they used knives and adhesive tape. And the victims were women—at least the two last night. That's about it. Oh, yeah—one of them might have had her wrists slashed. But why don't you give the sheriff out there a call? You could get the whole story. His people won't talk to me. All I know is from another reporter at the scene."

"I'm about to do that. I just wanted some idea of how the land lay. Thanks for the information, Hilton." He sounded like he was ready to hang up.

"Uh . . . Walt? . . . I wasn't suggesting that you call him purely for your own benefit. If you find out anything interesting I sure could use a break. I helped you out on this, y'know, calling last night."

Walt chuckled. "I realize that. But Rose didn't tell me there were strings. She thought you were calling as a friend."

"That's right. I'm your friend. You're my friend."

"You have a gift for explaining things. I'll do what I can for you but you have to understand there are certain . . . "

"Ethical considerations. I know. I'd never dream of asking you to violate your ethics. Not even for a war buddy."

Next Walt called his office. Storm Lake hadn't been in touch with them. Maybe that was a bad sign but it might just mean they hadn't gotten around to calling yet. Matt Vollmer had heard about the killings on the car radio driving to work but it never occurred to him that there might be a connection between a knife murder in one county and one in another. It figured. At least Matt was able to get him the Buena Vista County sheriff's name and phone number.

Dialing the number, Walt realized his nerves were tingling like an excited schoolboy's. He felt he was on the verge of a breakthrough and this phone call would clinch it.

But all the call did was take a little of the wind out of his sails. No one working on the case could come to the phone. That was understandable. He talked to a sergeant on duty, who promised to relay his message to the sheriff as quickly as possible. Walt made him repeat it twice to make sure he had it straight and to underline the urgency of the matter.

For the next two hours Walt paced anxiously in his study. What was taking them so long? If his intuition was right, it was as important to their case as it was to his own.

Rose came in with his breakfast—grapefruit, toast, corn flakes and coffee. No eggs. She was watching the cholesterol again.

"What d'you call this?" he said. "This isn't a breakfast."

"If you don't want it, don't eat it. Just sit down and behave yourself. You won't make the call come any faster by wearing out the floor."

He didn't understand her tone. "You don't seem to realize what this could mean," he said, though he was in no mood for an argument.

"Oh, yes I do. I also realize three people are dead and you're acting like I should invite in the neighbors to celebrate."

That stung. It brought him back to the ground immediately. "I don't think you're being fair," he said sheepishly.

She turned and walked out without answering him. She was being fair all right—and he knew it.

Around ten-thirty Storm Lake finally called. It wasn't the sheriff himself but his top deputy. He let Walt know right away that he was the top deputy.

"Now what can I do for you, Sheriff Taliaferro?"

Walt explained again his interest in the Storm Lake murders.

"Well, that's certainly an interesting theory," the deputy said dryly, "but you know it's quite common for crimes like the one in your county to trigger copycat imitations. These crimes often . . . "

"I understand that," Walt cut in sharply. "But I think it's worth checking out until we know for certain one way or the other."

"Possibly," the deputy condescended. "But right now we're working on the theory that the perpetrator was a person or persons known to the victims. The house shows no sign of forcible entry."

Walt couldn't believe what he was hearing. He swallowed hard to keep his temper under control. "Tell me something," he said. "Have you interviewed the husband yet?"

The deputy seemed taken aback by the question. "In . . . in what connection?"

"In connection with whether the . . . *decedent* always kept the door locked when she was at home."

"No. We didn't ask him that," the deputy confessed, the starch gone from his manner.

Walt couldn't forbear rubbing it in. "Well, you know it's quite common, young man, to find no sign of forcible entry when the door is unlocked."

There was silence from the Storm Lake end. "Listen," Walt went on quickly, "let me get a few things straight. You suspect more than one person was involved? They used knives, and one of the women's wrists were slashed? They used adhesive tape?"

"Yes."

"Then if you have no objection I'd like to come down there and check things out for myself."

"I have no objection, Sheriff. I'll look forward to seeing you." His tone was icy.

Walt waited for him to hang up, then slammed the receiver down in its cradle. "Go fuck yourself," he said to it softly.

Walt called Matt and told him to go home and pack a few things. He'd pick him up in an hour. They were going to Storm Lake and might be there a few days.

They checked into a motel and drove immediately to the sheriff's office. It was located in a single-story lath-and-plaster building on the outskirts of town. After some difficulty with the duty sergeant—not the one Walt talked to in the morning—they were finally directed to a tiny cubicle in the rear.

All the while Matt beamed like a new father. The outfit he worked for had a great deal more class.

Sheriff Andy Vandenberg was seated at his desk looking over some photographs while he munched on an unhealthily grayish roast beef sandwich. He was a florid, silver-haired man whose mouth curved permanently downward as if he was always troubled by gas.

"Would you believe this is my breakfast?" he said for openers. "Four-thirty and I'm just having breakfast."

Walt had to explain the purpose of his visit from the beginning. He got the distinct impression that no one in this department communicated with anyone else. But at least Vandenberg was interested in his theory, whether any of his men had thought it worth their while to brief him on it or not. The questions he asked indicated he was totally baffled by the case and would welcome just about anything that could give focus to his investigation.

"Well," he said when Walt completed his presentation, "I suppose you want to get out to the house and have a look around for yourself. I'll give you a ride as soon as I finish eating. Here, you might want to look at these."

He handed Walt the sheaf of pictures he had been studying. They were lab photos and blow-ups of the victims as the police had found them. In one, the tablecloth covering Joyce had been removed and her eyes stared hideously into the camera. The handle of the knife still protruded from her chest.

Walt glanced wonderingly at Vandenberg. He had finished his sandwich and was peeling back the top of a wedge-shaped Tupperware pie container.

A notice sealing off the Heynen home hung from a piece of string festooned across the front door. Vandenberg lifted it up for Walt and Matt Vollmer to duck under.

Walt stopped inside the door. The sense of being in the presence of death struck him as soon as he stepped over the threshold.

Vandenberg said, "Yeah, I know. You should have been here before they took the bodies away."

Walt surveyed the room, trying to account for the feeling. Except for the bookcase that had been tipped over and partially blocked the door to the hall, everything seemed perfectly normal. It was just an empty house. The bookcase was the only sign of violence.

"C'mere. Take a look at this," Vandenberg said. He had gone into the dining room.

There was a small, slightly discolored patch on the carpet under the table. It looked like a stain that had been washed out incompletely.

"She was tied to the leg right here—like this." Vandenberg demonstrated with his hands behind his back. "But look at that. She dragged the table a good two inches. It's amazing. Try lifting it." There was a note of awe in his hushed voice.

"Hmmh." Walt and Matt each hefted a corner in turn. It was heavy.

"There's not much blood," Walt said, indicating the spot on the carpet.

"It ran down inside her shirt."

Walt nodded. "What happened over there?"

"The bookcase? Hold on a minute." Vandenberg went back into the living room and called someone down the hall. Two men appeared. The thin-faced one with the neatly trimmed moustache Walt guessed immediately to be the top deputy. His name was Frank Parker. The other was introduced simply as Bob. He seemed to be the Department's resident criminalist. He was wearing civilian clothes.

Walt asked him about the bookcase.

Bob shrugged uncertainly. "It must have got knocked over while they were struggling. She grabbed it at some point . . . "

"She?"

"Yeah. I don't know which one though. Let me show you." He stood the bookcase back against the wall. It was a light, flimsily constructed piece used only to display knickknacks and family pictures, now strewn on the floor. There was a smudge of graphite powder on the slat frame at about chest level. Evidently he had righted it before to dust it for finger prints and then laid it back on the floor the way he had found it.

"See," Bob went on, "this here's a palm print. It's not readable—smudged. But it's too narrow to be a man's hand."

"No others?"

"No, not here. I picked up a few possibles so far around the house but we still have to check them against members of the family. I got a pretty good thumb and partial forefinger off the knife in the bedroom. The murder weapon—the Buck knife. Not enough for an I.D. but if you get your man you can nail him with it."

"Terrific," Walt said. *"If* we get our man."

"Sorry, Sheriff, but it's not like the movies. To take a good print you gotta roll the finger over the pad. In real life people don't handle things like that."

"I realize that," Walt said abstractedly. He was examining the print with some curiosity. The black powder brought out the main creases of the hand but, even without magnification, he could see that the smaller lines were little more than a blur. "I don't mean it's your fault," he said.

He wrapped his hand around the slat frame right below the smudge. It was strange. The balls of his fingers pressed into the wood. No matter how he positioned his hand, the act of grabbing should have left marks from the fingers as well as the palm.

"The way my hand is now," he asked, "would that leave fingerprints—even if I did it quickly?"

Bob peered at his hand. "It should."

"It's really quite simple, Sheriff," Parker said, seeing his perplexity. "The victim was probably knocked against the case and grabbed onto it for a moment to keep from falling. Something like that. Precisely how she grabbed it is immaterial."

Walt eyed him coldly. He was no less insufferable in person than he had been on the phone. "The question isn't how, it's when," he said. He turned to Vandenberg. "I thought you told me they fought with the assailants after they were tied up—after their hands were tied?"

Vandenberg's habitual scowl deepened. He sensed that Walt was trying to make things even more complicated, which he didn't need. He pushed his cap back and scratched his temple as he considered what new light Taliaferro's question threw on his prior assumptions.

"That's right," Parker said, not waiting for his boss to formulate a response. "The women had several lacerations on their torsos but none on their hands, where you would expect to find them if they were warding off a knife attack. It seemed to me . . . "

"It seems to me," Walt interrupted, "that she couldn't grab the bookcase if her hands were tied already."

Vandenberg said, "That's a good point. But where does it leave us?"

"Where we were before," Parker said definitively. "Except that the victims put up resistance before they were tied as well as after."

Walt gnawed doubtfully on his lower lip. "I guess you're right," he said. "But it's kind of hard to believe—starting to fight again once they've been subdued."

"Well, it's what the evidence shows. You see it yourself," Parker said. He turned on his heel and walked triumphantly back toward the bedroom.

"Don't mind him," Vandenberg said. "He has strong opinions."

"I want to show you something else. Over here," Bob said, thinking they were finished by the bookcase and wanting to get back to business. He went to the front door and swung it closed.

Walt took another look at the puzzling fingerprint and then joined the others in the corner of the room. There were two small charred holes in the carpet, hidden previously by the open door.

"Cigarettes," Bob said, squatting down on his haunches over the marks. "One of them ground out two cigarettes here just like it was a goddam ashtray. With his hand, not with his shoe. That little stain there—you can hardly see it, you have to bend down to catch it in the right light—that's beer. There was a quart bottle there, tipped over. Y'know, they're a couple of fucking hooligans—putting out cigarettes in the carpet."

Walt snorted. It was the first time he had seen any hint of emotion from Bob. Hooligans. He stooped down and fingered the blackened fibers. But he understood exactly what had stirred the deputy's feelings. For a moment he felt the same thing himself. It was funny, he thought, how different things affected you. You looked at a picture of a young woman with a knife sticking out of her chest and you thought, What kind of maniac did this? You thought about the tragedy, the waste. Still, you're investigating a murder—you're dealing with killers. You start taking what happened for granted. But then the burn in the carpet—it was such a peculiar desecration. For some reason it filled him with disgust disproportionate to its real significance. Christ, there were ashtrays all over the house.

"That bottle," he said, "no prints on it either, I suppose?"

"Nope. In this humidity cold things pick up too much dew. Same with the glasses in the kitchen."

"Shit," Walt muttered under his breath. "Even with the air conditioner going?" But it wasn't really a question.

Matt said, "You know what just struck me? If the guy put out those cigarettes by hand he must have been sitting right here on the floor." He sounded amazed.

Walt smiled, wondering what conclusion Matt drew from his uncharacteristic deduction. "Yeah. So?"

"So nothing," Matt said defensively. "The middle of a murder's a funny time for a cigarette break, that's all."

That's not all, Walt thought. It's a good point. How come the killers weren't in a hurry? It would be worth knowing whether the women were dead already when one of the men sat down to smoke and guzzle a beer. And what was the other one doing meanwhile? Did they know the husband wouldn't be back until late, or had they planned on waiting for him? He still had faith that the more of these questions he answered—the more he knew about these men, how they operated, the kind of people they were—the closer he'd be to an ultimate solution. So far the killers hadn't made any crucial mistakes. They hadn't left behind any clues that pointed straight at their identity. But they left riddles—riddles about their behavior and character if not their names. Solve enough of them and then maybe—just maybe—you'll get the one break you need to tie everything together. He believed that.

"That's nothing," Bob said. "You should see what we found in the kitchen. There were two glasses—one with beer, the other with milk—and a plate with crumbs of chocolate cake on it. Not what you usually find at the scene of a murder, I'd say."

"You sure it wasn't for the women—before the killers arrived? Maybe the little kid—what's his name? Jonathan?—had the cake and milk."

"It's possible but I doubt it. The women had coffee in the den. And according to a neighbor the kid was outside all afternoon."

"Maybe he came in for a few minutes."

"Maybe. But did you know the Manson gang fixed themselves something to eat after one of their jobs?" Bob said, nodding significantly.

"Was that Sharon Tate?" Matt asked.

"No, I think it was probably the other one."

Vandenberg whistled through his teeth. "Holy shit," he said, "you suppose we got another Manson case on our hands?"

"Whatever you got, I wouldn't mention the food to the press if I were you," Walt said. "Some reporter's bound to see the connection whether there is one or not."

"I just mentioned it," Bob said. "I'm not saying it means anything. But Parker's got this theory that the victims knew the killers—invited them in, served them refreshments. It's kind of interesting."

"I know Parker's theory," Walt said derisively. But he realized immediately that he wasn't being objective. As an explanation it had certain merit.

"No, listen," Bob said, warming to the challenge of Walt's skepticism. "I don't know if he'd want me to tell you this, but I think he might suspect the Miller woman's husband. Yeah, I'm serious. Y'know, no one called him till about ten-thirty. Now how come he wasn't trying to find his wife if she wasn't home by then?"

"That little cocksucker," Vandenberg said through his teeth, referring—Walt realized a moment later—to Parker, not Miller. "Howard Miller's father is a member of my lodge. Howard wouldn't do this kind of thing. Where does he come off with bullshit like that!"

"I don't know about lodges," Bob said, "but if you want to kill your wife it's not a bad way to do it—while she's at someone else's house. Nobody'd ever suspect it was done to get her."

"What're you talking about?" Vandenberg said heatedly. "If Parker figured it out, any asshole could figure it out. It's stupid. I don't even want to talk about it."

"Well, like I say, I just mentioned it for what it's worth," Bob said, backing down. "I'm not really sure that's what Frank had on his mind. All he said was . . . "

"Fuck what he said. It's getting late. What else you think we should show the sheriff here? He thinks it was the same guys that did that killing over in Arlington County. Now Howard Miller's got nothing to do with Arlington County."

Walt didn't like the sound of that. The last thing he needed was to find himself a pawn in the running battle between the arrogant top deputy and his rather fuddled but stubborn superior.

He had his own opinion about the Howard Miller theory but he figured he'd better keep it to himself for the time being. He let Bob conduct him to the bedroom where Georgia Heynen's body had been found and where Parker was still busily searching for clues.

Fortunately, Vandenberg decided this wasn't the time to bring matters to a head with his deputy. He contented himself with glowering at him malignly. When the blow-up came it promised to be spectacular but Walt wasn't in the mood for it now. He was getting tired.

There wasn't much to see in the bedroom that gave him a feel for the case one way or the other. He wanted a look at that Buck knife, which had been used to slash Georgia Heynen's wrists, but it had been taken to headquarters along with the rest of the moveable physical evidence. It was a good bet that it would prove to be the missing murder weapon from Lake Barrett. At any rate, it was the only bet. The paring knife that had been used on Joyce Miller came from a magnetized board in the Heynens' kitchen and so too, probably, did the wide blade that had taken Jonathan's life. It hadn't been found yet.

Vandenberg said he'd have to check with his D.A., but he saw no reason why Walt couldn't take the Buck knife back to Arlington for a few days to let his people run tests on it.

On the way to the kitchen Walt commented on the fact that the two killers apparently entered the house with only one weapon between them. To kill three people they had to "borrow" two knives. Like so much of the information gleaned from the evidence, it seemed to be trying to tell them something about the killers but its significance—if, indeed, it had any—was far from clear. It suggested, perhaps, that one or both of the men weren't prepared to commit murder. But maybe the fastidious one—the one who covered his victim with a tablecloth so as not to get squirted with blood—was reluctant to soil his own knife when others were at hand. Maybe he had a gun in his pocket but didn't feel like using it.

They looked briefly around the kitchen. When they were finished there, Vandenberg said it was too dark to bother going out to where Jonathan's body had been found. There wasn't much point anyway since the downpour last night had washed out all footprints. There wasn't any other evidence as far as he could tell. But Walt was welcome to come back and see for himself the next day.

He offered Walt and Matt a ride back to headquarters, where their car was parked. Bob said he'd stick around awhile longer. He and Parker still had a lot to do. He didn't suggest that the others go down to the basement. So far, it hadn't occurred to anyone to look around down there.

Walt dozed off in the car on the drive to headquarters. It had been a long day. But he went inside to have a quick look at the evidence they were holding and to see what else had come in during the evening.

It gave him a strange feeling to hold in his hand the knife that probably killed Kay Orben. From the cursory examination he could give it in the office there was no way to be sure. But it was exactly what he expected—a folding Buck knife with a four-inch blade, an extremely keen edge and a point that seemed fine enough to have inflicted the wound on the Orben girl's breast. He suspected there was no way to prove that this was the knife he had been looking for. All his lab would be able to say would be that it was "consistent with" the murder weapon. Still, that was progress.

The blood-soaked shirt was a disappointment. It was a light blue short-sleeved wash-and-wear Arrow shirt. There must be a million just like it. No laundry marks either. But now they knew that one of the killers wore a size sixteen collar. That really narrowed the field, didn't it?

There were the women's purses and wallets with no money inside and the jewelry case that had been found in the living room. If anything had been taken from it, it couldn't have been much. That would have to be checked with the husband and daughters, who might have a pretty good idea of what pieces were missing. Maybe robbery was the motive, or maybe it was incidental, but either way Walt wasn't going to let it bother him. Just because they hadn't robbed Kay Orben, it didn't mean they wouldn't need money sooner or later.

Copies of the coroner's reports on two of the victims were waiting on Vandenberg's desk. They didn't bother looking at them. It was too late in the day and everyone was too tired to pick his way through medical prose. But they glanced briefly at the reports that had come in from the investigators in the field. They seemed to be doing a good job. The neighbor across the highway who had noticed Jonathan playing outside several times during the afternoon hadn't seen anyone entering or leaving the Heynen home or hanging around suspiciously. Around seven o'clock—she wasn't sure of the time—she had heard yelling from the direction of the road. She didn't go look because she assumed it was just children playing. Now she wondered.

Another interviewer had traced Joyce Miller's whereabouts that morning. She had run into a friend while she was shopping in town. The friend remembered Joyce saying she was going to call on Georgia Heynen. She didn't think she said anything about anyone else being there.

There was a note from one of the deputies saying he had talked briefly with Jack Heynen and Howard Miller, but out of decency he had held off questioning them in depth. Was that all right?

Vandenberg initialed an "o.k." across the bottom and gave the note to the desk sergeant. He Xeroxed the other reports and gave copies to Walt.

"I think I'll go home now myself," Vandenberg said with a groan. "I'm bushed. See you tomorrow."

At the motel Walt found a note under his door asking him to call room twenty-eight as soon as he got in. So Hilt was staying in the same motel. Was it a coincidence or had he moved during the day to be closer to his source?

Walt phoned him reluctantly. He was exhausted but he felt he owed it to Hilt to give him whatever he could in exchange for his tip. He left the door open.

When Hilt walked in a moment later he was loaded down with a bucket of ice, a fifth of Cutty Sark and three preposterous sand-wiches that must have been built to his robust specifications.

Walt laughed good-naturedly. He didn't feel like eating but the scotch was a temptation. "Did you put that stuff on your expense account?" he said.

"Fuck that," Hilt said, his tone almost surly. "I had to file a couple hours ago. Where were you guys till now?" It was apparent that he had already been drinking. Not from that bottle though—the seal hadn't been broken. "Why don't you call Matt? I got him a sandwich too."

Hilt poured out three stiff drinks while Walt went to the phone.

"Let's get one thing straight," Walt said as soon as he hung up. "Whatever you hear tonight, you got to clear with me before you use it. Understand?"

Hilt looked astonished. "No deal. That's like in Red China. I can't give you approval on my stories."

Walt opened his hands. "All right. Then everything's off the record. I have no control over what Vollmer might say."

Grudgingly, Hilt accepted the terms.

It took them a while to get around to discussing the case. First they had to listen to Hilt griping about what a raw deal it was to get assigned a story like this. Part of his complaint was that his paper was notoriously cheap when it came to sending reporters out in the field. When he came back from Arlington he had to haggle with them over every penny on his expense account, including a few little items that had no business being on it. He was pretty funny telling the story but his humor had a cutting edge to it. Walt got the impression that something was eating him.

"I thought reporters loved this kind of stuff," he said. "A spectacular murder—big headlines."

"Ah, it's a lot of bullshit," Hilt said, gesturing contemptuously with his whiskey glass. "It's all right for some guys. But what do they expect me to do, solve the fucking case? It's nothing but a lousy rewrite-man's job. Some dude gives me an official handout at the sheriff's office. 'This is your story, gentlemen.' You're gonna tell me, Here, Hilt, you can write this, you can write this, sorry old buddy, but I can't let you write that." Mimicking Walt, his voice rose to a sneering falsetto. "It's a pile of shit. The whole thing's gonna peter out in a couple days anyway, just like at Arlington."

Walt's eyebrows shot up. He didn't expect effusions of gratitude for the information he had to offer but certainly Hilt's derisive attitude was way out of line. He was going to call him on it but then he figured that Hilt had been drinking. There was something else bothering him as well.

Matt wasn't inclined to be so tolerant. "If it's such a pile of shit," he said belligerently, "I suppose you don't want to hear about it. And what makes you think we're not gonna catch these guys?"

Walt couldn't prevent an explosive guffaw. "Matt! What makes you think we *are* gonna catch these guys?"

Matt stared at him incredulously like a kid who's just been told there wasn't a Santa Claus. "Didn't you tell me the same guys did this as Lake Barrett?"

"Yeah, but that doesn't mean I know who they are." He turned to Hilt. "What's the problem, Hilt? Something bothering you?"

Hilt fluttered his hand in front of his face. "It's nothing. It's personal."

"You don't want to talk about it?"

The corners of Hilt's mouth worked nervously but he didn't say anything. Walt got up and freshened their drinks. When he had stretched back out on the bed, Hilt blurted, "All right. Why not?"

He took a long pull on his drink. "You know why I got this goddam assignment?" he said. "It's a tryout."

"I don't understand."

"A tryout. If I do a good job there'll be other choice plums coming my way," he said sarcastically.

"That doesn't make sense," Walt said. "You're a top reporter. What happened?"

"Watergate—that kind of thing. I'm an investigative reporter, Walt, but my beat was always local stuff. THE FAMILY THAT RUNS ADAMS COUNTY. All of a sudden everyone's gunning for big game. I'm an anachronism. I didn't catch on until it was too late. The editor sticks me back on the feature page. 'Gosh, Hilt, it was a big news day. We didn't have room up front.' You remember that series we did on state mental hospitals? They didn't even give me a piece of it. I don't even remember what I was working on at the time. It was so chickenshit, I can't even remember."

His voice was choked with tears. Walt didn't know what to say. "I'm sorry, Hilt."

"Yeah. So listen. You really think it's the same guys? What makes you so sure?"

Walt tapped his chest. "I'm sure," he said. But he didn't want to come on too strong, to sound like he was right on top of his job while everything was going so poorly for his friend. Besides, he didn't actually know it for a fact. "Call it a hunch, I guess. I keep seeing the same patterns over and over again."

"Slashed wrists, you mean?"

"Yeah, for one thing. But there's other stuff that's more—what?—psychological. Like all three women were positioned so that the killer didn't have to look them in the face." He ticked them off on his fingers. "Orben. Heynen had her head stuck under the bed. And the one in the living room had a tablecloth thrown over her. Now what does that suggest to you?''

"I dunno. That they're squeamish? A guilty conscience? What about the kid?''

"Squeamish—right. But they're incredibly ruthless. The kid's a different story. The guy was struggling with him. Even so, his arms must have been pinned to his sides since he had no defensive wounds. The killer must have been holding him from in back. Unless they were both there, and one held him while the other stuck the knife in.''

"Jesus!''

Walt stood up and paced about the room as he elaborated on his theory. At first he had thought the two men they were looking for were opposite personality types. One was explosively violent—the one who vandalized the car at Lake Barrett. The other was absolutely cold-blooded. He tied up his victim and let her die slowly. There were insects that killed like that.

Now he saw it wasn't that simple. The same traits appeared in both crimes but he couldn't separate them so easily in his mind. For the brutal one, there was the cigarette in the rug, the knives plunged into the heart, maybe the bookcase. No, there was some other explanation for the bookcase. Still, there was the car and the rug and the little boy. But with Joyce Miller he was incredibly fastidious, covering her chest to contain the flow of blood. And the job on Georgia's wrists had been butchered. It was her blood on the discarded shirt. Yet this was the man who had killed Kay Orben with such surgical precision.

"You see what I mean?'' he said. "Unless I'm missing the boat completely, they're more alike than I imagined. They run to extremes all right, but the same extremes in each one. I don't know how else to put it. It's like each has a part of the other one's personality. Does that make any sense to you?''

"Yeah it makes sense. They're traveling together. They're partners. It's weird though. . . . But even if you're right, I don't see how it does you any good. Are you trying to catch them or psychoanalyze them?''

Walt laughed soundlessly and sat down on the corner of the bed. He looked over at Matt, who sat in an armchair with his head tipped back and his mouth hanging open. He had fallen asleep.

"It doesn't help necessarily," he said softly, wanting to make sure that Matt didn't hear what he was about to say. "Maybe there's a clue to their identity in all this and I just don't see it yet. Maybe there's a clue to what they'll do next. The thing is this, Hilt." He was whispering now, pointing a forefinger steadily at the reporter. "If I'm right, they're on the move. That means they're vulnerable. They're visible. But they're killers first and thieves only second. They robbed those women because they needed the money . . . and they didn't get very much."

Hilt exhaled in a long, sibilant hiss. "You're telling me you're sure you'll catch up with them sooner or later. It's only a question of how many people they're going to kill first."

"That's right. Listen—print what you want, but use a little discretion."

CHAPTER 14

WEDNESDAY.

Roger got on Jimmy's nerves all morning. He slept late and then showed no inclination to get out of bed. He lay there smoking cigarettes while Jimmy asked him repeatedly when they were going to get started. Each time he promised to get up in a minute. Around eleven the boy got tired of hanging around the motel. He pulled on his sneakers, took a few dollars from his father's pocket, and announced defiantly that he was going out for a walk. He slammed the door behind him.

He started toward town but, out of curiosity, turned off at the road that led to the grain elevator. In back, a railroad siding ran past a loading platform that jutted out to meet it. Jimmy walked along the tracks. There was no one around to mind him wandering about.

At close range the size of the elevator was overwhelming. Jimmy looked up a sheer, unbroken wall of concrete well over a hundred feet tall. The building was more than a block long, constructed like smokestacks clustered together. Quietly—though he didn't know why he had to be quiet—he pulled himself up to the platform. In front of him were four huge corrugated metal doors that must have raised from above. There was a normal-sized door at the far end of the platform. He tiptoed over to it and tried the handle.

Surprisingly, it turned. Opening the door, he found himself inside a large, noisy machine room. Most of the sound came from something that looked like a giant vacuum cleaner. Workmen in twos and threes were dismantling equipment. There were several compressors, the drive mechanism for a conveyor and two huge fans set into air ducts—all in various stages of being taken apart.

Fascinated, he stood in the doorway absorbed by the activity. He had no idea that so much went on inside a grain elevator. He had always thought of them as big, hollow tanks.

Five or ten minutes passed. Suddenly he felt a hand on his shoulder. Startled, he turned and saw an old man smiling beside him. His tiny, close-set eyes were bloodshot. He said something unintelligible in what sounded like a foreign language. It was hard to hear over the din of the vacuum.

"The . . . door wasn't locked," Jimmy stammered, drawing away. Despite the old man's reassuring smile, he was frightened and confused. He felt he had to justify his presence there.

The little Dutchman nodded vigorously. "Not locked. Dis is okay. You see before?" he gestured expansively, taking in the entire room.

"No. No. I've never seen this before," Jimmy said hastily, speaking over the noise with exaggerated precision.

The old man took him by the hand and led him forward. Jimmy followed him meekly to the head of the conveyor. By this time several other workman had noticed him and stopped what they were doing. They were all smiling at him. Nevertheless, the boy felt like an alien, an intruder in a secret place. Yet he knew the old man simply wanted to show him around.

Jimmy took his eyes from these men and glanced down the conveyor, which ran in a tunnel the length of the building until it disappeared in darkness.

The man's arm shot past him, pointing in the direction he was already looking. "Ya, *snel*," he said. "Goes quick." Then he spoke rapidly in Dutch to another workman, who was hunkered down on the floor beside a compressor. The man looked up, grinning with wide gaps showing between yellow teeth. He wiped his hands on an oily rag and reached back to throw a switch. The belt lurched into motion, gaining speed quickly.

Without thinking, Jimmy yanked his hand out of the old man's grasp and fled to the door. He was in a nightmare world where the terror was real though no threat was apparent.

It wasn't far to the door. As he pulled it open, the sunlight poured in. Behind him, the gap-toothed worker bellowed to the old man in English, "Your red nose frightened him, Papa. Your big nose frightened him."

The others joined in a chorus of hearty laughter.

Outside, he knew immediately that no one was following him. He hopped down from the loading platform and walked briskly along the tracks in the direction of town. In the time it took him to catch his breath he had put the whole bizarre episode out of his mind.

The tracks angled across the highway that was the main street of the town. Jimmy looked around to get his bearings. Almost a mile behind him the elevator rose like a monolith on the flat landscape. No doors or windows were visible. He had the feeling that if he told anyone he had seen people inside working on machines, they would never believe him.

He stopped at a Dairy Queen and bought a thirty-five-cent cone. Licking it slowly, he walked back the highway toward the motel. His father had to be up by now and ready to go. It was close to noon already, a perfect day for driving. The temperature was down, probably in the low eighties, and the air was light and fragrant. Overhead, the sky was truly blue, not the pale, parched gray they had been traveling under for more than a week.

When he opened the door, his father was lying on the bed in his undershorts. But the bed had been made up since he left.

"Shit," Jimmy said, "aren't you ready to go? We should have checked out of here by now."

"The woman was in to make up the room," Roger said. "The owner or whatever she is. Guess what she talked about."

"How would I know? Let's get going."

"Guess."

Jimmy gestured vaguely back down the highway. "The . . . uh . . . those people?"

"That's right. Do you know what she said?"

Jimmy's mouth twisted maliciously. "Yeah. She said, 'You killed them, didn't you, you creep? That's why you're hanging around this ratty motel like you got no place to go.' " He tensed up as soon as he said it. He had meant it as a joke, he was about to explain.

But Roger, inexplicably, seemed to hear nothing in the boy's response beyond the fact that the answer was wrong. "No," he said evenly. "She called it the crime of the century. She said that's what they called it on the radio. She said it's getting so a person isn't safe anywhere. She said a person had to be sick in the head to kill a five-year-old boy."

Jimmy blanched momentarily. That last remark was leveled at him, as if his father was insinuating that what he did was worse. "What did you say?" the boy asked warily.

"What do you think I said? I said it was probably niggers."

"Niggers!" Jimmy chortled. "There's isn't a nigger within two hundred miles of here."

Roger laced his fingers together and put his hands behind his head. "Well," he said laconically, looking up at the ceiling, "it won't be the first time I've been wrong in my life."

Jimmy broke up laughing. His father's delivery was perfect. The boy sat down on the one uncushioned wood chair in the room and leaned back against the dresser, rocking lazily on the balls of his feet. He started laughing again every time he thought of his father telling the woman it was niggers.

"C'mon, Dad," he said coaxingly after a minute or so. "It's getting late. Why don't you get dressed so we can get the hell out of here?"

"We're staying another night," Roger said. "I already paid the woman."

"Here? What for?"

"I'm sick of driving, for one thing. That's what for."

Jimmy was at a loss for words. There was nothing to do in this godforsaken place. Beyond that, he knew that the driving wasn't really the problem. He could drive the car himself if necessary. No, his father simply—stubbornly—didn't want to do anything except lie in bed. The boy had no idea how to cope with him when he was like that.

He picked up his father's key ring from the dresser and flipped it back and forth impatiently between his two hands. There was no point in arguing, not if Roger had already paid for the room.

Roger said, "Go into town and buy a paper. I want to see what it says."

"I was just in town," Jimmy said sullenly. His father had shown no interest in reading about it the first time.

"So? Go again."

"The papers didn't have anything about it," Jimmy lied. He was in no mood to be treated like his father's lousy errand boy. "They must have found them too late."

"Those were the morning papers. Get an afternoon paper. Get a carton of cigarettes too. There's money in my pants."

"I have money. Why can't you go?"

" 'Cause you're going for me."

"Can I take the car."

"No."

For the second time that day he slammed the door behind him. He took his time walking to town. There was so little traffic on the highway that it wasn't worth hitchhiking. At the drugstore, the evening papers weren't in yet. From the spaces on the rack he could see that they carried two—one local and the other from Omaha. There were few copies of the morning Des Moines *Herald* left. In the upper right hand corner of the front page there was a small, black-bordered box that told of the murders. All it said was that the bodies of two women who had been stabbed to death had been found last night at a farm near Storm Lake. Their names were withheld pending notification of the families. There was no mention of a boy as either missing or dead.

He hung around the drugstore for a while, browsing through the magazines until a clerk started watching him. Out on the street again, he wandered around listlessly.

Eventually he came to a school building at the far end of town. A girls' gym class was playing field hockey out in the yard. He watched them idly through the cyclone fence. They were about his age, wearing short green uniforms they made even shorter by rolling up their pant cuffs over their thighs. They squealed like little animals whenever the ball moved toward one end of the field or the other. He got a kick out of seeing them run up and down, their little tits barely jiggling under their loose-fitting blouses. One fat girl had big ones that flopped all over the place. She was a pig though. She actually looked like a pig.

The bell rang and they stopped playing immediately and ran into the building. Jimmy considered waiting around to see if another class came out. He had nothing better to do. Then it occurred to him that he might get in trouble loitering around the school. Somebody might ask him what he was doing outside. What if a cop insisted on taking him back to his father? He'd think there was something funny about a guy checking into a motel last night and then not leaving the next morning though he had no business in town.

He left his place by the fence and went back to the street to check out the drugstore again. See, that was the problem with staying so close to Storm Lake. Everyone was bound to be jumpy and suspicious, especially where strangers were concerned. His father had picked a hell of a time to start acting weird.

The local paper was in. A huge headline covering half the front page said GRISLY TRIPLE MURDER AT STORM LAKE. Jimmy's head jerked back when he saw it. He looked around quickly to see if anyone had noticed his reaction.

Underneath, in progressively smaller type it said MOTHER AND SON, AGED FIVE, SLAIN and BODIES DISCOVERED BY TEEN-AGE DAUGHTER and POLICE HAVE NO LEADS.

Jimmy smiled faintly and picked up a copy. At the counter he asked the clerk for a carton of Winstons. The clerk eyed him suspiciously.

"They're for my father," Jimmy said.

Back at the motel, Roger apparently hadn't moved since he left. The boy tossed him the paper and lay down on his own bed. Roger got up and went into the bathroom to take a leak and rinse his face in cold water. He lit a cigarette, stretched out on the bed again and began reading aloud.

Jimmy only half-listened. His father droned on, reading the words without inflection. According to the paper, it didn't seem they had anything to worry about. The police hadn't a clue where to start looking.

He must have dozed off. The next thing he knew his father was jostling his shoulder. When he opened his eyes the electric lights were on in the room. "What is it? What time is it?" he said in confusion.

"Nine-thirty. We're getting out of here. Come on."

"Now?"

Jimmy saw that his father had showered and shaved. His scraped jaw looked pinkish and shiny. With his damp hair combed back neatly in place, he seemed very young—younger than Jimmy ever remembered seeing him. He had his blue gym bag in his hand.

The boy dropped his feet over the side of the bed and sat up, rubbing his eyes. He yawned. Despite his nap, he felt tired.

"C'mon."

Jimmy rolled down his window and leaned close to it to let the wind blow in his face. It was a gorgeous, still night and they were alone on the road. It was a good idea, driving at night for a change.

Roger stopped for gas at a station that was just closing in the next town down the road. Jimmy said, "I'm gonna get a Coke. Do you want one?"

"No, thanks."

Jimmy finished his drink as soon as they got moving. He pressed the cold aluminum can against his eye sockets. "I can't seem to wake up," he said.

"You want some coffee?"

"Coffee?"

"Yeah, I got a thermos." Roger motioned with his head to the back of the car. "In fact, get me some, will you?"

Jimmy thought, He's really going in for this night driving in a big way. He actually left the motel to go shopping. Amazing.

Beside the thermos was a paper bag stapled shut. The cash register slip was on the outside. He tore it open. It was a box of shotgun shells.

"You want to try it?" Roger said.

"Sure. Where?"

"Here. Take a shot out the window. There's no one around. Just get me my coffee first."

Jimmy filled one of the plastic cups that came with the thermos halfway to the top and handed it to his father. He got the shotgun from where it was wedged in next to the tire well and slid a single shot into the breach. Coolly, he handled the gun for a minute, trying to develop a feel for its heft and its balance. He had never fired one of these things before. Then he rolled down the back window on his father's side and poked out the barrel.

"Wait a minute," Roger said. "A car's coming."

Jimmy pulled the gun in. The road was straight and flat here and you could see oncoming headlights miles away. He kept looking off to the side though. It was a long time before he saw the lights on the pavement. The beam flicked to low. Then the car whooshed by.

Roger said, "Okay. There's a sign coming up. I'll tell you when it gets close. Hold the gun firmly. It's got a pretty good load. It's gonna have a lot more kick than the carbine. And squeeze it off slow. . . . All right. . . . Just up ahead. . . . Now!"

Sighting along the barrel, Jimmy saw the road sign pop into view out of the corner of his eye. He was ready to follow it. The gun swung around like at a shooting gallery as his finger gently pressed against the trigger.

The explosion came unexpectedly, echoing through the car. Through it Jimmy heard the rattle of pellets striking the sign.

"I hit it!" he shouted.

"It's hard to miss with that thing at close range," Roger said disparagingly. "Now put it away."

Jimmy replaced the gun and climbed over to the front seat. That shotgun was a hell of a weapon. Marty's little carbine was a toy compared with it. He wondered if his father had any special reason for buying the shells.

Roger held his cigarette and the coffee cup in the same hand. He looked over to Jimmy a few times. When he finished the cigarette he said, "Say, Jim, I talked to your mother this afternoon." He was trying to pass it off as the most natural thing in the world but he was obviously reluctant to bring up the subject.

"What'd you do that for?" Jimmy said peevishly.

Roger shrugged. "She *is* your mother. I just didn't want her to get the cops looking for us."

"I suppose." Jimmy knew that wasn't the reason. "Did you tell her where we were?"

"Of course not."

Roger fell silent. He finished his coffee and lit another cigarette. "She said I could still get that check I missed if I told them I was out of town looking for work."

Jimmy's lips started to quiver. He didn't feel angry though—just terribly let down. "When would you have to be back?" he said softly, making an effort to keep his voice steady. He didn't want his father to know how badly he felt.

"Friday."

"Are you gonna go?"

"I don't know yet. I haven't decided. How long can we go on this way, Jim? We have to stop somewhere."

Jimmy finally nodded his head. He knew what his father meant but it was a point of logic he preferred not to face. "Boy, that's a bummer," he said after a minute, his bitterness starting to surface. "You really want to go home, huh?"

"I didn't say I wanted to," Roger said defensively. "It's just . . . "

"Shit!"

Roger turned and glared at him, not watching the road. He took a deep breath. "Try and understand," he said, meaning to be conciliatory but letting an edge of impatience creep into his voice. "What choice do we have? How long do you think . . . ?"

"You didn't have to call her," Jimmy broke in again, harping on the point. That was what it was all about—his father was copping out on him, no matter what kind of face he tried to put on it. "There are a million things we could do."

"Listen to me!" Roger shouted him down. "How many times can we do it before they're on to us! Before we make a mistake!"

"Well you didn't have to call her!" Jimmy screamed. "Nobody's after us. What did we hang around all day for if you're so scared?"

"I'm not scared. I'm just trying to be sensible."

"Bullshit! You were scared shitless before you even did it!"

Roger whirled around savagely, taking a backhanded swing at the boy. He still held his coffee cup. Jimmy jerked his head out of range as a few drops of liquid splattered his face. He grabbed the empty Coke can on the seat and flung it furiously out his father's window, missing his face by just a few inches.

Roger slammed on the brakes, locking the wheels. The car skidded erratically down both lanes and then the rear end broke loose, spinning hard to the right. A back tire came around and hopped the curb, stopping the car immediately as it sunk into the soft turf by the side of the road.

Jimmy, facing his father, was hurled sideways off the seat. His head slammed into the windshield. When the car stopped he was sitting on the floor. A thin trickle of blood ran down the side of his face from a cut at his hairline. He was breathing hard but he was more stunned than hurt.

"Get out and get it," Roger ordered, barely opening his mouth.

"What!"

Roger leaned over him and shoved open the door. Obediently, Jimmy crawled out and trudged slowly up the road. He's crazy, he thought, but he wasn't afraid. More and more the past week he had been getting away with things he would never have dared to say before. He had noticed it without ever really putting it into words. This time maybe he went too far. But nothing was going to happen to him when he got back to the car. They could have been killed though if anyone had been coming when his father spun out. If he was trying to prove what an asshole he was, he had just done it.

He found the can lying in a clump of rushlike grass at the base of a telephone pole about sixty yards down the road. He took his time going back to the station wagon.

Roger restarted the stalled engine as the boy approached. Jimmy slid into the front seat and dropped the can contemptuously between them. "Is this what you wanted?" he said nonchalantly.

"Yup. We didn't get a flat tire, did we?"

"No. But don't ask me why not."

Roger eased the car back on the pavement. He drove slowly, well under the speed limit. "Let me see your head," he said a few minutes later. He switched on the dome light.

Jimmy showed him the cut. It had already stopped flowing. The blood had caked in a fine brown line from his sideburns to his jaw but it still glistened darkly in the pale hair over his temple. "It's just a cut," Roger decided, "but get it cleaned up."

He handed the boy his handkerchief. Jimmy wet the corner in his mouth and began daubing at the side of his face. He turned the rear view mirror to have a look at himself.

Roger said, "I told you, I haven't made up my mind yet. We'll see tomorrow. We just gotta be careful, that's all."

Jimmy studied his face in the mirror. He didn't let his expression change. He smiled inwardly.

⊂‡ ⊂‡ ⊂‡

Despite all he had drunk, Walt didn't sleep well after Hilt left. The case had been with him too long, too much new information had come in in one day to let him rest quietly. At seven o'clock, when the motel operator rang with his call, he vaguely remembered getting up in the night and pacing the room. If something had occurred to him then, he had no idea now what it had been.

He smoked a cigarette lying on the bed. There was Hilt too to think about—the poor bastard. He put in a call to Matt's room to see if he was awake yet. Naturally he wasn't. They agreed to meet in the coffee shop for breakfast in half an hour.

While they ate Walt read the paper. Matt couldn't have been

hung over but he wasn't too chipper. Then they drove out to the sheriff's headquarters.

There was no one in yet whom he recognized as being assigned to the case. He asked the duty sergeant for a desk he could use and for any new reports that had come in since last night. When he got settled in and had everything he needed, he lit a pipe and began reading, starting with the coroner's reports he had picked up yesterday.

There were no surprises in any of the material. How had the men gotten into the house? For the heck of it he asked Matt, who was reading through the reports, taking each page as soon as Walt had finished it.

"I dunno," Matt said as if Walt had just asked him to name Van Buren's vice-president. "Maybe they grabbed them outside—or the little boy, whatsisname? Then they could have forced the mother to open the door."

Walt nodded. It was certainly possible. "Or they just rang the bell," he said. "Rose always opens the door for strangers. Last month it was an encyclopedia salesman."

"Two of them?"

That was a point too. "Mormon missionaries," Walt said, smiling at the idea. "They always travel in pairs. Or Jehovah's Witnesses."

"I doubt if they looked like missionaries." Matt took the suggestion seriously.

"What do you suppose they looked like," Walt asked idly.

"Creeps, I'd say, but that's probably not right."

There was the problem in a nutshell. Walt flipped his sheaf of papers down on the desk. Despite all the information they had gathered, all the theories and evidence, the knives and fingerprints and patterns of operation, they still were back where they started when it came to the basics. The answers could be anything and everything. Who were they, after all? The data was all meaningless— planets drifting randomly without a sun to hold them together.

Walt stood up abruptly. "I'm going to take a walk. I'll be back in a few minutes," he said.

When he came back half an hour later the sergeant stopped him at the desk. "Your deputy's out looking for you," he said. "You're supposed to go out to the house. They found the third knife."

Turning into the Heynens' driveway, Walt saw Sheriff Vandenberg, Bob and a third man at the edge of the field on the other side of the road. Vandenberg waved to him. He stopped the car and got out, leaving Matt to park it by the garage.

"Morning, Walt," Vandenberg said cheerily. "D'you have a nice night?"

"Fine, thanks, Andy. Whatcha got here?"

Bob handed him the knife, holding it out by the tip. "It's all right," he said. "I already dusted it. It's from the set in the kitchen."

Walt took it by the handle and ran his thumb lightly over the edge. "Whew!" he whistled softly through his teeth. It was a stainless steel, German-made carving knife with a blade eight inches long—a gorgeous kitchen utensil but an awesome weapon. The graceful ebony handle was attached by three shiny rivets.

"How'd you like to carve a turkey with that?" Vandenberg said. "You know anything about knives? That's the finest one made. Trident. Must have gone in him like butter."

Walt said, "D'you look at the coroner's report yet? It came within three-sixteenths of an inch of going right through him." He shook his head in amazement. There was a grisly fascination in these numbers—in Vandenberg's commonplace metaphors—as if the mind balked at accepting the atrocity for what it was and sought solace in measurement.

The third man pawed nervously at the ground with his foot. "Well, if you don't need me no more, Sheriff, I oughtta get back to my work," he drawled with a faint accent.

"Oh, excuse me, Karl," Vandenberg apologized. "This is Sheriff Taliaferro from Arlington County. They had a killing over there that might be connected with this one. Walt, Karl Vandermeer. Karl here found the knife."

"Sheriff."

"Pleased to meet you. Could you show me where you found it?"

"It was right over here." Vandermeer led him across the field, angling down toward the drainage ditch. "Actually, it was my dog that found it," he said as they went. "He must have smelled the blood or something. I wondered what he was sniffing at. Figured it was prob'ly a ground squirrel. Soon as I saw what it was, I got the dog out of there and called up the sheriff." He stopped and pointed to a white circle painted on the ground at the edge of the ditch just a few yards ahead.

The ditch was a narrow culvert less than three feet deep. Weeds and wild grasses grew irregularly up from the bottom and lapped over the sides, running out a few yards to meet the land under cultivation. It was in this narrow untilled strip that the knife had been found. Evidently, Bob had circled the spot with lime so it would show up better in photographs.

"It was sticking out of the ground, point down," Bob said. "In about halfway."

"Any prints?"

"Clean as a whistle. We had a real downpour, you know."

"Yeah. You're not having much luck."

"I'm not having *any* luck," Bob corrected.

"All right. Now, where was the boy's body?"

"Just about straight across the highway," Bob said, pointing. "He was in the ditch on the other side. But he seems to have been killed in the field about ten yards away. You want to have a look?"

"Sure. There's nothing more to see here."

They all thanked Vandermeer for his time and trouble and for having the presence of mind not to move the knife before the police got there. He said he only hoped it helped them catch the fellas who did it. "The Heynens were neighbors, y'know."

They walked along the edge of the field back toward the driveway so as not to have to scramble up and down the culvert and then crossed the highway to the Heynen farm. Matt joined them coming from the opposite direction. Something bothered Walt about the killer throwing away the knife. Here they had found all three murder weapons. At Lake Barrett they hadn't found one. Again, the evidence raised more questions than it answered.

Bob showed him where Jonathan's body had been deposited in the ditch. The area was also outlined in white. "But he was killed over there." He pointed across several broken furrows to a small patch of ground that had been roughly trampled. From where they stood, the gaps in the furrows pointed straight to the spot.

"Huh," Walt snorted thoughtfully. "He dragged him from there to here? Is that how you figure it?"

"Yeah," Bob said. "By the hands. We found a lot of dirt inside . . . ." But Walt had wandered away without waiting for him to finish his sentence.

He went to the spot where the killing took place. From the condition of the ground it was obvious there had been a scuffle. He stooped down and picked up a handful of dirt, sifting it idly through his fingers.

"What's up, Tolly?" Matt said, walking over.

"See, he killed him right here," Bob said, joining them, pressing on with his explanation. "Then he heaved the knife as far as he could and hid the body in the culvert there."

Walt stood up abruptly. "Are you sure of that?" he asked sharply, his eyes narrowing to thin slits.

"Of course I'm sure. . . . Sure of what?"

"Can I see the knife again?" Walt asked, not hearing Bob's question.

Bob handed it to him, a puzzled expression on his face. Walt reached back with it in his hand like an old-fashioned pitcher and brought his arm up in a powerful sweep. The knife went sailing into the air high across the road. The four men stood together and watched its trajectory, the steel blade glinting brightly in the sun as it tumbled end over end.

When it dropped out of sight below the highway no one moved for a full second. Then Walt broke toward the drainage ditch at a full run. The others followed after him. He leaped across, falling a little short and having to scamper part of the way up the soft dirt wall. He raced across the shoulder and over the hump of the road. He stopped at the other side, panting hard.

In less than a minute his three companions straggled up behind him. Curiously, their eyes looked where his looked. They saw it but they didn't understand.

There, across the culvert, was the white circle where the knife had landed when Jimmy Mapes threw it. Beyond that spot, out in the bare field a good thirty yards, the Buck knife stood now, its point embedded in the ground, its handle still quivering.

CHAPTER 15

A T T H R E E - T H I R T Y P.M., Wednesday, May 21, the Buena Vista County Sheriff's Department issued a bulletin requesting the cooperation of other jurisdictions in detaining Roger and James Mapes for questioning in connection with the deaths of Georgia Heynen, Jonathan Heynen and Joyce Miller in Buena Vista County, and of Katherine Orben in Arlington County. The bulletin gave the year, make and model as well as the license number of the car they were driving and a brief physical description of Roger Mapes and his twelve-year-old son.

"This is the most amateurish piece of police work I've ever seen in my life!" Frank Parker screamed across the office as he rushed toward Vandenberg's desk. One of the deputies had just called him at home and told him what Taliaferro wanted to do. "A kid! Come on, Vandy. I don't believe it!"

Vandenberg lowered his eyes.

Walt glared at Parker. He had no intention of giving him an explanation. He turned to Vandenberg. "What's it going to be, Sheriff?" he said evenly. He had outlined his theory as they drove in from the farm. He had no proof—just a lot of facts that suddenly became comprehensible when you thought of a father and son. Everything from the failure to consummate the rape of Kay Orben to the milk and chocolate cake in the Heynens' kitchen. The palm print on the bookcase. Would a man have dragged Jonathan's body ten yards or carried it? And so on. There was even a witness, he suddenly remembered, who had seen a man and a boy behaving erratically at Lake Barrett the morning of the murder. The tag from a boy's bathing suit. The ease of access the killer evidently had to the Heynen home.

Roger Mapes was not a stable man. Shiftless. He had a violent argument with his wife the day he left home. As for Jimmy—he knew nothing personally about Jimmy. His half-brother had committed suicide about a year ago. The Mapeses were a sick family. The apple wouldn't fall far from the tree.

"I got two sons," Walt had said in the car. "It's not an easy thing to think about. I wish there was another way."

"I'm sorry, Frank," Vandenberg said without lifting his head. "We got to bring them in for questioning."

"Questioning? All right. But if you're going to do it, why stop halfway? Give their pictures to the media, for chrissake! Why just an A.P.B.?"

Vandenberg looked over at Walt, whose expression didn't change. They had just been over all that and Walt wasn't about to go through it again for Parker's benefit.

"It seems best, Frank," Vandenberg said hesitantly. "We'll probably catch them quicker if they don't know we're looking for them."

Parker stomped toward the door, then whirled around and came directly toward Walt. "This is just brilliant," he fumed. "What if they ring another doorbell in the meantime and another woman lets them in the house? Have you thought about that? I sure as hell wouldn't take that responsibility."

Walt returned Parker's stare coldly. This time he didn't wait for Vandenberg to handle his deputy. "I thought about it," he said grimly. "What the fuck do you think I thought about?"

Will Schroeder had been a member of the Dundee, Minnesota, Auxiliary Police for seventeen of his thirty-five years. That included the three years he spent in Vietnam. Since the Auxiliaries were unpaid volunteers, no one minded when he asked to have his name left on the roster while he was over there. He was single and his parents were dead. The Auxiliaries were his only tie with "the world."

There were eight of them. They met regularly Monday evenings, wearing their uniforms, for drill and target practice. Other than that, their duties consisted of turning out a contingent to keep order at football games and policing Main Street every Friday night in the summer. In theory, they could issue citations to the kids who were cruising, but they rarely did. The way Will saw it, their job was to make sure that if anyone asked for trouble, he got it.

Wednesday afternoon he knocked off work a little early and drove out to the State Police Barracks to kibbitz with the boys for a while. He poured himself a cup of coffee in the lounge and sauntered over to the corner table where he knew the three guys. Their tours started in forty minutes. They greeted him perfunctorily and continued their conversation, making no effort to include him. They faced long, tedious shifts, isolated in their cars. With each passing minute their talk grew more desultory, their eyes more sullen.

Will didn't mind. He liked hanging around.

A boyish-looking officer just getting off duty came over and joined them. He put his helmet down on the floor. "Man, my ass is draggin'," he said. "Whatchew guys think of that A.P.B. from Iowa? Isn't 'at sumpthin'?"

"What A.P.B. from Iowa?" No one knew anything about it.

"Jeez, it's right up there on the board. You'll get it at roll call. Christ, the lieutenant was funny about it."

"What A.P.B. from Iowa?"

"Them killin's. Y'know who did it? A twelve-year-old kid."

"No-o shit!"

"Yup. The other one too—a couple weeks ago."

"So what the lieutenant say?"

"Somebody ought to tell that kid's mother on 'im."

"He's doin' it with his father. Two of 'em."

"They s'posed to be around here? What they come up here for?"

"Nah. That's why they call it an *all-points* bulletin, turkey."

"Where's the mamma? Home sharpenin' knives?"

"See? Who says the family's fallin' apart?"

"Manson family, you mean."

"Yeah. Right."

"So what the lieutenant say?"

"He was talkin' to Andersen about it out in the hall. So I stop to listen. He gives him the whole skinny, see—car, description, what they done—really lays it on how bad these guys are. Dangerous, y'know. Then he puts his hand on Andersen's shoulder, looks him right in the eye. So you tell your men to keep a sharp lookout, he says. You could be in on making p'lice history. Andersen's head's goin' up and down. He's really impressed. Yup, the lieutenant says. First time I ever heard of a manhunt where the fugitive wasn't allowed to cross the street."

They all laughed.

Around the room chairs started to scrape as clusters of men finished their coffee and headed for roll call.

Someone said, "Yeah, but it wasn't as funny as the time that hunter went crazy, started shooting at anything that moved. Remember that? Remember what he said?"

They started laughing again. "Sure. But let's get goin'."

"Betcha Andersen's not gonna crack any jokes."

"Are you kiddin' me?"

Will was left alone at the table with the boyish officer who just came off duty. They chatted for a couple minutes.

"Gotta get home, Will. I'm tellin' ya, my ass is draggin'. See ya around."

"Yeah, take it easy."

On his way out, Will stopped at the bulletin board and copied down the information about the Mapeses in the small spiral notebook he always carried in his shirt pocket.

Walt Taliaferro knew it was a race against time. Find the Mapeses before they killed again. It was anyone's guess when that might be.

The question was where they were now. They had a headstart of almost forty-eight hours. They had gone west from Lake Barrett but that didn't mean anything. It had taken them over a week to cover three hundred miles. Either they weren't traveling directly or they weren't traveling fast.

Till now. At that moment they could be anywhere within two days' drive of Storm Lake. It was way too late to put out roadblocks. And every hour that went by without a sign of them, the radius of the circle increased sixty miles.

As soon as the two sheriffs agreed on the bulletin, Walt and Matt Vollmer took off for Arlington. There was nothing more Walt could do at Storm Lake and he had to get started building his case.

That was another race against time. In a way, it put even more pressure on him because the brunt of the work was primarily his. He had suspects but no proof.

The partial thumb- and fingerprint found on the Buck knife were the only reliable physical evidence so far linking the Mapeses with either crime. Hardly enough—especially as they had no value whatsoever in regard to the Orben killing.

If they were lucky, they might find incriminating evidence in the suspects' possession. But maybe they wouldn't.

Driving at top speed, he made it home a little past nine. Rose greeted him like a conquering hero. One of his men's wives, thoughtfully, had called to tell her that Walt cracked the case. If she resented the fact that he didn't take a minute to call her himself, she never let on.

Walt tried to downplay her applause. It wasn't over by a long shot. He had been surprised himself that finding the solution hadn't given him even the most fleeting sense of elation. He felt drained, in fact. Maybe it was because part of him wanted so desperately to believe he was wrong. How could it be a twelve-year-old-boy?

So he was in no mood to hear himself praised. "Seriously, Rose, it's no great accomplishment," he finally said when she persisted in fawning over him. "The answer was there all along. I just wouldn't let myself see it. Then it just hit me 'cause of the stupidest thing." It ruffled his professional pride that there had been no long string of complex deductions leading inexorably to the solution. The way it happened seemed almost accidental.

Rose frowned for a moment, then brightened again. "You're wrong, Walt. Sherlock Holmes is a character in a book. Seeing the truth—that's what makes a great detective. You made yourself ready for the truth when it came. You should be proud of that."

He smiled faintly despite himself. Rose really believed that.

"Where do you think you're going?" she snapped. She had just realized he was putting on a fresh shirt.

"There's something I have to do. It shouldn't take long."

"Oh no you don't. Not tonight. Not after the day you've been through."

"I have to see Sheila Mapes."

Sheila was wearing a bathrobe that wouldn't stay closed. Her hand clutched at the fabric between her breasts.

"Mrs. Mapes, I'm sorry to bother you so late. May I come . . . ?"

Sheila's eyes began narrowing as soon as Walt started to speak. "Something's going on, Sheriff," she interrupted him. "I have to know what it is. The two men at work today wouldn't tell me anything. They wanted me to give them some pictures."

"That's what I want to talk to you about, Mrs. Mapes. May I please come in?"

The question, not being part of her own train of thought, seemed to puzzle her for a moment. Then she walked away from the door and let him follow her into the house.

"You'll have to excuse . . . " she mumbled, her gesture taking in everything.

Walt nodded as he cleared a place on the sofa to sit down. "Mrs. Mapes, have you heard anything from your husband yet?"

"No," she said, but it wasn't in answer to his question. "Oh no. You tell me what's happened to him. Something's happened, hasn't it?"

He could tell she'd been drinking—not heavily, but enough to make talking to her even more difficult. "We think he might know something about a case we're investigating."

Sheila wasn't satisfied. She stared at him fixedly, waiting for him to go on.

"The girl who was killed at the lake, a week ago Saturday. Another case in the western part of the state."

Shelia shivered violently. She wasn't able to stop, as if the house had suddenly grown cold. In her confusion she remembered her son. "Jimmy?" she asked softly, her eyes pleading with him to give her something to hold onto. "Is Jimmy all right? Where is he? Has anything happened to him?"

Walt forced himself to look in her eyes. "We think he's still with his father, Mrs. Mapes."

She cupped both hands in front of her mouth, turning her face to the floor. Aren't you mistaken? she struggled to say, but she hadn't the strength it would take to have doubts. She knew it wasn't a mistake. Her head shook slowly from side to side as if the pain she felt was beyond her comprehension. She started sniffling. She wanted to cry but the tears wouldn't come.

Walt's heart went out to her. He gave her time.

Her robe had fallen open, partially uncovering her breasts. After a while she noticed. "Excuse me," she said as she pulled the two sides together. Somehow there was comfort in the irrelevance of decorum.

"Mrs. Mapes," Walt said gently, "I'll try to be brief. I have to ask you a few questions. Have you heard from your husband since he left?"

"No." She wasn't lying. Her mind was a blank.

"You don't know where he is?"

"No."

He unfolded the top of a brown paper bag and took out the closed Buck knife. He held it toward her. "Do you know if your husband owned a knife like this, Mrs. Mapes?"

The object overwhelmed her. "Oh, my God, no, no, my God, no," she wailed, losing all control of herself. She began whimpering hysterically, her body rocking back and forth.

He put the knife away quickly. The sooner he got this over with, the better for her. He fumbled inside the bag and pulled out the shirt just as far as the collar. He didn't want her to see the blood.

"Do you recognize this shirt?"

She looked at it a few seconds, then turned to him dumbly.

"Is it your husband's shirt?"

"No, it isn't his shirt," she said, shaking her head in frantic denial. It meant so much to her—being able to deny.

Walt was confused. He didn't think she would lie. "Are you positive, Mrs. Mapes?"

"Of course. I iron his shirts!" she screamed, her voice breaking in sobs. She grabbed the collar and pulled it toward her but he wouldn't let go. "It isn't even his size—you want to look in his drawer?" she said, the words barely articulate through her crying.

He accepted her answer. "That won't be necessary. I'm sorry. I wish there was something I could say."

Tenderly, he removed her hands from the collar and slid the shirt back into the bag. He stood up and walked slowly to the door.

Her eyes followed him but she didn't get up.

"Just one more question," he said. "Did Jimmy have a new bathing suit—one he hadn't worn yet?"

"No," she said quietly. "He hadn't outgrown the one from last year."

Walt nodded. There was nothing to say. He showed himself out.

⇔ ⇔ ⇔

"Hilt called twice," Rose said as soon as Walt walked in the door. "He sounded really upset. He couldn't understand how you left without telling him what was going on. I said I'd ask you to call him the minute you got in."

He walked away from her. "Yeah. All right," he muttered half to himself. "I'll call him first thing in the morning."

⇔ ⇔ ⇔

Jimmy slept off and on while his father drove through the night. By morning they were about ninety miles due north of Arlington.

They came to a town with a funny name that Jimmy remembered from the trip with Marty. In utter detachment, he wondered what Roger was going to do.

Roger turned left at the main intersection. He was going north. The boy wasn't surprised.

They stopped under a red signal. Roger drummed on the steering wheel, craning his neck as he looked around at the town. He laughed nervously. "Well, here we go, Son," he said with forced heartiness. "You remember this place from a couple years ago? Maybe you were too young." Underneath, it embarrassed him that he was giving in to the boy. Any wisecracks from him, he said to himself, and I'll turn right around.

"No, just the name," Jimmy said.

The light turned green. Roger eased along in the flow of morning traffic. There was some kind of industrial park a few miles outside of town.

Jimmy said, "This is the smartest thing. If we went back right now, it might look suspicious."

"Yeah. That's what I figured," Roger said.

Toward the Minnesota border the land got hillier and more thickly wooded. When they stopped for gas, Roger had them change the oil and he and Jimmy went in for breakfast. He bought a paper. There was a small story inside about the Storm Lake murders. It didn't say anything that gave him reason for concern. He folded back the paper and handed it across to Jimmy. The boy skimmed the article and nodded smugly.

After they ate Roger stopped at a supermarket and bought a few groceries. About an hour later they crossed into Minnesota. Soon they saw a small pond up ahead from the crest of a rise. It was less than half a mile wide, its margin ringed with white spruce. It looked beautiful reflecting the sunlight.

"Let's stop there," Roger said. "I'd rather drive at night anyway."

They circled the pond once. The only road down to it had a chain strung across it and a No Trespassing sign.

"Fuck it," Roger said the second time he came to the road. He turned into it and stopped the car. Jimmy got out and took down the chain. They drove in and parked right by the edge of the water.

For Jimmy it was a fabulous afternoon. They went for a swim together in the icy blue water, not even bothering to put on their suits. The place was absolutely deserted. All the tensions, the ill-will that had been building up between them ever since they broke into that house in Missouri seemed to vanish in the warm, sweet air. This time he had no illusions that this peace, this intimacy, would last. He had seen sides of his father he wouldn't have thought possible two weeks ago. Roger wasn't the god he had thought him to be, he wasn't a man in whose shadow the boy could be happy forever. Right now was an interlude, but no less pleasant for the knowledge that soon they'd be fighting again.

As they lay together, naked in the soft duff between the pond and the trees, an odd thought crossed Jimmy's mind. He loved his father. It was the first time the notion ever occurred to him.

Roger was content to drowse in the sun as the day wore on. Late in the afternoon, Jimmy got dressed and asked him if he wanted to go for a walk. "Just around the pond."

"I don't think so, Jim. Don't go too long. I'm gonna fix dinner pretty soon."

"Okay." He got the shotgun out of the car and put in six shells. "Is it okay if I take this?" he asked his father.

Roger sat up to see what he was talking about. "Sure. But don't take too many shots. I only bought two boxes of shells."

"I took six."

"That's fine." He lay back down, his head on his arms, watching the boy lope down the shore, the gun slung over his shoulder.

Will Schroeder didn't know what he was going to do for his dinner. There was one Fiesta Mexican Dinner left in the freezer. They were good but he just had one the other day. He couldn't remember if there was anything else in the house.

He'd probably stop at Tiny's. Or maybe that smorgasbord place—Larsen's. Why not? Payday in two days. Tonight's

Wednesday. Nothing on the television except reruns of shows that were lousy the first time.

He drove slowly down the twisting road. He was hungry but he was in no hurry to get to dinner or to get home afterward.

The chain was down on the road to Coe's Pond. He drove past it, then stopped and backed up. It shouldn't be down. The car was perpendicular to the road. He leaned across the seat and peered out the passenger window but he couldn't see anything.

He cut the wheel and backed up again, then drove down to have a look. He pulled up behind a dirty white Chevy station wagon with Iowa plates. Hmmh! He expected to find high school kids skinny-dipping in the pond. But there was no one in sight. Shit—it was the ones with knockout bodies who ran around naked, too.

Wait a second, he thought. He took his notebook out of his pocket and leafed through it from the back to the last page he'd written on.

Jesus Christ! That was it all right. His hand began trembling as he tried to think what to do. If only he had a fucking radio in the car.

Shit, it didn't matter. It was just a man and a boy. He had a gun, they didn't. He'd get the drop on them easy. Imagine that. They were looking for these guys in at least six states probably and he was going to bring them in.

After re-reading the entry in the notebook to make sure, he dropped it on the seat and got his revolver out of the glove compartment. It was fully loaded with a round in the chamber.

He opened his door quietly and got out, leaving it opened. Crouched low like in Nam, he ran to the side of the station wagon, using it for cover. There was a man in the pond swimming parallel to the shore. No sign of a boy. Will decided to wait for him to come out on his own. He ducked down even lower, keeping one eye on the man and the other peeled for the boy.

In a few minutes Roger swam a few strokes toward shore and then began walking in through the water. He was stark naked. What a way to catch a killer, Will thought. He cocked his gun and waited.

Roger pulled himself onto the bank in a sitting position and stood up. Will stepped out from behind the fender.

"Are you Roger Mapes?"

Roger looked at the gun, pointed at him. For some reason he didn't feel anything, only a second or so of surprise. "No," he said.

"Is this your car?"

"No."

"Don't shit me, mister. I'm a police officer. You're wanted for questioning."

"Questioning? In connection with what?"

"You'll find out—as if you don't know already. Where's the kid?"

"The kid? He just took a walk around the pond. He should be back any minute. You mind if I put my pants on?"

Will considered a second. He wasn't going to take him bare-assed. The guy might as well put them on now as later.

"All right. But don't try anything. I'll use this if I have to."

"I won't try anything." Roger couldn't get over the feeling that all this had nothing to do with him. He reached down and slowly pulled on his undershorts and his pants.

"Come on over here," Will ordered him, stepping off to the side of the car. He told Roger to bend over the hood with his legs spread so he could pat him down. He wasn't about to put a killer in the car without checking first to see that he didn't have a knife in his pocket.

Roger did as he was told. Will stooped behind him and ran his hand up his leg.

"You know I don't have anything under my pants," Roger said calmly. "Just check my pockets."

"Shut up," Will said. He completed the frisk the way it was done in the book.

As soon as Jimmy saw the car he saw there was someone with his father. He stopped in his tracks, then ducked behind a tree, making sure he was out of sight. They were about thirty yards away, well within his range. He knew immediately what he was going to do.

The gun wasn't primed. He stuck the barrel tightly between his thighs to muffle the sound and inched the slide forward. He held his breath. If that turkey heard anything, it was all over.

The shell snapped into the firing chamber with a sudden click but the cop didn't turn.

Jimmy raised the gun and took aim from behind the tree. The cop was standing beside his father now, their heads less than a foot apart. The cop was saying something to Roger but he didn't try to hear what. He concentrated on his target, which hardly moved at all.

It had to be now!

"Dad!" he screamed. "Down!"

Will Schroeder whirled toward the boy just as Roger threw himself to the ground. Jimmy fired, aiming at the very top of the man's head. Any lower and the scatter would get Roger too.

Will flopped to the ground like his legs had been yanked out from under him. A good part of the load caught him right in the face.

Roger pulled himself to his feet as Jimmy raced up. For a moment they stood over Will's body. From the nose up, his face was covered with gore. His arms and legs twitched spastically as blood poured from his mouth. If he was still alive, he wouldn't last long.

Jimmy pumped the shotgun again and aimed the muzzle point-blank at Will Schroeder's head. He squeezed the trigger and blasted it away.

CHAPTER 16

W E D N E S D A Y N I G H T Walt couldn't sleep. He dozed fitfully off and on but even those few minutes gave him no rest. He was haunted by the strange and self-destructive Mapeses. Some time before dawn he climbed out of bed and went downstairs to stretch out on the sofa.

It was a family that should never have been. What did they bring to each other but misery? He thought of poor, helpless Sheila and tried to imagine a time, a set of circumstances, in which she might have been happy. She was addicted to her unhappiness—though she got more than she bargained for. He remembered—vividly— the solemn-eyed child who hovered in the background during the two visits he made after the older boy's suicide. That was Jimmy. He seemed awed by his half-brother's death. A boy couldn't find love in that house—or if he did, it was a poisonous kind.

Outside the window, the sky lightened. He closed his eyes, thinking of all the things he had yet to do. If only it would end quickly. So many police were looking for one man and one boy. How long could they hide?

Like an infection Roger's madness spread to them all. As long as their violence turned inward, on themselves and each other, nobody cared. Nobody cared when Mapes beat his wife, when she found ways to retaliate. When children grew up in this home . . . and did away with themselves. How many other families in his town tortured themselves secretly behind drawn curtains? A seventeen-year-old boy had taken his own life without anyone so much as raising a hand. No one knew what went on in that house, and afterward no one asked.

Then the violence spilled over. Jimmy, the frightened boy, became a killer. He was still a boy. Roger was a killer. Suddenly their need to inflict suffering was cause for concern. A thousand police officers mobilized to punish them.

No, there was nothing wrong with that. The state had to protect itself from the Rogers and Jimmies. It just started too late, that was all.

Walt got up and went to the window. In the east, the morning star was already beginning to fade. Rose would be up soon. Barefoot and in his pajamas, he wandered out to the kitchen and watched a jay gorging itself at the backyard feeder. In its zeal, it spilled more than it ate over the side, where it was snatched up greedily by a family of sparrows. It was the middle of May. When the feeder was empty, it wouldn't be filled again until winter.

Rose came up behind him quietly on her slippers. "Walt? How come you're up? Is anything bothering you?"

"I just couldn't sleep."

She fixed him breakfast. They didn't talk while he ate—she could see he was preoccupied. Afterwards, she reminded him to call Hilt.

He said he would from the office.

He showered and shaved while Rose woke the boys and fed them. Then he waited around so he could drive them to school.

⚟   ⚟   ⚟

Roger and Jimmy decided they had better ditch their car. Finding Will's notebook convinced them.

Jimmy said they couldn't leave the body there. He opened the tailgate and told his father to put it inside.

"I'm not gonna pick it up," Roger said.

"Then drag it. I'll help you."

They each took a heel and pulled him around to the back of the car. Then Roger got in and tugged the body up after him. It was sickening work. Both of them went to the lake and vomited when they were finished.

They transferred what they wanted to take to Will's little Camaro. Roger backed their car up as far as he could and still leave it pointed straight at the pond. He wedged a small branch under the gas pedal to keep the throttle wide open. Then, standing next to the car, he released the handbrake and jerked the gear shift into low. The tires spun momentarily on the slippery duff before taking hold. Roger flung himself out of the way as the car bolted forward, its back end fishtailing wildly as it picked up speed. It was angled to the water when the front tires hit the grassy rim at the edge of the bank. The car flipped onto its side as it struck the water with a thunderous splash. Slowly, it rolled over bottom up and settled into the mucky bed of the pond.

It hadn't carried as far as they hoped. The tires and one end of the chassis stood out like the carcass of a dead animal in the desert.

"Damn," Roger said. "There's a shelf just a little way further."

"Well, we can't push it," Jimmy said, not entirely sure that they couldn't.

"No, I suppose not."

The cop's car was low on gas but Roger went as far as he could before stopping. Someone around there might know the car and wonder why they were driving it. He stayed on small county roads, running a zigzag course more or less to the northwest. He figured they had a day, two at most, until someone went down to the pond and the Camaro was hot. He was scared. They'd have to keep stealing cars.

It got dark. The Camaro was a responsive little machine but he didn't dare open it up. A traffic ticket was the same as turning himself in. He glanced at the speedometer every few seconds, making sure not to get more than a mile or two over the limit. He made up a little game with himself. When they'd gone a hundred miles they'd be safe from anyone recognizing the car. The magic number was twenty-four thousand six hundred and thirty-eight point seven.

He didn't round off. Each time the seven approached he did the arithmetic in his mind. Forty-four eight . . . forty-four nine . . . forty-five down, fifty-five more to go.

When he made it he lit a cigarette but it didn't relax him. It had no taste at all.

"Jim? You awake? I was just thinking," he said. "They're looking for a man and a boy traveling together."

"Yeah? So?"

"So I was just thinking, that's all. We stick out like a sore thumb. D'you think we'd be safer if we split up?"

"I think you should go fuck yourself," Jimmy said bitterly. "What could I do? I'd get picked up like that."

"I'd put you on a bus, say, for California. Drive out and meet you there. Kids take buses all the time, especially now with school almost out."

"Forget it."

"Why don't you think about it? If you want to stay, I'm willing to risk it. But just think about it."

"Thanks," the boy said sarcastically.

The car hit the shoulder, spraying gravel up under the chassis. Roger guided it back onto the pavement. It was the third time he had fallen asleep at the wheel. He muttered something to himself and fiddled with the radio. It was losing the station. Jimmy was sound asleep.

"I'm gonna stop at the next motel. Okay?" Roger said. No more camping out in the open. Next time they might not be so lucky.

Jimmy didn't answer. Why doesn't he talk? Roger thought. It would help me keep my eyes opened. He just sleeps and expects me to take care of everything.

There was a Quality Court outside a town called Montevideo. Its sign was still on. He used the name Albert Becker on the card. Albert was his brother, Becker was Sheila's maiden name. He made up an address in Minneapolis. The pen stopped when he came to the blank for the car license number.

"That's all right," the clerk said. "I can never remember mine either."

The room was by far the nicest they had been in. It was clean and bright with pictures over the beds.

"Jeez, how much did this cost us?" Jimmy asked, flinging himself down on his bed.

"Just twelve bucks."

"That's not too bad."

"No, it's not bad at all."

They went to sleep right away. During the night Roger had another nightmare. He saw the body of the cop they had killed sticking out the back of a car. Its shattered head hung down over the tailgate. It was bloodless but smashed like a doll's. The broken features changed into his own and then into Marty's. He groaned and tossed on the bed. In the next bed, Jimmy stirred. The body began to move. It sat up, the head flopped limply to the side. Roger began to scream.

Jimmy flew over to him and clapped his hand over his mouth. Instinctively, Roger grabbed him and threw him down to the floor. He was sitting up now, panting, his eyes bulging in terror as if that hideous face waited in the darkness of the room.

"I'm sorry, Jim. Was I screaming or . . . ?"

"Yeah. You were having a nightmare."

"Are you all right? Go back to sleep."

Roger pulled himself slowly to his feet and staggered into the bathroom. He turned on the cold water and ran his eyes under the faucet. Then he sat down in the armchair and put on the desk light. Its amber shade sent a gentle glow to the corners of the room. He tipped his head back and fought against sleep.

ⅭⱫ　　ⅭⱫ　　ⅭⱫ

Five major oil companies joined in the manhunt. Through a check of bank records, Walt found out what gasoline credit cards Roger Mapes carried. Contacting each company's regional manager, he dictated an urgent circular to be sent to all dealers, requesting them to notify local authorities if Mapes' card turned up. The wording emphasized that under no circumstances were they to attempt to apprehend or detain Mapes or to discuss this request with him. The dealers were instructed to honor the card.

Walt also asked that Roger's accounts be flagged so that any purchases he made since leaving Arlington could be reported as soon as the vouchers came in. Surprisingly, one company called back within minutes to inform the sheriff that Mapes had bought gas in Barnard, Missouri, on May 17.

Walt drew a circle in red on the map on his wall. What the hell were they doing in Barnard, Missouri? It was about two hundred and fifty miles due south of Storm Lake. Maybe a pattern to their movements would begin to emerge as more purchases were· reported, but the big payoff would be a voucher from Storm Lake dated May 19.

He assigned a man to find out whether Ben Hargrove could identify Roger and Jimmy as the ones who had been abusive to him that morning in the parking lot. Other deputies began canvassing every store that sold bathing suits in Arlington itself and on the way to Lake Barrett. If Sheila wasn't mistaken, Jimmy must have bought a suit the day he left home. Maybe somebody remembered selling it to him. With any luck, they'd soon have hard evidence placing the Mapeses near the scene of the crime.

All morning long Walt put off calling Hilt. He was too busy, he rationalized, but the real reason was that he didn't want to talk to him. He knew Hilt would badger him for information he couldn't give out. Of course Hilt wouldn't take it personally and there was no call for the sheriff to feel he was letting down an old friend. Still, Walt couldn't face the prospect of playing through that charade—the appeals to their long-standing relationship, the careful explanations that didn't explain too much. He was harried enough as it was, and exhausted. He didn't need the aggravation of having to justify what he did.

Instead, he called Sheriff Vandenberg.

"Andy? Walt Taliaferro. What's happening?"

"Plenty. I was just going to call you. Looks like they got a gun."

Walt made a sucking noise through his teeth. He waited for Vandenberg to go on. There had to be more to the story than that.

"We're not sure yet. There's an empty rack in the cellar for a rifle or shotgun. Just noticed it this morning. We're still hoping it was empty before."

"Ask him. Heynen."

"The funeral's right now. We will though, first chance we get. I guess we have to assume that they're armed."

"I guess we do. And if they got a gun, they'll use it."

"Uh-huh." Vandenberg hesitated. "Y'know, Walt, I was thinking. Maybe we ought to release what we got—pictures and everything. Get the whole country looking for them." He said it like a question. It was evident that Parker was leaning on him.

"I still don't like it," Walt said. "Every cop in the area's after them and they don't even know it. That's our one big advantage. What's the chance some little old lady's gonna spot them if they're trying to hide?" He didn't mean to sound so abrupt but they had been over all this yesterday. Nothing changed now just because they had a gun.

"That's true," Vandenberg conceded. "But I thought maybe an announcement might scare them—sort of flush them out. Parker was saying . . ."

"It's not Parker's decision," Walt interrupted. "It's your case as well as mine. I can't tell you what to do. But what does Parker think they'll do if they get scared—give themselves up? What if they go on a rampage? They can disappear if they want. They can change cars. What if they split up?" They were good arguments but Walt questioned how well they'd stand up when Vandenberg tried them on Parker. That was really the issue.

"I wasn't asking you to tell me what to do," Vandenberg said, getting his back up. "I just wanted to hear your thinking on it, that's all. Okay then. If you feel that strongly about it, let's keep the lid on one more day. But that's the limit."

"Fine with me," Walt said testily. It annoyed him that Vandenberg was wriggling away without having to stand up to either side.

He gave a little to Walt, a little to Parker, and took no responsibility for the resulting decision.

Walt filled him in quickly on what he was doing at his end. Vandenberg said he'd keep in touch.

It was almost one o'clock. Walt went out to get a sandwich and a decent cup of coffee. When he came back he found two messages waiting on his desk. Ben Hargrove had identified the picture of Roger and Jimmy. A woman had called. She wouldn't leave her name.

It was probably Sheila. For some reason, Walt realized, he had been more or less unconsciously expecting to hear from her. He tried calling her home.

He was about to hang up when she picked up the phone.

"Oh, Sheriff. It's you. Excuse me. I was just lying down." She sounded terribly distraught and confused. Walt couldn't tell whether she'd been drinking again.

"Did you call me, Mrs. Mapes?"

"Uh . . . no. I probably should have. I . . . there's something I didn't tell you yesterday. Could you please come out here? It's . . . it's . . . it might be important."

"Couldn't you tell me over the phone?"

There was silence. "Please?" she murmured, as if asking a favor she had no right to expect.

Walt drove to the Mapeses' residence on the outskirts of town. Last night he hadn't seen how badly the house needed paint. In many places it had peeled down to the wood.

Sheila was sober but not very coherent. It took Walt several minutes of prompting to bring her around to the ostensible point of his visit. Obviously, she wanted someone to talk to and was using the promised information as bait.

What she hadn't told him yesterday, it turned out, was that Roger had called her. Tuesday, she thought. He didn't say where he was. She had asked him to come home—pleaded with him, in fact—but he had said no, it was out of the question.

Walt wondered what it meant. Tuesday was the day after the

killings at Storm Lake. Roger must have been at least toying with the idea of coming back if he thought about calling his wife. Or else he was just trying to find out if the police had been asking about him.

"Did he say whether he'd call again?" Walt asked.

Sheila shook her head. Still, it was worthwhile ordering a trace on her phone.

Although his business with her was finished, Walt made no effort to leave. He sat in her living room, hardly saying a word as she spilled out a long, rambling monologue about her unhappy life. Surprisingly—or perhaps not—she never asked him why he suspected her husband and son of terrible crimes. At first he thought, Could there be stronger evidence of their guilt than the fact that Shelia never doubted it? But that wasn't the point. Whatever she said, she was talking about herself really, not about them. She seemed almost to welcome the sheriff's insinuations—he had never specifically mentioned Storm Lake or accused them of murder—as if they were the ultimate indignity toward which her whole life had been building. He sensed her relief in finally knowing where it would end.

Her vulnerability touched him deeply. Tired as he was, he didn't want to leave her. He saw no hint of the aggressiveness that had set him on edge that day in his office.

She talked about how strongly Jimmy was attached to his father. Somewhere along the line, she had forfeited the boy's love. She smiled thinly, as if her son's indifference somehow validated her own opinion of herself.

Listening to her, Walt found himself trying to think of them as simply a family. "It doesn't mean anything," he said, hoping to comfort her. He hadn't spoken in quite a while. "Boys are drawn to their fathers."

She looked at him curiously, as if surprised by his voice. "Are yours? Drawn to you, I mean. Do you have sons?"

He laughed. "I have two. Yes, somewhat. But they're younger. The oldest is seven."

She nodded. "Well, they should be," she said, and he was

moved by the compliment. "But it wasn't like Jimmy really admired his father. He fawned on him, you know what I mean? Marty did too, kind of, but he was rebellious."

Her eyes looked past him, puzzling with thought. "Jimmy . . ." she went on, "with Jimmy, the harder his father was on him, the more desperately he clung. It's funny. I see a lot of myself in him that I never saw before. It was almost like he goaded Roger sometimes—pushed him to get mad. Then he'd be hurt when he did. But Marty was just like his father. He had Roger's temper."

She tossed her head back, brushing her hair from her brow. "I think he did it because it was the only way he knew to get back at him. I don't know if it worked. He never let you know if anything touched him."

Walt didn't follow her at first. He had been struck by the way she talked about all of them, not just Marty, in the past tense. It took him a few seconds to realize she was talking about the older boy's suicide.

"Did Marty always live with you?" Walt asked.

She shook her head. "Off and on. Most of the time, I suppose. See, his mother was very sick—some kind of blood disease. Sometimes she couldn't take care of him. I think Marty resented having to come here. He and Roger fought all the time."

"Is that why you . . . ?"

"Yes. That last night was terrible."

Walt furrowed his brow. That wasn't the way he remembered the story. "Are you sure of that, Mrs. Mapes?"

"Of course. Marty threw an ashtray at his father and ran out of the house. Roger tried to find him but he couldn't."

"That's not what you told me."

"I know. When he didn't come back and we reported him missing, it didn't seem right to say they'd been arguing. So we said he was depressed—which was really the truth, too. After, there was no point in changing it."

"Whose idea was it to say he was depressed?" Walt leaned forward on the couch. He felt like he was cross-examining her.

"I don't remember. It just seemed better at the time." She

paused and looked directly at Walt. "I know what you're thinking, Sheriff, but it isn't true. The same thing occurred to me. But Marty was his son. It just isn't possible." She said it firmly but with no rancor, as if she was settling a reasonable question.

Walt didn't know what to think. For a moment he was confused, he thought he must have misunderstood something. But no. They were talking about whether a man had murdered his son. And she had said, I thought the same thing myself.

The enormity of her statement began to overwhelm him. It felt like a heavy weight had lodged in his chest. She said Roger hadn't done it. Maybe he hadn't—that wasn't what mattered. But how was it conceivable she had even wondered about it? . . . her own husband?

Suddenly he had to get away from the house. It wasn't her—he pitied her with all his heart. He had to clear his mind. He felt hemmed in, oppressed. He stood up and walked slowly to the middle of the room, his leg accidentally kicking the coffee table.

He turned and looked down at her. "Sheila," he began, not knowing what he would say. He couldn't think of anything. Each second he stayed he felt more and more lost.

"Sheriff?"

"It doesn't matter. I have to be going. I'll let you know as soon as there's any news."

She followed him to the door.

Outside in the fresh air, he felt some relief. The weight had lifted but his mind was still numb.

When Walt got back to his office—it was only four-thirty—he closed his door and pulled the file on the Martin Mapes suicide. There were only four pages and he sat down heavily at his desk and read them slowly. Even knowing the Mapeses had lied, he found nothing that tended either to confirm or refute his suspicions. According to the coroner, death had been caused by drowning—which didn't necessarily rule out homicide. The body had been in the water too long for a complete autopsy.

There were meaningless reports from the two officers who answered the call and found the boy's body.

Walt smiled sardonically as he re-read the three-quarters of a page of single-spaced type he had submitted himself to the coroner's jury. He held his head cradled in his hands and stared at the sheet on his desk until the words blurred before his eyes. It was all there in front of him but he hadn't seen anything.

Conclusion: *In light of the decedent's mental condition, apparently aggravated by an unstable home life, the sheriff recommends a finding of suicide.*

Finally, Walt flipped the folder closed. He felt strangely empty and alone. He buzzed for Matt to ask him for a ride home.

"When'd you get back? I didn't see you come in," Matt said excitedly as he entered the office. "What d'you think of that?"

"What?" Walt picked up the memo Matt was pointing to on his desk.

"This woman called from Missouri," Matt started to explain what the note said. Walt stopped reading and listened. "Uh, Phyllis Hedlund, her name is. Said she suspected this guy of the first murder but figured she was crazy. When she read about the others, she had to tell someone."

"Mapes?"

"Yeah. He had scratches all over his back."

"Hunh!"

"That's not all. I just talked to the sheriff down there. Seems they had a house broken into about the same time. I said to him, They get any sports shirts? He says, Yeah, as a matter of fact. But it's not the guy you want unless he's a midget. He got in through this window that's way too small for a man."

Walt grinned at his deputy's enthusiasm. He had done a good job. It had never occurred to Walt to call the sheriff at Barnard, the other town where they knew the Mapeses had been. "That's good work, Matt," he said. It was all coming together, winding itself down. When they got their hands on the suspects they'd have a strong case.

Matt beamed at the praise. "Thanks, Walt. I figured you'd want to go down there," he said. "So I checked. There's a morning plane from Cedar Rapids to St. Louis. It's not much of a drive from there."

Walt nodded. "That's terrific," he said, but his voice suddenly sounded thick with fatigue. "But why don't you go instead? You wouldn't mind, would you? I know you can handle it."

CHAPTER 17

T H E N E X T M O R N I N G , again, Jimmy couldn't get Roger to leave the motel. He acted like he was in some kind of trance.

Finally the boy gave up pleading with him. This time they couldn't wait till Roger got ready to move. It wouldn't be long before the cops were looking for the Camaro. Jimmy took the keys and started the car. He went back into the room.

"You gonna come?" he asked. " 'Cause I'm leaving anyway."

Roger, still in the armchair, stared at the boy mutely for a minute. His eyes seemed to be covered with some sort of film. They looked as if no light got through to them. Then he stood up and followed Jimmy out to the car. He got in the passenger side.

After Jimmy had driven a few miles he came to his senses. "Better pull over and let me drive," he said. "Cops see a kid driving, they'll stop us for sure."

Jimmy signaled right and steered onto the shoulder. As soon as the car stopped he threw the transmission into park and ran around to the other side.

"What's the matter with you?" he asked when Roger was back on the road. "You sick or something?"

Roger said, "Nothing. We're in big trouble, you know that? How long you figure until they catch up with us?" He said it like it was all the boy's fault.

"I don't know. Not long if you keep acting like that."

Roger snapped his head around toward the boy. "Sure. You think that's funny?" he said. "You're a kid. They'll just put you in a home or something. You ever wonder what they're gonna do to me?"

Jimmy felt the blood rise to his face. Since the cop yesterday, he had thought about getting caught but he never thought of the consequences beyond that. Getting caught was the end of it. He never thought that the consequences would be different for the two of them.

He shrugged his shoulders. "Listen," he said. "Maybe they won't get us."

Thursday afternoon Roger tried to steal a car.

He and Jimmy sat in the diner in a booth by the window. They kept an eye on the used car lot on the other side of the highway. So far they had seen only one man in the place. He was sitting behind a desk in the little shack that served as an office. The front door was opened and they could look right at him.

Jimmy leaned across the table toward his father. "Don't act so nervous," he whispered. "It's gonna be easy."

"I'm not nervous," Roger said. "I'm just trying to think if there's some other way."

Jimmy sat back. "Well, go ahead and think," he said. "But that's the best idea we've come up with so far."

They ordered hamburgers and kept watching the lot. No one went in or out. Obviously, the man worked alone. There was almost no pedestrian traffic on the street. The only chance of being spotted was from the diner but there were trucks passing back and forth between it and the shack all the time. It seemed pretty safe.

Roger paid for their meal and they went out to their car. Coming out of the parking lot, he headed straight toward the shack for an instant, then turned left onto the highway and took the first right. He pulled over to the curb.

Jimmy said, "Better give me fifteen minutes." He started to open the door.

Roger reached over and grabbed his shoulder. Jimmy turned and looked at him suspiciously.

"We're gonna meet right here?" Roger asked.

Jimmy nodded curtly. "That's what we said. You sure you can do it?"

"Don't worry. I'll do it."

Jimmy strode easily toward the center of town and turned down the sidestreet right past the department store. Two blocks further he came to the school. There was no one around the faculty parking lot. It took him less than five minutes to sneak in and unscrew the license plates from one of the cars. He put the plates inside a newspaper and tucked it under his arm.

On the way back to the rendezvous point he crossed to the other side of the highway. He was early and he didn't want to pass his father. When he got near the used car lot he saw Roger standing out front. He was checking out some of the cars from the sidewalk. There were no more than twenty-five or thirty. His father didn't see him. The boy went straight to the Camaro and got in to wait.

Roger decided on a '69 Pontiac that didn't look too bad. He hitched up his shoulders and walked up to the door of the shack. He hesitated, then stepped inside.

The salesman stood up immediately and flashed a pleasant smile. He was a balding, paunchy man of around forty. "How d'ye do? What can I do for you today?"

"I'm looking to buy a car," Roger said.

The man nodded his head as if Roger had just cleared up a mystery. "Well, I guess we can help you," he drawled, his inflection carrying faint traces of a Scandinavian accent. "Have any specific idea of the kind of automobile you'd like? Here—why don't we step out on the lot and have a look around?" He walked around the desk. "Tell me—you're not from around here. I can't seem to place you."

"No. Actually, I know the car I'd like. That rust-colored Pontiac. Sixty-nine, I think."

"That's a fine-lookin' car. Probably the best on the lot. For the price, y'understand. If you'd be interested in something a little newer . . . "

"No, the Pontiac seems fine. Any chance I can take it out for a drive?"

"Sure thing. Let me get you the keys. It's a clean car—top condition. I can let you have it . . . "

"Why don't you let me drive it first," Roger interrupted. He laughed nervously, trying to cover what he was afraid might sound like too much impatience. "That way I'll have my own idea what it's worth."

"Makes sense," the man said. "Here, lemme see . . . " He turned to a pegboard behind his desk where sets of keys were hanging.

While his back was turned, Roger kicked the door shut behind him. He pulled Will Schroeder's revolver out of his belt under his shirt and aimed it at the salesman's back.

The man heard the door close. He looked over his shoulder toward Roger, a questioning frown on his face. Then he saw the gun.

He spun around, holding up his hand in front of him like a cop stopping traffic. "Now wait a minute, mister," he said.

"Shut up," Roger snapped.

"C'mon, mister. Look. I got a family."

"Shut up, I said! Do what I tell you and you won't get hurt."

The man couldn't stop babbling. The words poured out of him as he drew back toward the wall. "Whaddya want? Money? I don't keep money here. You can have what I got. I got a wife and two kids, mister."

He reached into his pocket to pull out what money he had. Roger thrust his arm forward, menacing him with the gun.

The man jerked his hand away from his pocket. "Just money," he whined. "I was just reaching for my money. Here—a car? Is that it? You wanna car?"

He turned quickly toward the pegboard, his hands groping for keys, as if he'd suddenly discovered what magic would appease this man. "Here, look, I'm . . . "

The rapid movement startled Roger. His body tensed as his arm instinctively followed the man. Then he heard the gun go off and felt the recoil like a wave moving up his arm.

The shot hit the man above his right shoulder blade, slamming his body into the wall. Roger watched, frozen for a second while the man seemed to be stuck to the wall. Then he began falling. His hands reached for the pegboard and held on until he toppled over backwards, pulling it down with him. The keys clattered faintly against the floor.

Roger took three steps forward and he was standing over the man, who groaned in pain and clutched the front of his shoulder. Blood spilled over his fingers from the exit wound. Roger stooped down and turned over the pegboard. The keys were all loose, uncoded, lying around him. He picked up one, then another in panicky confusion.

It was no use. Someone might have heard the shot and come bursting through the door any second. The man's groaning got louder as he writhed on the floor.

Roger flung down the keys in his hand and raced out the door, leaving it wide open behind him.

Jimmy, watching anxiously out the back window, saw his father come running around the corner. Automatically, the boy flung open his door before realizing that something had gone wrong. There was no other car. His father ran funny as if he'd been hurt. He held his arm pressed close to his side.

Jimmy leaned over quickly and opened the door for him. Roger slid in and began fumbling in his pocket for the keys to the Camaro.

Jimmy saw the gun tucked under his father's arm. He was all right. "What happened?" the boy shouted while Roger's hand shook trying to get the key into the ignition.

"What happened?" he shouted again. "Why didn't you get it!?"

Roger started the engine and sped away from the curb. He was panting hard in short, rapid gasps. He circled the block, the tires screeching on the corners, and turned right at the highway.

In two minutes they were well past the town.

"All right! Slow down," Jimmy barked, turning around to face front. "No one's after us. Now what happened? Why didn't you get it?"

Roger was still panting. "I couldn't," he gasped. "The keys . . . they were all over the floor."

Jimmy's head wobbled in confusion. "You mean you tried? You fucked it up! Did he see you? Did you kill him?"

"I shot him," Roger shouted. "I don't know!"

"Did you kill him?" the boy yelled again, thrusting his face right up to his father's.

"I don't know! I don't know! I shot him!" Roger screamed even louder, the veins standing out on his temples and his face turning purple with rage.

Friday morning Walt didn't go into the office. Rose didn't like the way he looked the night before and turned off the alarm once he had fallen asleep. As soon as she got up she phoned headquarters and told Jerry to be sure to call the house if anything happened on the Mapes case.

No one called. Walt woke up a little before noon. He pretended to be mad at her but she could see that he was grateful for the few extra hours.

He didn't rush to get out of the house. They had a quiet, pleasant lunch together without once discussing the case. After a second cup of coffee, he said he'd better go in for a while just to see how things stood.

No luck yet in finding the store where Jimmy bought the bathing suit. Walt rang up the sheriff in the county where Bradford was located and spent about twenty minutes trying to explain to him what he wanted. The sheriff couldn't think offhand of any house-breakings or robberies around the time in question, but he promised to make inquiries among local police. Walt figured that was a county he'd never hear from again.

Just as he was about to leave, Matt called from Missouri. The man whose house had been robbed positively identified the shirt. At least one just like it was stolen. And that Phyllis woman was fantastic. Of course she identified the Mapeses from pictures and she said how they were hard up for money and even took food from her. She described the scratches on Roger's back down to the sixteenth of an inch.

If there was nothing else Walt could think of for him to do there, Matt said, he'd stay overnight and catch a plane home the next morning.

Four high school kids cut their last class Friday afternoon and drove out to Coe's Pond. They noticed the overturned car in the water but thought nothing of it. People ditched cars just about any place.

They killed a couple of six-packs as they lay by the water's edge. The boys kept suggesting they go for a swim and the girls kept reminding them that they didn't bring bathing suits. Finally the girls conferred together, giggling, and came back to announce that they'd get undressed if the guys did it first. Negotiations almost broke down at that point. Eventually they all stripped at the same time and the girls raced into the water.

One of them swam over to the abandoned car. She posed seductively with one arm draped over the tire, her glistening breasts no longer hidden under the water. Her boyfriend chased after her. She scurried away to the far side of the car. He followed her and almost caught her but she dived under the surface. When she came up, her mouth was wide open in a soundless, horrified shriek. Through the window she had seen part of a human body.

They were crazy to drive around in a car the cops might be looking for.

That's what Roger said. As soon as it got dark Thursday night, he said he was going to check into a motel. Jimmy didn't like it. He wanted to get further away from that car lot. They weren't even at the South Dakota border yet.

Suddenly Roger cut off the discussion. Whatever Jimmy said, he just wouldn't answer. The boy got tired of arguing with himself and shut up. He glowered sullenly at his father.

Roger drove past several motels but then pulled into one that was more to his liking. He registered using the same alias as yesterday but this time he knew the license number—the one from the plates Jimmy had stolen.

"Are the units in back any quieter?" Roger asked the clerk before he reached for a key.

"I suppose. It's pretty quiet out here anyway."

"I don't like the highway noise. I've been listening to those semis all day."

"Okay then. In the back it is."

When they closed the door behind them, Roger said, "First thing in the morning we've got to figure out what we're gonna do. We're all right for now right here. They probably haven't even found that goddam car yet."

Jimmy nodded. "D'you have any ideas?" he asked.

"I said first thing in the morning. Now let's get some sleep."

When Jimmy woke up his father had already showered and shaved. He had that scrubbed, boyish look again. He was sitting up on his bed smoking a cigarette.

"Okay, Jim, this is the way I figure it," he said without even waiting for the boy to get his mind clear. "If we keep going west, we're dead. We stick out like sore thumbs. I say we try to make it to Minneapolis. In this car. We'll ditch it once we get there. It's easier to keep out of sight in the city. We can decide later what we'll do from there."

Jimmy got out of bed and went to the window. Outside, the land stretched away flat to the horizon. His father was right. Their only chance was some place like Minneapolis. He guessed that his father planned on ditching him as well as the car. That explained why he came on so cool, like, Here's what I think, and, How does that look to you? But it wasn't as if they had any real choice.

Besides, he thought, I'll be all right without him.

"Okay," he said indifferently, still looking out the window. "Let's try Minneapolis."

Shortly after three-thirty a swimmer from the local Minnesota Highway Patrol barracks pulled Will Schroeder's body out of Coe's Pond. He was able to identify him even though half his face had been blown away. He made the car as the one that was listed on the A.P.B. from Storm Lake.

Sheriff Vandenberg was contacted immediately. He asked Minnesota to notify all units of the change in the car and to cover it with local jurisdictions.

"They're still not moving as fast as they could," he told the captain he spoke to. "Maybe they're trying to lay low. It's possible they're still in your area."

The captain said, "Well, if they are, Sheriff, we're going to nail them."

Vandenberg phoned Arlington to tell Walt the news. He finally got him at home.

"Where the hell is this place?" Walt said. "I'm going up there."

"You're crazy. It'll take you a day and that's not where they are now. Sit tight. There's no way you're going to catch them yourself."

Walt drummed impatiently on the telephone stand with his cigarette lighter. "All right. But let me know as soon as you hear anything else. I'll be in the office."

An alert small town cop just checking in the station house pulled the latest A.P.B. on the Mapeses from the wire. The man fit the description he had taken that morning from the wounded used car salesman. When he notified the Highway Patrol, they intensified the manhunt. Men were asked to stay over their tours. For the first time they knew they were within twenty-four hours of their quarry.

They were closer than that but they didn't know it. Roger and Jimmy had gone west almost to the South Dakota border before stopping for the night. Now they were heading east, skirting to the north of the highways they had already traveled, trying to keep out of sight on two-lane county roads.

Walt sat by the phone in his office, feeling worse than useless. He thought of calling Sheila but there was nothing he could tell her. That her husband and son might be gunned down any minute?

Five minutes after Andy told him about the used car dealer, Walt called him back. "I bet they're not heading west," he said. "They're too smart to stay in the open. What's the nearest big city?"

"Minneapolis. The people up there already thought of that. Take it easy, Walt. They got everything under control."

Around dusk a highway patrol car fell in behind Roger and Jimmy. They had to stay on bigger roads now and they had been noticing cops all over the place. Jimmy sat scrunched down in the seat, keeping his head below the window. The car followed them about a half a mile and then turned off. He had been fooled by the license plate and the single occupant.

Another one picked them up about twenty miles later. He turned off too.

Roger rubbed his hand hard over his lips. "We're not gonna make it," he said.

"How d'you know? How many miles we got left?"

"I know. The next one's probably stopping every yellow Camaro."

Jimmy felt his stomach tighten. "Just keep driving," he said, but his voice carried no assurance.

Roger kept one eye glued to the mirror. Jimmy, with nothing to look at except his father, watched him grow more frightened with each passing second. The corners of his mouth began to twitch violently.

The next town they came to, Roger pulled into a sidestreet. He stopped the car and turned to his son. "I'm sorry, Jim. This is it," he said. "You can go with me or not. I don't give a shit."

Jimmy's eyes widened. "Where?" he asked.

"One of these houses."

The boy shook his head. There was no question in his mind what his father intended. Why not just give themselves up? What good would it do? But he knew it was even more pointless to argue.

"I'll go with you," he said. Nothing made sense anymore.

Roger drove up a few more blocks away from the main street. He stopped the car and looked around. It was dinner time and there was no one outside. He gave Jimmy the revolver and got the shotgun out of the trunk.

Jimmy followed him at a run to the back of a two-story house. Roger pounded on the back door.

"All right. All right. I'm coming," a surly voice called from inside.

They listened, poised, to the sound of footsteps approaching. A man opened the door without asking who was there.

Roger leveled the gun at his chest. The man tried slamming the door but Roger hurled himself against it, driving him back. They stepped in quickly and shut the door behind them.

They found themselves in a small entryway. "Do as you're told," Roger said. "Understand?" He motioned with his head for the man to turn around.

Roger prodded him in the back with the shotgun, forcing him into the kitchen. One by one, the four people at the table stood up, their mouths hanging open.

"What do you want?" the man asked.

"Nothing. We're just gonna stay here awhile. No one has to get hurt."

The woman stared at Roger's gun uncomprehendingly. Then, as its reality sank in, her lips began to tremble. Suddenly she started to scream.

Roger jumped forward, raising the gun butt, and brought it crashing down on her face. She crumpled to the floor. It happened too fast for the husband to react. Instinctively, his first move had been toward his wife. By the time he turned to Roger, the gun was pointed at him again.

A boy about fifteen bent down to his mother. He was crying.

"Look, I mean business," Roger said through his teeth. "Everyone . . . out there." He pointed to a hallway toward the front of the house. The boy helped his mother to her feet and they made a slow procession into the living room. Roger ordered them to lie down on the floor.

Roger got the man's car keys and handed them to Jimmy. "Move it out and put ours in the garage," he said.

The boy was back in a few minutes. His father had pulled the front curtains and turned on the lights. The two of them paced the living room, not talking to each other, keeping their guns trained on the hostages. The woman moaned quietly from time to time.

"You better shut up," Roger warned her. But she didn't stay quiet for more than a minute.

The next-door neighbors heard the woman's scream. One of them went to the window to see what was wrong. She couldn't see anything so she went back to her dinner. In a few minutes she heard a car start so she took another look. A strange boy was moving one car out of the garage and putting a different one in. She discussed it briefly with her husband and they decided to call the police.

Within minutes of the time the Highway Patrol units began to arrive, Walt Taliaferro got word the Mapeses were trapped. But they had hostages. He knew the case as well as anyone but he couldn't even guess what they were going to do.

The Highway Patrol took their time getting in place. They surrounded the house with eight teams of men, half of them armed with rifles and the others with shotguns. The men were under strict orders not to risk injuring the hostages.

A crowd began to gather. The local police were assigned to keep them at a safe distance.

When the Highway Patrol was ready, their commanding officer spoke to Roger and Jimmy over a bullhorn. "Mapes. Listen to me.

You're surrounded by the police. Don't make this any harder on yourself. Throw out your guns and come out with your hands up." He paused. "Think of your boy, Mapes. There are innocent people in there with you. No one has to get hurt. Throw out your guns and come out with your hands up."

He lowered the bullhorn and waited for a response.

Several minutes passed. He was about to try talking to them again when a quick volley of gunfire exploded from inside the house. The Highway Patrol responded with a short salvo of their own, aimed carefully for the sake of the hostages. But it was important for the two inside to see the police were willing to use force.

"Mapes. It's no use. You can spare a lot of lives."

This time Roger and Jimmy didn't wait for the end of the message before firing from inside. Their shots were returned.

"Why doesn't he talk?" the captain said to the officer beside him. "It don't make no sense." He turned around and addressed a sergeant who had taken cover behind a parked car. "Anyone get hit?"

"No."

"Shit. We're gonna have to go in and get 'em. Tell Phillips to get over here."

The sergeant scurried away, keeping low to the ground.

The captain made no more announcements. All they seemed to do was provoke a gun battle. He and Phillips laid plans for an assault on the house.

An hour dragged by. It was getting dark. It had been a long time since the last shots and the crowd now filled the sidewalk across the street from the house. Phillips had his men ready in helmets and flak jackets. They had been briefed on the plan and awaited only the captain's order to move. But he seemed reluctant to take the responsibility for turning them loose. He was willing to try one last appeal.

"No," Phillips said. "They had their chance. We go in, they're the only ones gonna get hurt. I guarantee it."

"All right. Take your positions. Go on your signal."

Unexpectedly, a few moments later a boy's voice called out from the house. "Okay. I'm coming out."

The captain raised his hand to stop the assault in case Phillips was ready. "All right," he shouted. "Come to the front door with your hands up. Drop your guns on the porch." Then he remembered what he was holding in his hand and repeated the message over the bullhorn.

The front door opened and Jimmy stepped out, keeping his hands high over his head. He held the shotgun by the barrel.

"Drop it," the captain yelled.

"Okay. Where's your father? Is your father coming too?"

"My father's dead," the boy said, speaking hardly any louder than in normal conversation. His voice carried easily across the quiet street.

The captain and the officer looked at one another. The officer's eyebrows went up, forming a question.

On the porch, Jimmy's head pivoted slowly from side to side, his eyes scanning the shadowy faces surrounding him in the gathering darkness.

In Arlington, Walt Taliaferro picked up the phone before it finished one ring.

"They got 'em. They got 'em, Walt. No one got hurt. Mapes is dead but the kid is all right."

Walt didn't say anything. He nodded his head slowly and returned the phone to its cradle.

"Walt? They got 'em," Sheriff Vandenberg repeated before he realized there was no one on the line.